When Our Stars Aligned

The Starboard Beach Series

Tracy McJames

Heart on Paper LLC

When Our Stars Aligned

The Starboard Beach Series, Book 1

Copyright © 2023 by Tracy McJames All rights reserved by author.

This book is licensed for your personal enjoyment only. No part of this book may be reproduced or transmitted in any form by any means, electronic or mechanical, including photocopying, recording, or by any informational storage retrieval system without written permission of the author, except for the use of brief quotations in a book review. Thank you for respecting the hard work of this author.

This book is a work of fiction. Names, characters, places, brands, media, and incidents are either the product of author's imagination or are used fictitiously. Any similarities to persons living or dead is purely coincidental.

Cover design by Kari March

Edited by Erica Russikoff of Erica Edits

Proofread by Emily Lawrence of Lawrence Editing

To all those who brave the storms and come out stronger.

Contents

1. Aly — 1
2. Jax — 8
3. Aly — 13
4. Jax — 16
5. Aly — 21
6. Jax — 29
7. Aly — 32
8. Jax — 37
9. Aly — 41
10. Jax — 45
11. Aly — 51
12. Jax — 55

13. Jax	60
14. Aly	66
15. Jax	70
16. Aly	72
17. Jax	75
18. Aly	81
19. Jax	85
20. Aly	95
21. Jax	103
22. Aly	110
23. Jax	120
24. Aly	124
25. Jax	129
26. Aly	133
27. Jax	141
28. Aly	152
29. Jax	156
30. Aly	166
31. Jax	175
32. Aly	189

33. Jax	196
34. Aly	201
35. Jax	207
36. Aly	216
37. Aly	220
38. Jax	224
39. Aly	232
40. Jax	235
41. Aly	238
42. Jax	242
43. Aly	252
44. Jax	257
45. Jax	262
46. Aly	268
47. Jax	272
Epilogue	279
Bonus Epilogue	284
Acknowledgements	290
About The Author	292

1

Aly

Fifteen Years Ago, Virginia

"Woo-hoo! Way to go, Aly!" one of my sisters cheered as I raised myself out of the pool. We weren't sisters by blood, but in the last four years, we had become like family. As soon as I neared the stands, Sophia, Claire, Mia, and Lyndsey embraced me in a hug. I stood out like a sore thumb in the middle of their circle. All four of the Parker girls took after their mom, who was straight off the boat from Italy. Their olive skin, inky black hair, and dark brown eyes were quite the contrast to my fair Irish skin, blondish hair, and light blue eyes. I also stood about four inches taller than them.

"*Sei stato fantastico!*" Sophia gushed.

"*Grazie, bella*! But I only came in second and you know what they say about second place."

"Second place is *not* first loser, Aly! You put too much pressure on yourself," Claire scolded. She was always looking out for me. All the Parkers looked out for my well-being. It's why I cared about them so much, why I considered them more like family than my own.

"You're also forgetting my relay team came in seventh."

"Oh, please!" Mia snorted. "The only reason your team came in seventh was because of that girl Ariel. She can barely swim to save her life. I'm surprised the lifeguard didn't have to go in after her."

"Yeah, you'd think with a name like Ariel, she'd be a better swimmer," Lyndsey added.

"Stop!" I laughed. It was true that Ariel was a terrible competitive swimmer. She was also a nasty human being in general. The only reason why she made the team was because her mom was the coach.

"Ms. Winters!" my coach barked.

"Crap, I gotta get back over there," I said to my sisters as I ran toward my coach.

"Ms. Winters, I am very disappointed in you," Coach Harris scolded. She kept her eyes trained on the pool and had a death grip on her clipboard.

"I'm sorry, ma'am. I'm not sure what I did wrong."

"I put you as anchor for the relay so you could pick up the slack for everyone else, but you still came in seventh."

"I'm sorry, ma'am. It wasn't easy. Most of the teams were already on their last twenty-five before I even got into the water." My body began to shake. I hated to disappoint anyone.

"Well, I'm pulling you from the hundred-meter back."

"What?!" I yelled and quickly covered my mouth. I knew I shouldn't yell back, but the backstroke was my best stroke. I always placed in the top three.

"You heard me," Coach Harris hissed. "From now on, I want you on freestyle all the time. It doesn't matter if the rest of the team practices butterfly, back, or breast, you're going to live and breathe freestyle until you can pick up your pace. If your relay team places at the next meet, I'll put you back in for backstroke."

"Th-th-that's not fair!" I squeaked, my shoulders slumping, as hot tears welled up behind my eyes. I refused to let them fall. I didn't want her to see me cry.

"I'm the coach and I make the rules. I can speak with your parents about this, but"—she pretended to look around the bleachers, knowing full well my parents were nowhere to be found—"it looks like they're not here."

I pivoted on my feet and headed for Mamma M and Papa C. They were my ride home, and since I was removed from my last heat, there was no sense in staying for the rest of the meet.

"That's bullshit, *bella*!" Lyndsey yelled as we piled into the Parkers' minivan. It was typical for all five of us to call each other *bella*, or beautiful. It was our little way of lifting each other up.

"Lyndsey! Language!" Mamma Maria scolded.

"Sorry, but you know Coach Harris was wrong! She was trying to use Aly so her daughter could place!"

"We know and we filed a complaint with the rec center, although it probably won't do much of anything," said Papa Chris.

"You didn't have to do that for me," I said softly. Though deep inside it warmed my heart that this family cared for me. I honestly didn't know what I'd do without them.

"Of course, we did! No daughter of ours is going to be penalized for someone else's actions."

My sixteen-year-old heart swelled. The Parkers really did consider me to be an extra daughter. They had come to every swim meet to cheer me on while my own parents were busy schmoozing clients and making business connections. Dollar signs were more important to them than anything else.

"What am I going to do without all of you?" Tears once again pricked behind my eyes.

"We're going to miss you so much, Aly. We love you and we wanted to provide you with an opportunity to keep you happy and busy once we're gone." Mamma Maria reached back from the front seat and handed me a long envelope with a gift certificate inside. "We know how much you love swimming and we are so proud of you for sticking it out as long as you have with that horrible coach. We think we may have a way you can keep swimming, but you won't have to beat yourself up with competition."

My eyes went wide as I read the contents of the envelope. "You're paying for my lifeguard training?" It was my dream to become a lifeguard, but the training cost over three hundred dollars and there was no way my parents would shell out that kind of money for me. I mean, they had the money; we weren't poor by any means. They just wouldn't put the money out for me.

"There's even enough for you to buy a few uniforms," Papa C added as he pulled into their driveway.

"I don't know what to say. Thank you!" Excitement filled me as I thought of all the possibilities this would bring. I could get a job and save up some money before I headed off to college in two years.

"You're welcome, Aly. We love you, you know. These past four years have been so wonderful with you in our lives." Mamma M choked up. "We're going to miss you terribly. Just know that even if we are not physically next door to you anymore, you will always be in our hearts."

I nodded and wiped away the tears trying to break free. I jumped out of the van and embraced Mamma M. She held on to me a little tighter than usual, and then I noticed she was sniffling.

"Come on now, Maria, you're acting like we're leaving today. We still have a few weeks left," Papa C said, trying to comfort both of us. He turned to me with a look of sadness on his face. "Someone is waiting for you out back. She's a little upset right now and I think she could use some company."

I nodded and walked towards the back porch to where one of the sweetest women I had ever met sat. Nonna Grace was in a rocking chair, gazing out into nothingness. Her silver hair was tied back in a neat bun and a flowery blue housedress peeked out under the blanket she had resting on her lap. It could be a hundred degrees outside, yet she was always cold.

I didn't know my grandparents, but Nonna Grace was the epitome of what I thought every grandmother should be. She was a soft-spoken nurturer who loved her family fiercely, and I longed to be part of her family. Even though the Parkers considered me one of their own; in truth, I was just the girl next door.

"Hey, Nonna Grace," I said softly so as not to startle her.

"Aly! How are you doing, sweetheart? Mia just ran by and told me you had a rough time at your meet today."

"Yeah, today was a tough day." I sighed and sat down on the top step next to her chair.

"Well, I guess misery loves company." She reached out and patted my knee. "I didn't have the best day either."

"No? Why is that?" Nonna Grace was always happy. I didn't think I had ever seen her in a bad mood.

"My other son, Mark, and his family were supposed to come out and visit, but my grandson was horsing around with his friends and broke his leg."

"Oh, no!" I gasped. "Is he okay?" I had heard about Nonna Grace's other grandchildren, but never met them. Nonna Grace and Nonno Steven lived near their other son, Mark, and his family, but visited the Parkers here in Virginia often. I wondered how much traveling they would be doing out this way since her son, Papa C, and his family would soon be leaving for their next duty station overseas.

"He'll be fine in time." She gave a sad smile. "I really wanted my Jaxyboy to meet you."

"You did?"

"Yes, and his sister Emmalyn too. Call it a feeling, but I just know you and Jaxyboy would be perfect for each other."

"Nonna Grace!" I gasped. "I'm only sixteen!" I had yet to have a boyfriend, mainly because I was so busy hanging out with my sisters. The five of us didn't have time for boys. Plus, I was sure Papa C wouldn't approve of any of his daughters dating.

"I know and so is he. He's a swimmer just like you and I will have you know I met my husband at fifteen, so you're already a year late." She chuckled. Nonna Grace and Nonno Steven had been married for forty-five years and they still acted like teenagers at times. "I was so looking forward to you two meeting, but with Chris and the girls moving, that's not going to happen. Now—" She paused and once again stared out into nothing. "I just have a feeling that something bad is going to happen to him."

I stood up and pulled Nonna Grace into a hug. "I'm sure everything will be fine. I'm going to miss you, you know."

"I know, sweetheart." She pulled out of the hug and cradled my face with her hands. "I'm going to miss you too. Maybe one day I'll be able to get you and Jaxyboy together."

Three weeks later, I stood on the sidewalk watching the only family that ever loved me drive away to the airport to start their new life on a new continent. I hoped and prayed we'd stay in touch. I wasn't allowed to have a phone, so we would have to make do with e-mails and old-fashioned letter writing.

I stayed on the sidewalk until the van turned the corner and was no longer visible. I never realized how lonely I was until the Parkers came into my life. Now that I knew what unconditional love felt like, I never wanted to lose it again. I walked next door to my house. It was unnecessarily big and impersonal. While my house was filled with fancy artwork and designer furniture, the Parkers' house was filled with love.

Love.

That's what I wanted more than anything in the world.

2

Jax

PRESENT DAY, OREGON

"Are you going to come back to bed, baby?" the redhead with the fake boobs and caked-on makeup coos.

I cringe at the term *baby*. Terms of endearment are bullshit, much like everything else in life.

"Don't call me baby," I say harshly and gather up my clothes.

"Well, you refused to give me your name. You can stay the night, you know. Are you up for another round?" She bats her fake eyelashes and I swear one is about to become unglued.

"Nope. That's not how this works." I zip up my jeans. "Was I not clear at the bar?"

She gets up on her knees and runs a finger over my abs. The smell of her trendy perfume nauseates me. "You were, but I thought once you got a sample, you'd come back for more."

I recoil from her touch and pull my shirt over my head. "I told you I don't do repeats."

I don't do overnight stays.

I don't do cuddling.

I don't do hand-holding.

I don't do cutesy names or names at all for that matter. The less I know, the better. Sex is a means to an end. That's it. End of story.

"So that's it? You're just gonna leave?" She pouts.

"That's exactly what I'm doing."

"But my roommate won't be home for—"

"What are you not getting?" I snap. "I laid out all the rules ahead of time. One time, no names, no repeats. I got what I wanted and now I'm leaving."

"Screw you!" She hisses from the bed.

"No, thanks. I already screwed you!" I slam the door to her room just in time to hear a loud thud from the opposite side. It's not the first time a girl has hurled something at my head and it probably won't be the last. I've gotten good at predicting and ducking out of the way over the years.

I hop in my truck, grumbling to myself about how I need to shower and get the scent of this girl's nasty perfume off me ASAP. I grab my phone out of my jeans and stick it in my center console, noticing that I missed a call from my sister. Shit! There's only one reason why Emma would call me at two in the morning.

I make the hour-long drive to the hospital in record time and sprint down the sterile-looking hallway towards the familiar voices around the corner.

"Jax!" My cousin Claire wraps her arms around my neck. She's clearly been crying for a while. I look up to see her husband, Bradley, who gives me a solemn nod. I haven't seen any of my cousins in a good year or two. I really need to make more of an effort to visit, but not this way. I may be an asshole to most, but I do have a soft spot for my family.

"Is she—"

Claire shakes her head. "The doctor said it's almost time. She's been asking for you. Go on in. Your mom is with her now. Your dad is with Emma outside. Emma had a bit of a breakdown and needed some fresh air. My parents and sisters are on their way."

I try to pull myself together before walking through the door. I'm not prepared for this, but I will never be prepared to say goodbye to one of the best women in my life. I push back the curtain and a pair of sparkling blue eyes meet mine.

"Jaxyboy! My favorite grandson! Come here, come here!" My gram's voice is breathier than usual. She still looks like herself, just a bit frailer. Her gray hair looks wispier, and her skin coloring seems so pale against the stark white linens of the hospital bed. It breaks my heart to see her fading away.

"Hey, Gram, how's my favorite girl?" I try to sound as causal as possible, but the realization that this is probably our last conversation puts a huge lump in my throat.

My mom clears her throat and motions for me to take her seat beside Gram. She puts her hand on my shoulder, squeezes it, and leaves without saying a word. I watch her wipe away tears as she walks through the door. Even though Gram is my father's mother, she and my mom have always been close.

"Jaxyboy, look, the doctor said I don't have much time left."

"Gram, don't say that."

"Hush, I'm fine! I've lived a good life and I've always been surrounded by love. I'm okay with meeting my maker and I can't wait to be with your grandfather again." Her lips curl into a smile and I take comfort knowing that Gram and Pop will soon be reunited. They had the most amazing marriage and I know a part of her died the day he passed nearly eight years ago.

"There's only one thing in my life that I regret," she begins, and I know what's coming. I do not want this topic to be the last thing we ever discuss.

"Gram, I'm fine," I say, but she holds a shaky hand up to cut me off.

"You deserve happiness, Jaxyboy. I don't like the cards you were dealt in life, and it never should've been this way, especially if I had my say. I've known in my heart who you were meant to be with for a long time. I tried to work some magic here on Earth, but it didn't happen."

Now, this part is news to me. I know Gram always wanted to see me settle down, but she knows who I was meant to be with? Bullshit! I think the drugs they've given her have addled her mind. Besides, I tried to settle down and it epically blew up in my face. I've since sworn off all romantic relationships. You can't get hurt if you don't get involved.

"Gram, that's impossible. I don't need anyone in my life. I am okay. I will be okay," I try to argue.

"That's enough!" she says with all her might. "You deserve to be happy and I'm going to make it happen. I wasn't able to make things happen while I was alive, but I'm not going to stop when I'm dead."

"Gram! Don't talk like—"

"Hush!" she cuts me off again. "I'm getting tired and I need to say this to you. I'm going to make sure that you finally meet the girl you're supposed to be with—your other half, someone who will reignite that spark you once had. You have been walking around like a shell of a man for much too long. You have a whole life ahead of you that can be filled with love and happiness if you just trust and let it happen."

"Okay, Gram, I think you need to rest." I try to fluff her pillow a bit. Her speech seems to have taken a lot out of her.

I hate that in her final hours, she's more concerned about the quality of my life.

She leans her head back against the pillow. "Your pop has been visiting me lately. We've been talking and working out a plan." A mischievous grin spreads across her face. "She's already on her way."

"Okay, Gram." *Those must be some really good meds.*

I adjust her blanket and notice the chain she wears with her and Pop's wedding bands is no longer around her neck. After Pop passed away, Gram wore his wedding band on a silver chain. She eventually added her engagement and wedding band to the chain, stating that the arthritis in her fingers made it hard to take them off and put on. She never took off her chain. I wonder if the hospital needed her to remove it for some reason.

Gram closes her eyes and I know one thing is for certain. I'm going to miss her like hell.

"I love you." I give her a quick kiss on her forehead. I grab her hand and watch as she falls into a peaceful sleep.

Take care of her, Pop.

3

Aly

GEORGIA

I take a deep breath and look around my empty classroom one last time. I've been calling Beaute, Georgia, my home since I stepped foot on their college campus thirteen years ago. I left Virginia as soon as I graduated high school. There was no point in staying once the Parkers moved away. While I haven't heard from any of them in years, I still consider them my family and the best part of my childhood.

"So, this is it, huh? You're really leaving?" Amelia says, startling me. She is the coworker I am going to miss the most. The one who freely shares lesson plans or brings me surprise cups of coffee. I'll miss everyone I work with, especially the kids, but for now, I need to distance myself from this town.

"Yeah." I sigh. "The district is holding my place for a year, so who knows? I might be back next year to annoy you."

"And you can't tell me where you're going?" She cocks her head to the side. Her strawberry-blond locks are a frizzy disaster in this Georgia heat.

"No." I shake my head. "You know I trust you, but the fewer people who know, the better."

"I get it, truly, I do. I'm not mad at you or anything. I'm just going to miss you like crazy. I mean, seriously, who is going to pass me sarcastic notes and chocolate during our in-services now?"

This makes me laugh. "Yeah, maybe this break will be good for the both of us. At least you won't get in trouble for disrupting meetings anymore."

"What should we tell the kids when they come back next year and their beloved first-grade teacher isn't here?"

"The vocabulary word is *sabbatical* as in Ms. Winters is taking a year sabbatical to try new things."

"There are going to be rumors."

"Oh, there will absolutely be rumors! Do me a favor and write them down so we can laugh our asses off later."

"Hell yeah! I think I might start some of those rumors just to mess with everyone."

"Go for it! I can only imagine what you'll think up!" We might as well make light of the crappy situation I'm in.

"Hmm." She taps her chin. "I'll tell the kindergarten team that you ran off to join the circus and the first-grade team that you followed your dream to be a burlesque dancer in Vegas."

"Well, I guess that's classier than a stripper, right?"

"Totally!"

"The second-grade team will think that the FBI recruited you for some special mission, and I'll tell the third-grade team that you went off to study with Buddhist monks."

"Are women allowed to be monks?"

"Hell if I know." She shrugs. "Oh! Then, I'll tell the fourth- and fifth-grade teams that Jeff Bezos recruited you to go to space in his rocket ship."

"Isn't that the one that looks like a giant—"

"Dildo, yes."

"God, I'm going to miss you!"

"And if you don't come back, I will tell everyone that a handsome prince swept you off your feet and are living happily ever after."

"Thanks, Amelia, but I probably have a better chance of going to space in a giant penis."

4

Jax

I lean against the brick wall outside of the funeral home, in need of some fresh air. Gram slipped into a deep sleep shortly after our talk. She never regained consciousness and passed away three days later with a huge smile on her face. I'd like to think the smile was because she was finally reunited with Pop. I'm going to miss that woman fiercely, but I also know that at thirty-one, I was blessed to have her in my life for as long as I did.

"Needed some fresh air too?" my sister, Emma, interrupts my thoughts. She moves next to me and mimics my position against the wall.

"It's standing room only in there," I say, looking straight ahead towards the parking lot.

"Gram was a special lady and made quite the impression on a lot of people."

"Not to mention our cousins have quadrupled in size over the years."

Emma snickers. "Yeah, you can say that again."

Gram and Pop had two sons—my dad, Mark, and our uncle Chris. My uncle Chris met my aunt Maria while he was in the Navy. He was on liberty over in Italy and got lost trying to make it back to his hotel. He spotted Aunt Maria who, thankfully, was fluent in English. She took pity on him and not only helped him find his way back to his hotel, but became his personal tour guide for the remainder of his time over there. They kept in touch, and a year later, they were married and living in the States. They have four daughters. My cousins are all married now with a bunch of kids of their own. They're great girls. Growing up, we didn't see them much due to my uncle's career traveling all over the world, but we always have a good time when the family gets together. We try to have a family reunion every two years or so, and I swear the next generation of cousins keeps multiplying every time I see them.

Emma and I are the only ones without kids, although I am sure that will change for her now that she's married. I'm the only male of the Parker family and the only one to carry on our last name. Once upon a time, I fully expected to do just that, but not anymore.

"Did Gram, umm, I'm n-not sure how to put this..." Emma stammers. "Right before Gram passed, did she say anything kind of odd to you?"

I stiffen as I think back to our last conversation. It may have been the last conversation we ever had, but the topic wasn't entirely new. Gram always made it clear that she wanted to see me in a relationship. She hated that I live alone and away from the rest of the family. The commute to see my family is only about an hour-long drive. I love my parents and sister, but I have no desire to live back in the town I grew up in. Going back to my hometown means a chance I'd run into people I have no desire to see.

"She basically told me she hoped to see me settle down. You know, the normal Gram stuff." I shrug. I don't want to get into the other things she told me.

"That's it? Nothing, you know, else?" Emma squints at me.

"Why are you being all weird, Ems?"

Emma looks around to see if anyone is watching us, like she has some top-secret government information she needs to share. "You can't tell anyone."

"Umm...okay?"

"Please, Jax. No one knows about this yet."

"Okay, seriously, Ems, what's going on? I won't say a word."

"Remember when everyone was at the hospital, and we took turns talking to Gram? Well, when it was my turn, Gram told me that she had been seeing Pop, like he was visiting her."

I nod. "Yeah, she said something similar to me. You know, it's not uncommon for people who are dying to claim they see loved ones who have already passed."

"Yeah, I know and honestly, it's comforting to think she's back with Pop."

"Same, so what's the big secret? It can't be that."

"She told me she was excited to hold her twin great-granddaughters."

I give her a quizzical look.

"She told me I am going to have twin girls."

"Okay, well, I mean that could happen. Especially once Grant is finally out. Twins do run in the family," I say, referring to our cousins, Mia and Lyndsey.

Emma shakes her head and leans in closer to me. "That's not what I'm saying. I mean, I don't know. Ugh, this is so confusing. I'm just gonna say it. I'm pregnant, Jax."

I suck in a deep breath. "You're pregnant?"

She nods.

"Like right now?"

She nods again.

"When?"

"Well, I don't think you want to get into details, but remember last month when Grant came home on leave? I guess we weren't as careful as we thought."

"Oh my God, Ems, this is great news!" I hug her. I knew Emma and Grant wanted to start a family as soon as he was discharged from the Navy. He has less than a year to go before he will be home for good. "Wait—does Grant know?"

"Grant and you are the only two people who know. And, well, I guess Gram too. That's the thing. I didn't even know I was pregnant when Gram told me. I just found out."

"Wow, okay, so Gram might've had some intuition thing going on. Is it twins?"

"My doctor said she will do an ultrasound when I'm eight weeks along and I'm only six weeks right now. I don't know, but I feel like Gram was right. I'm just so worried Grant might miss everything! I mean, we both wanted to start a family right away, but ideally, it would be when he is home for good."

I pull her into another hug and kiss the top of her head. "I know, Ems, but this will all work out. It will be hard, but Grant will be given paternity leave, and before you know it, he will be out."

"You think so?" She looks up with tears in her eyes.

"Of course! You and Grant are going to be awesome parents! Mom and Dad are going to freak out when they learn they're going to finally be grandparents." I know Mom has been a little jealous over the amount of grandchildren Uncle Chris and Aunt Maria have. I can't help but feel a bit guilty not giving my parents any grandkids. Had my life gone differently, I probably would've had at least one child by now.

"Thanks." She sniffles. "You can't say anything about this just yet. I didn't want to bring this up when the focus should be on Gram. I'll tell them once everything settles down."

"I understand. Your secret is safe with me."

"I know it is. Now tell me, what else did Gram say? I have a feeling you're not telling me everything."

I lean my head back against the brick wall, choosing my words wisely. "I'll tell you what," I say, coming up with an idea. "I really don't believe much of what Gram told me, but if you are, in fact, having twins, I will tell you."

"So, you mean I have to wait until my ultrasound to find out what Gram told you?"

"Only if it's confirmed twins. I don't think she was in her right frame of mind before she passed. I really wouldn't put too much stock into what she said."

"Fine!" Emma huffs. "But I'm sure she was right and you *will* tell me!" She pokes a finger in my chest.

"Yeah, yeah." I brush her off. "Let's get back inside."

5

Aly

OREGON

This is it—my chance for a fresh start. If someone had told me two years ago that I would be relocating to the West Coast for a new job that I received out of thin air, I would've thought they were nuts. Yet that's exactly what I'm doing.

Now, I'm off to start my life over in Starboard Beach, a small suburb on the Oregon Coast. I tried my best to familiarize myself with the area through internet searches. I know it's considered a small beach town, but it's nowhere near as small as Beaute, Georgia. The condo I will be living in was only built a few years ago, and according to Michelle, my future roommate and landlord, the beach is only about a ten-minute drive away.

I found Michelle through a wanted ad on one of Starboard Beach's community pages on Facebook. We hit it off quickly and she was very accommodating for my need to stay private. The deal was sealed when I discovered the condo has a private indoor pool.

My phone vibrates as I make my way down to baggage claim and a picture of my best friend Jess pops up on the screen.

"Hey," I answer.

"Hey, yourself! You were supposed to call me as soon as you got off the plane, and according to my flight status app, you landed five minutes ago."

I roll my eyes. "Are you stalking me now too? I'm headed towards baggage claim."

"You are my bestie for life. It's perfectly acceptable to check up on you," she says matter-of-factly.

I met Jess and her twin brother, Jacob, during our first semester in college. I quickly became friends with them both. We moved off campus to a shared apartment during our second semester and lived happily for several years. But a few years ago, Jess met her husband and moved up to Maine where he received a job transfer. Jacob still keeps an apartment in Beaute, but he's rarely there now that his modeling career has taken off. "Okay, so what's your anxiety level right now?"

"Honestly, maybe like a three. Isn't that weird? I'm actually having anxiety over not having anxiety. What is wrong with me? I just left my home, job, friends, and everything I know to move clear across the country for a new position I accepted over a Zoom meeting. A freaking Zoom meeting! I don't know anyone here and have never taught at the college level before. Why am I not panicking about this?"

"Well, Dr. Winters, I suspect you are not freaking out because in your heart you know this is the right move. You have always wanted to teach at the college level. Besides, you need this change."

"Okay, yeah, so I have always wanted to go into higher education, but I figured that would be *after* I retired from the school district. This wasn't in my life plan."

I can feel Jess roll her eyes through the phone. I set up my life plan at some point in high school. It was during some sort of class to get us prepared for the real world. I took my goals a little more seriously than the rest of my classmates.

Aly's Life Plan
Step 1: Turn eighteen and get my ears pierced.
Step 2: Graduate high school with college credits/move away from home.
Step 3: Earn my bachelor's degree by 21.
Step 4: Earn my master's degree by 24.
Step 5: Earn my doctorate by 28.
Step 6: Get married by 29/live happily ever after.
Step 7: Start having kids by 30/continue living happily ever after.
Step 8: Retire from the school district and start working as a professor.
Step 9: Continue living happily ever after.

I checked off the first five steps with no problem. I should've been through step 6 and living step 7 by now, but here I am at thirty-one moving clear across the country to put as much distance as possible between myself and step number 6... Okay, the former step number 6.

"Screw your life plan." Jess breaks me out of my thoughts. "Look, you accomplished more before you turned thirty than some people do in their entire lives. As for the marriage thing, people of all different ages get married all the time. There was the cute couple at my grandmother's nursing home; they met in the dining hall, fell in love, and got married at eight-nine and ninety-two."

"Is this supposed to make me feel better?"

"It should! Stop acting like your life is over when it's just beginning!"

"Look, I just don't think I can do relationships again. I'm pretty burned by everything that happened. I've already come to the conclusion that I will dedicate the rest of my life to my career and I'll adopt a bunch of cats." I sigh.

"Aren't you allergic to cats?"

"Okay, dogs. Instead of a husband and children, I will adopt a ton of dogs and become their pack leader. It will be great; I can let myself go and walk around my house in pajamas and dirty hair. They'll still wag their tails when they see me. Hold on, I can see my luggage on the carousel. I need to grab it and get to my rental."

"Clearly, we need to revisit this discussion again at another time. When will your car arrive?"

"It should be here by Tuesday. I'll have a rental until then. It will probably be too late to call when I get to the condo, so I will send you a text to let you know I made it."

"Okay! Be safe, breathe, and remember that I love ya!"

"Love ya too!" I grab my suitcase from the carousel and balance my carry-on on top of it. My life is pretty much all in this luggage I'm hauling. My contract is only for a year, so I put most of my stuff in storage and rented out my home.

I can't believe I will have roommates again. It seems like forever since I lived with Jess and Jacob. We had fun and all, but that seems like a lifetime ago. The two girls I will be staying with seemed nice when we spoke on the phone. I'm sure we'll get along just fine. Being the people pleaser that I am, I can usually get along with just about everyone.

I pick up my rental car and thank God everything goes smoothly. I drive for about an hour before I reach my temporary new home: the Woodland Condominiums. Michelle, my new roommate and the owner of the condo, told me she would meet me inside the front entrance. She's twenty-five and in law school. I know six years isn't a huge age difference, but I can't help but think that I was in kindergarten while she was still in diapers.

Thanks to our FaceTime chats, I recognize my petite blond-haired, blue-eyed roommate as soon as I enter the lobby. She greets me with a warm smile and offers to help me with my luggage. "It's so nice to finally meet you in person!"

"Thanks! I can't believe I'm actually here!"

"Let me give you the grand tour." She waves her hand around the lobby. "The building is set up as a square, so it's easy to navigate. The main floor has the pool, a small gym, a laundry room, and a mailroom." We head towards an elevator marked with an *E*. "Each side of the building is named after the side it faces. Our condo is on the third floor on the east side, so we live on 3rd East."

We step on the elevator and Michelle hits the button for our floor. The moment the doors open, I am hit with a delicious smell of something sweet—maybe vanilla? The scent increases as we walk farther down the hall.

"This is the best smelling hallway I have ever been in." I take a bigger whiff.

"Yeah, that's what brought the boys of 3rd East to our place." Michelle grins.

I give her a questioning look. She points to a door on her left. "This is 310, home to Alex and Carter." She then walks a few steps and points to a door on her right. "This is 311. Jax lives here, and this"—she opens the door to 312—"is our home sweet home. I do a lot of baking and the scent tends to drift out into the hallway. The boys can't resist; they come over all the time to eat our food."

"And when you say 'boys,' do you mean like little kids or—" The sound of laughter coming from a gorgeous woman in pink scrubs cuts me off. She's on the shorter side and is super curvy, with tan skin and curly dark brown hair. She must be Gabriella, my other new roommate.

"Hi! I'm Gabby!" She walks over to shake my hand. "The boys Michelle is referring to are actually full-grown men, but they still act like a bunch of teenagers. They have the ability to feed themselves, but they seem to prefer the stuff we make instead of the ramen they keep in their kitchen."

"I'm sorry." Michelle looks down at her feet. "I should've told you ahead of time. The guys come over a lot. Well, at least Alex and Carter do. We usually keep our door unlocked if we're home because they always come barging in here to eat or hang out."

I'm sure my eyes must be bugging out of my head at this point because I have so many questions.

"I know it sounds crazy," Gabby explains, "but we actually have a great thing going on. If one of us cooks, they do the dishes; if they raid our fridge, they usually leave some cash on the counter or replace the groceries...eventually. Plus, they help with random things like killing the occasional spider or taking the trash to the compactor."

"Oh, well, that doesn't sound so bad." The thought of waking up to a bunch of gremlins in the kitchen dissipates.

"Nope!" Michelle chirps. "In fact, they're the ones who helped set up your room. Carter installed the new ceiling fan. Jax put your bedframe and nightstand together, and Alex, well, he put a fresh coat of paint on the walls."

I chuckle at the last statement. Michelle told me that my room needed some restoration after their last roommate graffitied the walls. I take a look around the well-kept condo. It has a homey feel to it with light blue walls and white furniture. It's an open concept where the kitchen is visible from the living room and dining area. While it's not my home, it will do for a year.

Michelle shows me to my room and Gabby leaves for her shift as a nurse at the local hospital. I unpack a few things and send a text to Jess to let her know I'm all settled in for the night. Before I know it, the exhaustion from traveling catches up to me and I fall into a sound sleep.

***

I wake up the following morning just as the sun starts to peek through my curtains. I tiptoe around my room, looking for my bathing suit and goggles. I may be up with the birds, but the need to swim is necessary. I've suffered from anxiety most of my life, but it has been under control for the past few years.

I tried the typical suggestions of yoga or meditation, but I had too much trouble focusing. Swimming, however, has always provided me with a sense of collectiveness. Basically, I found the right combination that works for me.

I quietly slip into my bathing suit and pull-on shorts and a T-shirt. I grab my towel and goggles and head down to the pool. I push through the heavy glass doors, a rush of warm air and the smell of chlorine immediately putting me at ease. I take in the sight of the crystal-clear pool; it's large but not Olympic-sized like I'm used to. There is one lane dedicated for lap swimmers, with the rest open for families or anyone who wants to just relax.

I remove my T-shirt and shorts and place my towel on a hook. I ease myself into the shallow end, spit into my goggles (gross, I know, but it prevents them from fogging), and start with a few slow warm-up laps of breaststroke followed by freestyle. I don't have to watch my time today since I don't check in with the university until later this week. For now, I'll focus on getting used to my new surroundings and, more importantly, taking care of myself.

6
Jax

"Man, the first thing I'm gonna do when I get home is order a big-ass steak." Travis picks at his mystery meat from the galley. "And then, I'm gonna order another big-ass steak for a side. And for dessert—"

"Let me guess, a big-ass steak?"

"No, I was gonna say a hot fudge sundae from Dairy Queen. I don't know what it is that makes them so good. I think it's the ratio they got going between the soft serve and hot fudge."

I shake my head and push the food around on my plate. This is Travis's first tour and my second, so I was better prepared for regular meals of shit on a shingle.

"Lunchtime is over!" Our Senior Chief bursts through the door. "We have a partial building collapse with women and children trapped inside!"

We quickly throw our meals away and run towards the convoy of trucks preparing to leave. This is not our typical job, but as the Navy's Seabees, we have the knowledge and heavy equipment to assist in these rare situations.

Travis and I jump into the truck carrying small equipment while Goodwin and Taylor take the forklift. We roll out of base in silence. I love being in the Navy, but I can't wait to be back in the States. I never thought I'd miss seeing grass, but the monotonous color of sand gets to you after a while.

My gut starts to churn as we get closer to the scene. Something doesn't feel right. There is a building of some sort up ahead, but it doesn't look like it's collapsed. The locals seem calm. Too calm. Travis and I share a look.

"Does something seem—"

I wake up gasping in a cold sweat. It's been six years, yet it still feels like yesterday. I grab my phone to look at the date. Damn! It's like my subconscious knows the anniversary of my worst nightmare.

My phone buzzes while still in my hand.

> **Uncle Chris**: Thinking of you today. You know I'm always here to talk.

I reply with my usual response.

> **Me:** Thanks. I know.

My family means well. They have a ton of love to give, and I guess I used to when I was younger. But now? I usually just give my bare minimum. It's safer to keep everyone at arm's length.

Looking at the time, I see my alarm is scheduled to go off in twenty minutes. I shut it off; it's not like I'll be able to get back to sleep. I say an extra prayer for Goodwin and Taylor and remind myself to go easy on Travis today.

Forgoing my morning coffee, I change into my swim trunks and head down to the pool. I'll need to push myself extra to work out my nervous energy.

A ping of agitation hits me when I open the doors to the pool and see that someone else is already in there and using my lane. I'm always alone. No one ever comes to the pool at this hour. Sure, some of the senior citizens like to float around after lunch or some families come on the weekends, but I'm the only one up and doing laps at the ass crack of dawn and I like it that way. I like my solitude. I know it sounds petty, but I like the simplicity of my mornings. Hell, I like simplicity period. I've had several rocky years and need this solace; fuck, I *seek* it. I've been burned, literally and figuratively.

I walk towards the pool to get a better look at who is stealing my lane. It's hard to tell since her face is in the water, and the tilt of her head when she comes up for air gives me nothing to go by. She's in a dark blue racing-style bathing suit, which is typical of what a female swimmer would wear. That's good. I can't stand it when girls claim to be serious swimmers and then show up in a skimpy two-piece. Don't get me wrong, I appreciate tiny two-pieces just as much as the next guy, but that's for hanging out at the beach or a party, not for doing laps.

I begrudgingly dive into the area next to the lane and start my freestyle warm-up.

7

Aly

My hands cut through the water as I start to find my rhythm in the pool. I used to swim nearly every day after work at the gym near my home. It was a great way to decompress, but after weird things started happening, I became much more of a recluse. I went to work and came straight home. I even used a grocery delivery service, so I didn't have to go to the store. Jess was right; I really was losing myself in Georgia.

I feel a splash nearby, alerting me that someone else has entered the pool. My heart rate picks up out of fear, but I try to rationalize with myself. I'm three thousand miles away from home and only three people (Jess; her husband, Brady; and her brother, Jacob) know my location.

My fear quickly subsides as the swimmer passes me, flip turns, and continues. I can tell by the guy's swim trunks that he swims on a regular basis and decide he's here for the same reason I am. With my nerves calming, curiosity gets the best of me. He's fast, but his motions are seamlessly fluid. Some swimmers prefer speed over technicality. I suppose there's nothing wrong with that, but I tend to think it makes them look sloppy. This guy, though, has mastered both.

I straighten my head to get a better look as he does another flip turn. He has a sleeve of tattoos with some type of tribal markings on one arm and something else on his chest. It's hard to see smaller details when you're swimming next to someone, but I certainly take notice of his muscular arms, broad chest, and six-pack. Perfection. Not that I'm interested, of course. I'll probably never date again, but that doesn't mean I can't appreciate the sight next to me.

He switches his stroke to butterfly and I cringe. I hate swimming next to anyone doing the butterfly, especially a large guy. His movements become hard and angry. His testosterone-filled strokes create waves that inadvertently send a mouthful of water in my face every time I tilt my head for air. I fight against muscle memory to breathe in the opposite direction, but the mini tsunamis he makes nearly push me into the wall. I take back what I thought about him being a smooth swimmer.

I get out of the pool and let Angry Butterfly Guy attack the water. I notice a green towel hanging near my pink one. I wrap my towel around my chest, and for shits and giggles, take the green towel and move it two pegs over to the left.

I take the elevator back to 3rd East, disappointed my workout was cut short. The feeling wanes as soon I open the door to my new home and the sight of a muscular, half-naked figure sitting on the couch comes into view. His feet are propped up on the coffee table and he's eating what looks to be a bowl of cereal.

"Sup." The dark-haired, blue-eyed stranger tips his chin in my direction.

"Umm…hi. I'm Aly and you must be Carter, Alex, or Jax." I step farther into the room. I'm quite proud of myself that I remembered all their names so quickly. I make sure to keep my eyes focused from the neck up. I've witnessed many a woman fawn over Jess's brother, Jacob, and it's not a look I ever want to have on my face.

Before he can reply, a groan comes from the hallway. "Alex! What are you doing here so early? And for heaven's sake, put your clothes on!" Michelle pads down the hallway in a fluffy pink robe and matching slippers.

Alex stands up, revealing that he's only wearing a pair of red plaid boxers. He flashes a playboy of a smile complete with dimples. This guy is good-looking, and he knows it too. "I just wanted to be the first to meet your new roommate." He saunters over, grabs my hand, and places a kiss on the back of it.

"Is that the only reason you stopped by?" Michelle crosses her arms and raises an eyebrow.

"Well, that and I needed milk for my cereal." He shrugs.

"Of course you did." Michelle rolls her eyes.

Alex steps back and looks me up and down. "Damn, you're tall."

"You're observant," I reply sarcastically. I'm about five eight, but many people have told me I seem taller.

He leans in close to my ear and stage-whispers, "You do realize that you're now living among the fun-sized, right?"

"I didn't choose my living situation based on the height of my roommates," I quip back.

Alex's mouth spreads into a wide grin. "I like you. You've got spunk. I'm going to call you... Legs."

"Wow, original," I deadpan.

"Well, it's official, Aly." Michelle pours herself a cup of coffee. "Alex doesn't give nicknames to just anyone."

"That's right, Peanut. Notice I never called your old roommate anything."

"Carrie," Michelle answers.

"Which should've been your first red flag!" Alex waves his arms. Michelle gives him a look of confusion. "Seriously, how have you not read Stephen King?"

"Because I prefer to sleep at night!" Michelle responds.

The door opens and a sleepy-looking surfer guy shuffles in with a bowl of cereal in his hand.

"Dude! We're out of milk again," Surfer Guy looks at Alex, completely oblivious to me standing near him.

"Don't look at me." Alex puts both of his hands up in the air. "It was your turn to go to the grocery store. I just got off duty."

"Then you could've picked up some milk on your way home," Surfer Guy replies.

Their casual banter reminds me of the times Jess, Jacob, and I all shared a place.

"Carter! Where are your manners! Say hello to our new roommate," Michelle scolds.

Carter turns to see me standing off to the side. "Oops! Didn't see you there!" A warm smile spreads across his face as he puts his hand out to shake mine. Carter looks like the beach bum boy next door. He's long, lean, and probably muscular under the T-shirt he is wearing. His sandy hair is a little on the shaggy side and his blue-green eyes project a kind-hearted soul. Yup, I can see myself being friends with this guy.

"Nice to meet you," I greet and look down at the bowl in his hand. "Are you eating Lucky Charms?"

"Not yet." He gives a lopsided grin and looks over at Michelle, who grabs a carton of milk and passes it to him.

Michelle crosses her arms and shakes her head. "You boys are never going to grow up, are you?"

"Oh, come on, Michelle, they're magically delicious." Carter grins as he pours the milk over his cereal.

"Breakfast of champions!" Alex saunters over to Carter for a fist bump.

"And to think we trust this guy to save us from a fire." Michelle glares at Alex.

"You're a firefighter?" I ask Alex.

"Firefighter, hero, whatever you prefer." He winks. I respond by rolling my eyes.

"What about you, Carter? Are you a firefighter also?"

"No, but I've accidentally started a few fires." He gives a sheepish grin. "I'm an electrician."

"Wow, I wasn't expecting that one." I study him a little more. He certainly doesn't put out electrician vibes. Do electricians put out vibes? That probably wouldn't be good for them. Maybe that's how the accidental fires start.

"No one does." Alex snorts. "The guy should be a pro surfer, but instead he plays with wires and circuits and shit."

"The market for professional surfers is very small. The market for knowledgeable electricians is very high. I started my own business so I could make my own hours...so I can surf whenever I want." Carter shoves a spoonful of sugary cereal in his mouth.

"Smart, but what are you doing in Oregon? Shouldn't you be somewhere a little warmer?"

"I didn't want to be too far from my family." Carter shrugs.

That makes one of us, I think. My parents don't even know I'm living on the other side of the country. I tried to build a relationship with them, especially after the Parkers moved away. I desperately wanted to fill that void in my heart, but in the end, they chose their careers over me. So, I developed my life plan and stayed on course...until everything derailed. Now, I have no idea what life has in store for me.

8

Jax

There are only two bars in Starboard Beach, The Local and Bruno's. The Local has a friendly vibe to it. The décor is light with a nautical theme. They have a huge dance floor, plenty of pool tables, plus great burgers and wings. Bruno's is the opposite. It's much smaller, with dark décor, loud music, and sticky tables. You don't go to Bruno's to hang out with friends; you go to Bruno's to wash away your sorrows or find a one-night stand. Sometimes both. Tonight, Alex and I are at our usual sticky table at Bruno's.

"Slim picking tonight." Alex shakes his head.

"What about the two over there, the blonde and brunette at four o'clock?" I subtly aim my gaze over to the corner of the bar.

Alex squints his eyes. "Nah, the brunette's eyebrows are drawn on. I don't like women with fake eyebrows."

"Are you serious right now? I swear you're getting worse every time we come here." I shake my head in frustration. Alex has been my wingman for a little over a year. He sleeps around just as much as I do, but lately, something has been up with him.

"I think I'm getting too old for this shit, man," Alex announces as if he just read my mind.

"You're twenty-eight."

"My birthday is next month. Do you know what that means?"

"That you'll be twenty-nine?"

"Yes! I'm about to be in my last year of my twenties. That means in one year and one month from now I will be thirty. Thirty, Jax! I can't take it."

"I'm already past thirty, so what does that make me?"

"Old!" Alex yells. I flip him off. "I'm not ready to be like you."

"What am I like?"

"Alone!"

"I choose to be alone!" I say defensively. I haven't been in a relationship since I was eighteen and I'm completely fine with that.

Alex leans forward with his elbows on the table. "There are two groups of guys at the station. The married guys and the single guys. I am now the oldest of the single guys."

"So?"

"So, I used to enjoy being part of the single guys' group, but lately, I don't know. I look over at the married guys and they all seem so...happy and content. I guess I'm starting to feel a little restless. I think I'm getting ready to settle down."

"*All* the married guys are happy?" I find that hard to believe based on my short-lived experience.

"Well, all but Mickelson; his wife seems pretty bitchy. But anyway, I listen to the guys, and they talk about things they did with their wives on their days off. They show each other pictures of their kids learning to walk or their kids' little league games and shit. I want that too."

"Hey, guys!" Carter appears from behind me.

"What are you doing here? I thought you had a date with Kayla tonight." Alex takes a pull from his beer.

"Nah, we're done. She's moving up north to take care of her grandmother and we both agreed we're not long-distance relationship material. It's all good, though. It's not like she was the one, ya know?" Carter does not do one-night stands. Out of the three of us, he's the relationship guy.

"Please!" Alex scoffs. "You wouldn't know 'the one' if she was living right next door."

"Speaking of living next door, I spent a lovely afternoon with our new neighbor." Carter raises his hand to get our waitress's attention.

"No shit! You and Legs?" Alex raises an eyebrow.

"Legs?" I snort.

"You'll see!" Alex gives a wink.

Carter shakes his head at his roommate. "There's nothing going on between us. We have definitely friend-zoned each other. She had never seen the Pacific Ocean, so I offered to take her."

"Well, look at you being all kind and neighborly. What did she think of the Pacific Ocean?"

"She thought it was great. We took a walk along the beach and talked for a while. She told me a little about her life on the East Coast and her job at the university."

"You took a walk on the beach? Sounds romantic." Alex waggles his not-drawn-on eyebrows.

"Nope. She's beautiful and sweet, but we are most definitely just friends." Carter turns his attention to me. "Have you met Aly yet?"

I shake my head, playing with the label on my beer. "Didn't even know her name until you just said it."

"Aw, come on, your front doors literally face each other and you still haven't met her?" Alex sits back in his seat. "She's cute too. I'd ask her out but—"

"Yeah, yeah, we know the Alejandro Jones Clause," Carter teases. After the debacle with the girls' previous roommate, Michelle put in a clause stating that any future tenants would be evicted if they had sexual relations with Alex. "Pretty sure she's not interested in you anyway."

"What?" Alex feigns shock. "I'm a delight!"

"Anyway," Carter turns back to me. "You really should go over and introduce yourself. She just made a huge cross-country move and only knows the girls and me...plus the delight sitting next to you."

"I'll think about it," I lie. If I happen to run into her in the hallway or something, I'll introduce myself, but I'm not going out of my way to meet new people. It's a miracle that I go out with Alex and Carter or have the occasional dinner at the girls' place. Up until I moved into my condo, I had my family and my best friend, Travis. Throw in the occasional nameless one-night stand and that's the extent of my social life.

9

Aly

I step out of my car and take in a deep breath of fresh air. I swear the air smells cleaner out in Oregon. Beaute has a lot of farms, so the smell of cows and other livestock was always prevalent. Everyone said I would get used to it, but I never did.

Today is my first official day as an employee at Starboard Beach University. The summer semester doesn't start for another week, but I need to sign some paperwork and get my faculty ID.

I went for a swim this morning and pushed myself harder than yesterday. I purposely made myself tired to keep my nerves at bay. Also, Angry Butterfly Guy was back and I didn't want him to think I was a weak swimmer.

White and yellow daisies line the path that leads towards the administration hall and I hope the sight of my favorite flower is a sign of good things to come. I check in with the receptionist and wait for Dr. Conway, Head of the Education Department. She is the one who contacted me about the position after reading my dissertation online. We've spoken several times on the phone and through Zoom meetings. We seemed to click well during our chats, so I'm hoping things will go well in person.

While waiting, my phone vibrates with an incoming text.

> **Amelia:** Hope you are doing well wherever you are! Trent's been all over town asking if anyone has seen you. He saw me getting groceries and asked me too. I told him you left to be a burlesque dancer in Vegas. He was NOT happy. Also, if you really did become a burlesque dancer, I am so sorry for blowing your cover!

> **Me:** LOL! Thanks for the heads-up. I am definitely not dancing in Vegas, but I appreciate that you think I have those skills. Miss you!

> **Amelia:** Miss you too <heart emoji>

The sound of heels on the tile floor pulls my attention away from my phone. A tall middle-aged woman in a black pencil skirt and white button-up blouse heads towards me.

"Dr. Winters?" she asks as she approaches.

"Dr. Conway." I stand to greet her. "It's so nice to meet you in person."

"Same here, and you can call me Eliza."

"And you can call me Aly or Alyssa."

Eliza leads me to the back office where a mountain of new hire paperwork waits for me. "First and foremost, we need to get your ID, then I will show you to your office where you can fill out your paperwork."

"Sounds great!" I follow her to an adjacent office.

"Martha." Eliza looks at a gray-haired woman behind the desk. "This is Dr. Alyssa Winters, our new hire. Could you please get her set up with an ID?"

"No problem!" Martha replies. She hands me a stack of papers. "This is the form we need for your information to be on our website."

"Website?" I hesitate.

"Yes, all of our faculty are listed with their picture and credentials. You know, the basic stuff—what type of degrees you have, that kind of thing."

"Umm..." I bite my lower lip. I've uprooted my entire life to move across the country and in a mere few days, it might not even matter. "Is it necessary to add my information to the website? It's just that I have someone in my life that umm...well, I'd rather he not know where I am."

"You can check the box on the photo release form that says you don't want to have your picture published," Eliza states, sensing my discomfort. I'm grateful she doesn't press me for any more information.

"I'm also concerned about my name being published." *This isn't going to work. Why did I think this was going to work?*

"You don't have to use your real name. Many professors choose to go by different names for privacy purposes and other reasons," Martha suggests.

"Exactly," Eliza agrees. "Conway is my maiden name. I got married five years ago, but I was so used to Conway, I didn't want to change it."

"Okay, I guess I can do that." My nerves begin to calm.

"I do need you to give me a name today, so I can get all of this done." Martha shuffles a pile of paper. "And please do not choose Jones or Smith; we have too many of those. I can't tell you how many times students have signed up for the wrong class because they chose the wrong professor."

"Gotcha." I nod. I have zero attachment to my last name, so the thought of changing it doesn't bother me, but what do I want my last name to be? My first instinct is to change it to Monroe or Gray; those are Jess and Jacob's last names. As crazy as my ex is, he isn't an idiot. He would think to look me up under those names. I still can't believe I'm living through this ridiculous situation.

I look at the form Martha handed me and write down the only other name that means something to me. It's also something my ex won't know. I never talked about my childhood much. Maybe it will bring me luck. *God, I hope this works.*

10

Jax

"Am I here to meet the new girl or what?" I complain aloud to no one in particular. Michelle finally cornered me in the hall and proceeded to give me a speech on my shitty manners and how I should've met her new roommate by now. I help myself to a beer from the girls' fridge. I hope this night won't last too long. Maybe I can make an excuse to leave right after dinner. I still have to eat, of course.

"I just got a text from her. She's on her way." Michelle sets a large bowl of spaghetti on the table.

"Hey!" Gabby walks out of her bedroom. "Aly isn't here yet?"

"She's on her way," Michelle, Carter, and Alex say in unison. The hair on the back of my neck stands up. Why am I suddenly feeling so anxious?

I take a swig of my beer and watch Gabby and Michelle set the table. The girls always insist that they handle the setup, and the guys are in charge of cleanup. It doesn't bother me in the least. I'm just happy to get a home-cooked meal, and both of these girls know how to cook. Gabby is known for her Mexican-style food. Alex proposes to her every time she makes her famous empanadas. Michelle is a great cook but is more into baking. Her cakes and cookies could give any bakery a run for their money.

We genuinely like these ladies and think of them as sisters—except for their last roommate, but that's a whole other story and we blame it all on Alex. But it's an unspoken rule we don't fuck with them, in every meaning of the word. I have no doubt that it will be the same with Aly. What's that saying? You don't shit where you eat?

"Hey, guys! Sorry I'm late," I hear from the door. I look up to see the most beautiful girl—no, *woman*—I've ever laid eyes on, and she's standing no less than fifteen feet in front of me. Her dirty-blond hair is down, framing her angelic face. The hem of her light green wrap dress is slightly above the knee, revealing her long, lean legs. Her body is a mixture of athletic and soft. She's in heels, but I can tell that even without them, she is significantly taller than Gabby and Michelle. Now that stupid nickname Alex gave her makes sense.

Crash!

I drop my freaking beer. Pieces of glass shatter as soon as the bottle hits the tile. The amber liquid splashes all over the white cabinets and pools onto the floor.

"You okay, man?" Carter comes up from behind me with a roll of paper towels in his hand.

"Yeah, I don't know what happened. It just slipped from my hand."

"No worries." He hands me some cleaner. "I'll help you clean it up."

"Everything okay?" A sweet as sugar voice comes from beside me. I turn to meet two large sky-blue eyes looking at me with curiosity. Her face up close is even more beautiful than I thought. I open my mouth to speak, but nothing comes out. What the hell is wrong with me? I don't get tongue-tied when it comes to women.

"Yeah, we got it, Aly," Carter pipes up from the floor.

"Hi! You must be Jax." She puts out her hand to shake mine.

"Uh, y-yeah. Yeah, I am," I stammer, wipe my hands on my jeans, and stick my hand out to shake hers. An electrical current flows through my arm the moment our hands touch. I can write it off as my imagination, but I notice her eyes widen and her breath hitches before she quickly releases my hand and steps back.

"Thank God you're here, Legs!" Alex whines. "Michelle said I couldn't eat until you arrived. I was about to die of starvation."

"Oh, please, like you didn't have your second lunch a few hours ago," Gabby jokes.

"I'm a growing boy, baby girl. I got needs." Alex winks at her, earning a collective eye roll from all the girls.

Carter and I finish cleaning up my mess and head for the farmhouse-style table. While no one is officially assigned a seat, it's a habit for Michelle and Gabby to sit across from Carter and Alex. On the days I show up, I sit on the other side of Alex. The girls' old roommate, Carrie, used to sit across from me. Now that she is gone, Aly is in her place instead.

"So why were you late, Legs?' Alex asks, shoveling a forkful of salad in his mouth.

"Ugh, I got pulled over. I swear I wasn't speeding, but the cop said I was going five miles over the speed limit."

"No shit! Did he give you a ticket?"

"Yup."

"That's bull! For five miles over?"

"Seriously! I've never had a speeding ticket before or any kind of ticket for that matter."

"That's 'cause you got those Georgia plates still on your car. You stick out like a sore thumb. Why haven't you switched everything over to Oregon?"

"Uh..." Aly stiffens. "I'm only here for a year. I felt like it would be foolish to change everything over and then switch it back again when I return. I'm not considered a resident; I'm just visiting." Everyone else seems to accept that answer, but I can tell she's lying.

The subject changes to other random topics. I try to focus on the food on my plate rather than the beauty sitting across from me, but I keep feeling her eyes on me. Every now and then, I look up to find Aly studying me, like she's working on a puzzle and can't get the pieces to fit.

After the fourth or fifth time I catch her looking at me, I lean over the table. "Is something wrong?"

"No." She shakes her head. "It's just that you seem familiar and I can't figure out why."

"Never seen you before," I grumble and twirl the spaghetti around my fork.

"You've probably seen him in the parking lot or in a store," Michelle suggests.

"Yeah, maybe..." Her voice trails off.

I'm certain I've never encountered Aly before. I would've noticed her in the parking lot or in a store, and she's not the type of girl I pick up at the bar. The type of girls I pick up at the bar have a harder look; they wear too much makeup and too little clothes that leave nothing to the imagination. Aly is not that type of girl; she's the type of girl you proudly bring home to your parents.

As I reach across the table for more spaghetti, the long sleeve of my shirt lifts. I purposely covered up because I didn't want to be a spectacle for the new girl. I hate when people stare at me, or worse, take pity on my attempt to hide my scars. Too late. I watch Aly's eyes go wide as she catches a glimpse of my tattoos. They're probably too rough-looking for this good girl.

I contemplate saying something to her about the staring, but before I get the chance, she jumps a little in her seat and blurts out, "Angry Butterfly Guy!"

Everyone at the table stops what they're doing and shifts their focus towards us. *What the hell is she talking about?*

"You're Angry Butterfly Guy!" She repeats like this time I will magically understand, but then I put it all together. The butterfly—she's talking about my stroke.

"You're the one who's been stealing my lane?" I nearly yell.

"Seriously?" She scrunches up her nose. "I don't steal your lane. I'm always there first."

"But it's my lane. It's been my lane since this place opened," I argue. I can't believe I'm sitting across the table from the girl who has been disrupting my daily routine for weeks now. Why didn't I put it together sooner? I mean, sure, I can't really tell what she looks like while we're swimming, but I should've made the connection between the timing of the girls getting a new roommate and a new girl in the pool.

"Well, good for you, but I'm here now and I'm pretty sure the pool is open to anyone who lives here so..." She makes a shrugging motion.

"No, I've been here since the beginning; everyone knows that's my lane."

She throws her head back with a cackle. "Everyone? Who? I've never seen anyone else there and you, sir"—she points a finger at me—"are a royal pain in the ass!"

The rest of the table remains silent as they watch us volley back and forth. I hate the attention from them.

"Excuse me?" I cross my arms over my chest, hoping that my attempt to show dominance will make her back down... It doesn't.

"You have the most aggressive butterfly I have ever seen. Every time you get near me, you send a mini tsunami into my face. I swear you're trying to drown me on purpose. You really need to work on being more delicate."

"In case you didn't notice, sweetheart, there's nothing delicate about me." My tone is harsher than intended. Aly's cheeks begin to flush.

"Soooo... I take it you know each other?" Alex asks, breaking the tension.

"Apparently, we've been swimming next to each other every morning," I grumble.

"Wait!" Michelle chimes in. "Aly has been here for like two weeks. You've been swimming with each other the whole time and didn't know it?"

"Never saw a face," we say at the same time, causing an eruption of laughter from everyone at the table. Well, almost everyone. Aly remains stoic, but the light flush of her cheeks persists.

"Your flip turns suck," I finally say.

"Really, Captain Obvious, or excuse me, Angry Butterfly Guy, the pool is too short with no markings. I can't get my timing right. At least I'm not on a homicide mission every morning. Do you just wake up and think to yourself, today I'm going to choose violence?"

Muffled laughter erupts from around the table.

"I'm not a violent guy," I grit out.

"Well, your butterfly suggests otherwise." She gives a snarky little chin lift that makes me want to reach across the table and kiss that smirk right off her face. Wait. What?! This girl has me all bent out of shape.

11

Aly

"So, that was hot," Michelle says as she sits down on the couch with a caddy of nail polish.

"What was?" I ask innocently, although I have a feeling she's referring to my go-around with a certain dinner guest.

"That little exchange you had with Jax at dinner. You seriously didn't know who he was?"

I shake my head. "I'm in the water before him and I leave before he does. Our faces are always in the water. I can see some features, but not smaller details. It wasn't until I saw his tattoos that I put two and two together. I mean, what are the odds that the guy who's been swimming next to me lives across the hall?"

"So, you've seen his body, just not his face?"

"Correct." I never imagined he would have such intense steel-gray eyes behind the silver goggles he wears.

"Does he wear one of those little Speedos?"

I bust out laughing. "No! Thank God! No man, no matter how built they are, looks good in one of those things! He wears a tighter version of swim trunks." Normal swim trunks are too loose for swimmers. Plus, they can balloon up in the water. The type Jax wears helps him glide through the water but is less revealing than a Speedo.

"And how well built is he?" Gabby waggles her eyebrows as she takes a seat next to Michelle.

"Very. But I wouldn't tell him that. Honestly, he's built very similar to Alex, maybe a little broader in the chest, and of course he's got the tattoos."

The girls nod in understanding. In the few short weeks I've lived here, I've discovered that Alex is not a fan of clothes. That man has no shame in showing off his body. He does have a gorgeous, chiseled physique, but I swear I've seen him shirtless more times than not. Michelle finally made it a rule that he must wear a shirt while at the dinner table.

"Speaking of his tattoos, does he have any more than just the sleeve?" Gabby asks as she picks out a pretty shade of shimmery watermelon nail polish.

"Yeah. He has the Navy insignia on his chest." It took me a while to figure it out, but once I got a good look at it, I could see what it was. I'd know that symbol anywhere. As a kid, I grew up right outside of Norfolk Naval Base. My parents were civilians, but I went to school with a ton of military kids. I know most people called them military brats, but they never seemed like brats to me. Some of them were the nicest kids I'd ever met. Unfortunately, I lost a lot of friends as they moved all around the world while I stayed stagnant.

"Oh yeah!" Gabby perks up. "Alex told me Jax was in the Navy but got injured or something. I noticed he has some scarring on the arm where he has his tattoos."

"That's what it is!" I point a finger, realizing Gabby is right. "I noticed there was something different about the tattoos on his arm, but I couldn't figure it out. He's too fast in the water to let me get a long enough look."

"I've seen him a couple of times in short sleeves." Gabby shrugs. "I think it's the nurse in me that noticed it. The ink covers them up pretty well. I'm sure that was done on purpose, but I never felt comfortable enough to ask."

"How awful," Michelle interjects. "We really don't know much about him and it's not for lack of us trying. It's a miracle he comes to dinner every now and then. He's always so closed off."

"He didn't seem closed off to me," I say. Gabby and Michelle exchange a strange look between them. "What?"

"That's the most we've ever heard Jax talk," Gabby answers.

"Really?" I scrunch up my nose in surprise. He didn't seem to have an issue complaining about me.

"Oh yeah, he's always super broody and kind of mysterious. I know he was one of the first people to move into the condos when they were built and he was the last one I met on this floor. No one really knows much about him or what he even does for a living. He keeps to himself mostly, although I know he's friendlier with Alex and Carter. They hang out at the bar and sometimes work out together at the gym."

"No one knows what he does?" That's pretty odd to live right next door to someone and not know much about them. Then again, I lived in Beaute for the last thirteen years. Everyone there knows what kind of toothpaste your mom's uncle's cousin twice removed uses.

"Nope. I think the boys know, but they think it's funny that we don't. We've guessed everything from stripper to hitman for hire," Gabby jokes.

"Anyway," Michelle continues, "if I didn't know any better, I'd say there were some sparks flying between the two of you tonight."

"Oh, no. No way. He was just mad at me for hogging *his lane*." I use air quotes on the last two words.

"I don't know." Gabby shakes her head. "I thought I saw some sparks too."

"You two are crazy. There were no sparks."

Okay, I did feel something. Something happened when we shook hands. I tried to convince myself it's because I've gone so long without any physical contact. Although, I did give Carter a hug the other day when he took me to see the ocean and I didn't feel any weird sensations.

No matter what, I'm not going to act on it. I can't. I'm done with the whole dating scene. I have been hurt and humiliated. Ending the relationship with Trent was hard enough; being referred to as the runaway bride everywhere I went just added salt to the wound. I have no desire to open myself to something like that ever again.

12

Jax

I get back from my place and make a beeline for the liquor cabinet. I'm not usually big on the hard stuff, but I'm completely bent out of shape after whatever that was at dinner tonight. I called her sweetheart? What the hell? My phone vibrates with a text message from my sister.

Emma: You owe me, big brother!

Me: What do I owe you?

A picture pops up on my screen. It looks like an ultrasound. I'm not good at reading these things. They basically look like one of those inkblot tests, but I can clearly read the labels "Baby A" and "Baby B." Holy shit! Emma is actually having twins!

A picture of my sister pops up with Emma's incoming call. "Is that what I think it is?" I answer.

"Well, hello to you too!" she responds chipperly.

"Ems, seriously, are you having twins?" I pull out some whiskey and debate using a glass or drinking straight from the bottle. I take a swig from the bottle; no sense in wasting a cup.

"Yes!" she squeals. "I had my ultrasound this morning. Mom came with me, but the doctor allowed Grant to be on video. Mom is flipping out right now. Grant looked white as a ghost, but he'll be okay."

"That's...wow! That's incredible! How are you feeling?"

"I'm great! Mom was in shock, but I'm going with the flow. It wasn't a surprise. I knew I was having twins."

"Because of what Gram said?"

"Because of what Gram said. And you know what that means! You have to tell me what Gram said to you. I know it was more than she just wanted to see you settled down. I saw the look on your face when I asked you. She said something more. Spill it!"

"Didn't I say I would tell you if it was confirmed twin girls?"

"Nope. Our deal was you would tell me when it was confirmed that I was having twins. We didn't include the sex of the babies but trust me, they're both girls. I just know it. Don't try to get out of this."

"Fine." I sit down on the couch and take a sip of my drink. "Gram told me that she always knew who I was supposed to be with and that she was on her way."

Silence.

"Ems? Are you there?" I look at my phone to see if I lost the connection, then hear sniffling on the other end. "Are you crying?"

"Yeah, I am." She sniffs. "I really hope that's true."

"Ems—"

"If you say you're fine, I swear I'm going to come through this phone and slap you! You are not fine! You haven't been fine since high school, and that was over a decade ago, Jax. A decade! You have been going through the motions for years now like a robot. You never laugh anymore! I miss your laugh!" She sniffles again. "Can you humor me for just a bit?"

"Sure, I guess I can."

"Gram told you that she knew who you were meant to be with? That is a little weird. Does that mean you know her too? Do I know her? And how long has she known this girl? Wait! It is a girl, right? You and Travis aren't more than...you know...friends?"

"Hilarious, Ems, and yes, Gram was definitely referring to a female. Look, don't put much stock into this. You know her mind wasn't as clear towards the end. Maybe she was dreaming, or the pain meds were messing with her or something."

"But she was right about the twins," Emma counters.

"Yeah, yeah, I know." I lift my drink to my lips, but a thought occurs to me. "Do you know anyone from Georgia?"

"Umm... I don't think so. Why? Did you meet someone?"

"No, nothing like that," I lie. "Forget I said anything." I change the focus back to Emma's pregnancy and we talk a little longer before ending the call.

She's already on her way.

Those were the last words Gram ever spoke to me—to anyone for that matter. Her final words were about someone who may or may not even exist. I'd be lying if I said I haven't thought about what Gram said to me. I thought we knew all the same people. If it was someone I knew, why didn't she just come out and say it? She also said we were supposed to meet years ago. What does that mean? Did Gram not know where she was? If this girl even exists, who's to say she isn't married by now?

I shake my head and take another sip of my drink. Why am I wondering about some hypothetical girl? I've stood by my bachelor status for years. Though Emma was right about me not laughing anymore. I used to be a happy-go-lucky kind of guy, but that was so many years ago. Truth be told, I'm afraid to be happy again.

The next morning, I arrive at the pool a little earlier, hoping to get there before Aly and reclaim my lane. A mixture of disappointment and excitement hits me as soon as I see her well into her routine. I might not get my lane back, but at least I get to enjoy the view. I watch Aly propel herself through the water and crash her feet against the wall of the pool as she flip turns. I wince; been there, done that. While the pool at our condo is nice, it's smaller than the normal Olympic-sized pool and it doesn't have markers on the bottom to help time your turns. If you time them too fast, you can't properly push off the side, and if you time them too slow, you risk crashing into the wall.

As she makes her way towards the shallow end, I place my hand low on the wall with my palm facing her. It's a signal used to get the attention of swimmers since yelling doesn't exactly work. She slows her pace as she approaches.

"What?" She pops out of the water and moves her goggles to the top of her head. "Are you going to tell me that I'm hogging your lane again?"

"No." I roll my eyes and duck my head under the rope into her lane. "Come here," I tell her, but before she can respond, I place my arms around her waist and spin her so her back is flat against my chest. As soon as her body is flush against mine, an overwhelming and very foreign feeling comes over me. I can't quite figure out what it is, but I like it. I grab her right hand and place it up against the side of the pool.

"Wh-What are you doing?" she stammers. Shit. I think I accidentally scared her. It wasn't intentional, but I've quickly realized that being around Aly throws me off-balance.

"Put your hand right here." I slowly move her hand up and down the side of the pool. "Do you feel that?"

"I...umm...oh wait!" I feel her do a little hop when she realizes that the wall isn't as smooth as it should be.

"There's a flaw in the liner. It's faint, but once you know where it is, you can't unsee it. It goes straight down and ends near the middle." She tries to turn to look at me, but I can't let go of her waist...not yet. Even though we're surrounded by chlorine, I can still detect the scent of her shampoo, some type of coconut-vanilla mixture. I lean down close to her ear. "When that comes into view, start counting. It takes three strokes for me, but it might take five or six for you. As for the deep end, try using the filter as your guide. It's a bit of a pain in the ass since it's in your periphery, but you get used to it eventually."

"Thank you," she says in a near whisper. The sound of her soft voice and her body up against mine send me into overdrive. I release her waist and quickly duck back under the lane line to continue my swim. I don't stop until she finishes her workout and leaves the pool area.

13

Jax

Tonight, we are celebrating Alex's birthday. It's not for a few more days, but today is the only day everyone could get together. Gabby made Alex his favorite empanadas for dinner, then Michelle made him a double chocolate almond raspberry cake. Now, the girls are primping to go to The Local for a few drinks.

I managed to ignore Aly throughout dinner. I know I need to be careful; the girl is doing strange things to me. I got too close to her at the pool the other day. I could've easily shown her the mark in the pool without touching her, but something about her makes me want to be as close as possible. We ended up in the elevator the other day and I purposely reached for the button at the same time just so I could brush my hand against hers. Yeah, I find myself drawn to her, but this shit has to stop. There are a ton of reasons why we're not right for each other.

"So, what are your big plans for the actual day?" Carter asks Alex while we wait for the girls to get ready. He turns towards the counter and starts eating some baked stuff Michelle has made.

"Work, man. Smitty's wife just gave birth, so he's out on paternity leave. Everyone is taking turns filling in for him. But I'm going home to visit my family next weekend." He stretches his arms and places them behind his head. "My parents miss their golden child."

"Their golden child?" Aly asks as she walks out of her room. I notice she's a minimalist when it comes to her looks. She doesn't overdo her makeup and wears small, simplistic jewelry. That short denim skirt and the deep purple halter top that wraps gracefully around her neck do absolutely nothing for me. That's my story and I'm sticking to it.

"Don't you know? I'm the youngest of seven, Legs. My parents stopped once they had me...'cause why mess with perfection?" He gives her a wink.

"Yes, I'm sure it had nothing to do with the fact that your mom was exhausted after having all those kids." She spins around to face the kitchen area. "Geez, Carter! Are you eating again?"

Carter holds up a plastic container. "I saw these when I was cleaning. I figured it was fair game," he says with a full mouth of...what the hell is he eating?

Aly walks over to Carter and pulls out something that looks like a giant piece of male anatomy. She busts out in a fit of giggles. "Michelle! What are these?"

"Yeah, they are my latest Pinterest fail." Michelle sighs, coming out of her room. "They're supposed to be biscotti, but something went wrong."

"Oh, something definitely went wrong." Aly giggles, still holding the phallic cookie.

"Dude! Put that down! You're literally eating dick!" Alex yells at Carter.

"Well, it tastes delicious!" Carter takes another bite. I cringe. Something about this scene feels cannibalistic. "Try some, Aly!" he encourages.

I let out an audible gasping sound and everyone swings their head to look at me. For some reason, the thought of this wholesome-looking girl eating a pornographic cookie makes me cringe. Also, I think I may be jealous of the cookie.

Aly takes the cookie, looks me straight in the eye, and breaks off a piece. All three of us guys wince in vicarious horror. I take it back; I am no longer jealous of the cookie. She pops the cookie in her mouth and her eyes go wide. "Oh my God! Michelle, these are fantastic!"

"Really?" Michelle asks with wonder. "I was so disappointed with how they looked that I didn't even try one."

"Oh, yes," Aly gushes. "They're definitely not the texture of biscotti, but they could make a good butter cookie. Do I taste vanilla and...lemon?"

"Orange, actually!" Michelle corrects. "It was supposed to be like a creamsicle!"

Alex begins to choke on air.

"Oh, Alex, grow up." Aly rolls her eyes, takes another cookie, and hands it to him. "Here, try it." We watch as a small showdown goes on between Alex and Aly. Alex clearly does not want to try it, but Aly won't back down.

"Oh, come on, Alex." Gabby comes up from behind Aly. She must've been watching the shit show from the hallway. "I would figure a tough man like you would be secure enough in his manhood to try a cookie shaped like...well, his manhood."

Not wanting to disappoint Gabby, Alex takes the cookie and shoves the whole thing in his mouth. "I arur en I enood!" The girls burst into hysterical laughter. Alex, who has clearly bitten off more than he can chew, looks like a chipmunk storing acorns for the winter.

"Hey!" Alex says once he's finished. "That's really good, Peanut!"

"Told ya!" says Carter. "Do you think you could make these again, but you know, in regular cookie form?" he asks Michelle.

"I can absolutely make these again, and trust me, I will shape them differently next time," Michelle answers.

"You know there's a whole industry for this kind of stuff. Back in Beaute, we had two bakeries: a traditional one and an erotic one." Aly casually steps in front of me to grab her purse. "My best friend Jess had a crazy bachelorette party a few years ago. Her cousin, Britany, and I were co-maids of honor and Britany went all out with the decorations and food. We had penis-shaped balloons, sandwiches, and cupcakes."

"Yes!" Gabby says. "Back in Phoenix, I went to a bachelorette party like that for one of the nurses I worked with. Did you play pin the junk on the hunk?"

"Came in first!" Aly says proudly.

"Girl, me too! Although there was a five-way tie. Guess that's what happens when you get a bunch of nurses trying to accurately locate a male's appendage."

I tilt my head towards the ceiling, close my eyes, and silently count to ten. When I open my eyes again, I see Aly watching with me with an amused look on her face.

"I'm making you uncomfortable talking about this, aren't I?" A playful smile curls on her lips.

"I'm fine," I grumble.

"I'd ask if you want a cookie, but I already know the answer." She slips her purse over her shoulder with a smug look.

With the girls finally ready to go, we all head out the door. "Wait a minute!" I yell as we get to the parking lot. "How are we going to get there?"

"Do you want to hold hands and skip?" Aly says sweetly while fluttering her eyelashes. Her little teasing does things to me, things I like too much.

"I mean," I say through gritted teeth, "there are six of us and no one has a car big enough for all of us to go in one vehicle."

"Aw, crud," Michelle whines. "This means we'll need two designated drivers."

Originally, Gabby volunteered herself to be the designated driver, stating that she had an early meeting tomorrow.

"I'll do it!" Carter raises his hand like he's in school. "It's probably better that I stick to water since Michelle is going to have me dancing most of the time."

Michelle gives a wide, appreciative smile. I've been out to the bar once or twice with them. Michelle will stay on the dance floor all night and Carter always takes it as a challenge to keep up.

"Perfect! So, the girls will go in one car with Gabby as our DD and the boys can go in another with Carter as their DD," Michelle says in a singsong voice.

I huff as I climb into the back seat of Carter's Jeep. "I can't stand that girl!" I also hate sitting in the back of any vehicle. I'm six four; back seats aren't built for me. Alex is slightly shorter than me at six two; he wouldn't fit much better back here and the ass called shotgun before I did. Plus, it's his birthday, so I guess it's only fair to let him sit up front.

"Who? Aly?" Carters asks while putting his seat belt on.

"Yes, Aly." I lean forward between the front seats and place my elbows on each headrest.

"Why? She's terrific! I think she makes a great addition to the girls."

"Yeah, she's so much better than Carrie," Alex snorts. "And better looking too!"

Carter turns his head to look back at me. "Have you even tried getting to know her?"

That's my problem. I have a feeling that if I get to know her, I'll want to know more.

14

Aly

Everyone splits off in different directions as soon as we get into The Local. Michelle immediately pulls Carter onto the dance floor, Alex and Jax grab seats at the bar, while Gabby and I settle into a booth. I'm still full from dinner, but Gabby swears the nachos here are the best. It's my first time here, but I've heard from several coworkers that this is one of Starboard Beach's favorite places. It's easy to see why it's a popular place. There is a light, airy feel to it with beachy décor and reclaimed wooden tables and chairs. I take in a deep breath. I swear this place smells more like funnel cake than your typical stuffy bar.

"Oh! We have to order the buffalo wings and fried Oreos too!" Gabby does a little dance in her seat. "I'm so excited for you to try everything here."

"Are you sure we can handle all that food? I'm still pretty stuffed from dinner and birthday cake."

"Ah, it'll be fine. Just sample a little of everything. The guys will finish whatever we don't eat."

"I guess that is a perk to having them around," I reason.

Not only is this my first real outing since coming to Starboard Beach, but it's the first time I've gone out socially in about a year. It feels freeing to be out with friends again.

A few negative thoughts pop into my head, but I squash them down, reminding myself that I'm in a crowded bar and after all, there's safety in numbers. If anything were to occur, I feel like my roommates would have my back. I know Alex or Carter would step in too, if something were to happen. And then there's Jax. I turn to look at him sitting at the bar. I don't think he would sit back and let shit happen, but I still can't figure him out. Something tells me he has a history that he's not too eager to share with me or anyone else, and I can respect that.

A commotion near the dance floor has me turning my focus off my handsome, albeit aloof, neighbor and towards Michelle and Carter. Gabby and I both slide out of our booth for a better view.

"I cannot believe Michelle can dance in those five-inch heels!" I say to Gabby. Even though her heels give her nearly a half foot more in height, she is still several inches shorter than Carter.

"That girl is a beast on the dance floor! I've even seen her rock five-inch heels before. She's unbelievable."

I let out a low whistle. I'm not brave enough to go past a three-inch heel, but more power to her. The music changes into the infamous song from *Dirty Dancing*, and Carter and Michelle fall right into step. I watch the two in awe.

"Is there something going on between them?" I ask Gabby.

"I don't think so." She shakes her head, not taking her eyes off the dance floor. "I think they're just really good friends. Carter did have a girlfriend for a while, but I haven't seen her around recently."

The music continues, and Michelle and Carter have now gathered a small crowd around them. They're fantastic.

"Have they practiced this before?"

"Yeah." Gabby nods. "I've seen them do the whole routine in our living room, but it still gets me every time."

"Tell me he does the lift!" I grab on to Gabby's arm and start jumping up and down. I'm not a super girly girl or overly romantic person, but this is so exciting to watch.

The wide grin that spreads across Gabby's face is all the answer I need. We watch in excited silence as Carter and Michelle nail the famous lift. We whoop and holler as Carter slowly brings Michelle's feet back to the floor, both smiling brightly and looking at each other as if there's no one else in the room.

A ping of sadness hits me. I wish someone looked at me like that. I know I've said I've sworn off dating, but I'm not going to lie; the last year and a half has been tremendously lonely.

"Excuse me." A lanky, fair-skinned man with a delicious accent approaches. Standing next to him is a similar-looking man that's slightly shorter. "Would you two ladies be interested in a game of darts?"

"Nice accents! Are you from Ireland?" I ask. I'm a sucker for a foreign accent.

"Yes! We're from Limerick. I'm Declan and this is my brother, Shawn," the taller one says.

Gabby and I introduce ourselves and walk over to the dartboards with the two Irish brothers. They proceed to tell us that they are here in the States on business and work in marketing. Declan talks about the latest deal they just made—something about a big merger, which means lots of money. I pretend I'm interested because I'm too nice and don't want to offend anyone, but in actuality, I'm bored to tears. I have no interest in marketing and no interest in people who flaunt their money.

"I'm going to get a refill. Does anyone want anything?" Shawn shakes his empty glass. The three of us decline and Shawn heads to the bar. He comes back a few minutes later, sans drink. He whispers something to his brother and they both turn to face us.

"Ladies, thank you for the lovely game, but I just got a call from a coworker of ours. Something with work came up and we need to get going," Shawn says.

"We wish you all the best," Declan adds.

Gabby and I share confused looks but thank the guys and watch them hastily leave.

"Did you find that—"

"Strange?" Gabby responds. "Yeah, they already said they were done with work and then all of a sudden something comes up on a Friday night?"

I shrug it off. It's weird, but at least I no longer have to be subjected to listening to the latest trend in hamster toys.

"It looks like Michelle is taking a break. I'm going to grab a drink with her. Did I mention this place makes the best mocktails?" Gabby asks.

"I don't think so." I look around the bar. "I'm going to use the bathroom. I'll meet you over there."

As I make my way through the crowd, I can't help but get the feeling someone is watching me—but in a good kind of way.

15

Jax

Taking a sip of my beer, I train my eyes on Aly playing darts with Gabby and two guys who seem too cocky for their own good. The taller one keeps trying to show Aly how to aim just right. He lightly touches her arm and something deep within me begins to churn. I don't know what to think about Aly, but I know I don't like seeing someone else interested in her.

The shorter of the two breaks away from the group and makes his way over to where I'm sitting at the bar. I lean over into his space. "I hope you're not planning on getting some action with either of those two tonight," I tilt my head in the direction of Aly and Gabby.

"Now, that's none of your business, is it?" he responds with an Irish lilt.

"Look, I'm just trying to help a brother out." I feign innocence. "Those girls live in my building. We're neighbors. All I'm saying is if you're planning on taking them home tonight, you're shit out of luck."

"And why is that?" Smiley O' Jackass asks.

"They're girlfriends."

"I can see that." He rolls his eyes while trying to get the bartender's attention.

"No, I mean they're girlfriends—you know, lovers?"

Cocky McTightpants looks at the girls and then back at me. "You can't be serious!"

"I am serious. They don't like to put it out there, but I'm telling you. Those two are in love. Aly, the taller one, just moved in with Gabby about a month ago."

"She did say she just moved here from—"

"Georgia, I know. Apparently, they met on some sort of dating app and fell in love. Aly left everything behind to come out here so they can be together." We both look over at the girls. Gabby hits a bull's-eye, and the girls hug each other and squeal with delight. They're playing right into my spiel and don't even know it.

"Huh, thanks, man," he says as he walks away.

"No problem." I give him the fakest genuine-looking smile I can muster.

"You're going to hell for that." Alex chuckles and claps me on the shoulder. "I'm going to find Carter."

Alex no sooner leaves his stool than a bleached-blond woman in a tight red dress comes up to me. "Is this seat taken?"

I want to tell her yes. I'm not interested in hooking up with anyone tonight. But then my eyes fall on Aly walking past the bar. Maybe it would be better to have a distraction or else I may be tempted to do something I shouldn't.

16

Aly

"Dude, you just missed Jax epically cockblock the girls!" I hear Alex as I make my way out of the bathroom. I look around to see where his voice is coming from and notice the top of his head peeking out from the other side of the jukebox. I move my body closer and duck down a bit.

"What happened?" I hear Carter's breathy voice.

"So, Gabby and Aly were playing darts with these two guys. They were looking all happy and shit, but then one of them went over to the bar to get a drink. That's when Jax stops the guy and gives him this whole story on how Gabby and Aly are a lesbian couple."

That's why the guys took off so quickly! I had no intention of taking anything further with them and neither did Gabby, but I'm pissed that it wasn't our call. Why would he do that? Did he not like us talking to other guys? I don't think he has a thing for Gabby; it's clear that Alex is head over heels for her, and I don't think Jax would infringe upon whatever it is they have. Maybe it's me...probably because I annoy him.

I look over at Jax sitting at the bar. A busty blonde moves onto the stool next to him and they strike up a conversation. I make my way over to them. Two can play at this game.

"Hey, honey!" I croon as soon as I reach Jax. I wrap my arms around his shoulders and give him a quick kiss on the cheek. His five o'clock shadow tickles my lips, and his scent is a mixture of his bodywash and chlorine. I pull back and remind myself not to get distracted and stick to the plan.

He turns to me with a stunned expression.

"I have the best news!" I announce loudly, pretending not to notice the busty blonde next to him. "I found a local pharmacy that carries that special cream the doctor recommended."

"Umm...what?" Jax says, confused.

"You know"—I dramatically look down at his crotch and back up again—"for that situation."

Jax's mouth opens and closes like a fish out of water. I whip out my phone and pull up a random app, making sure no one around me can see my screen.

"It says here the redness and swelling may take a while to go away, but you should receive itch relief instantly."

"Aly," Jax says slowly like he's giving me a warning, but the lift in the corners of his mouth gives him away.

I feign complete ignorance and stare at my phone intently, trying to keep a straight face. "There are some side effects listed, but they don't seem so bad... What does chafing mean?"

I hear a thumping noise and look up to see that the busty blonde is nowhere to be found. Then I turn to Jax. His face is a magnificent shade of crimson, his eyes are the size of saucers, and his jaw is about ready to hit the floor.

"Well, my work here is done! Guess I'll head back to my lesbian lover now." I boop his nose and leave before he has a chance to respond. As I walk past the bar towards the booth

Gabby and I are sharing, Alex and Carter come up to me laughing.

"Good one, Aly." Carter puts his hand up for a high five and I reciprocate.

"That was awesome, Legs," Alex says, pulling me into a side hug. "Seeing Jax's face was the best birthday gift of the night."

"Glad I could make your day." We all head over to the booth where Gabby and Michelle are enjoying a smorgasbord of bar food.

"This looks amaz—" I start but feel a tug on the back of my arm. I stumble backward into what feels like a brick wall. A warm brick wall that smells like Jax. Oh, shit.

He holds me in place but looks around me to speak to the rest of the table. "Gabby, can Carter and Alex get a ride back home with you? Carter, can I have your keys? I think Aly and I need to go for a ride and have a little talk."

Gabby nods in agreement but gives a confused look.

"Umm...okay?" Carter says hesitantly. "Have you been drinking?"

"Only had one sip of beer. I'm completely sober." He lets go of my arm and places his hand gently on my hip.

"Are you okay going with Jax, Aly?" Carter slowly pulls out the keys to his Jeep and I realize he's holding them hostage until I give my answer. I have no idea what is going on in Jax's head, but the thought of being alone with him doesn't scare me in the least. If anything, I'm kind of excited and definitely intrigued.

"Yeah, I'm okay with that." I turn towards Jax and try to get a read on him, but his face is stoic as usual.

Carter tosses the keys to Jax, who leans down and whispers in my ear, "Let's go." He places his hand on the small of my back and guides me towards the parking lot and away from my friends, who looked just as utterly baffled as I feel.

17

Jax

"Where are we going?" Aly asks as she straps on her seat belt.

I'm surprised she agreed to go with me so willingly. It's not like I would've forced her to go if she didn't want to, but she did respond quicker than I expected.

"To the pharmacy to get that cream I apparently need," I say flatly.

Aly throws her head back against the seat in a full-on belly laugh. I bite my tongue, trying to keep a straight face, but dammit, her laughter is contagious. And really, the shit she pulled was funny.

"You should've seen your face!"

"Did you really have to give me some nasty disease?" I try to hide my grin.

"*I* didn't give you anything." She smirks. "And I never said it was a disease. I just said you had a rash with itching and—"

"Yeah, yeah. I know." I pull out of the parking lot and onto the main highway. I actually have no idea where I'm going. I didn't get that far into this plan of mine. All I knew was that I wanted Aly to myself.

"Well, I never would've done that if you hadn't told those guys that Gabby and I are lovers."

"How did you even know about that?" The answer pops into my head as soon as the words leave my lips.

"Alex," we both say in unison.

"In his defense, I overheard him telling Carter." She shrugs and looks out the window.

"No one has ever pulled anything like that on me before."

"Well, maybe it's about time someone gave you a taste of your own medicine," she says with a smug look. And I like it. I like her spunk. She gives as good as she gets.

This girl is nothing like what I'm used to. I typically get one of two reactions from women. They either find my hard looks intimidating and pretend I don't exist, or they throw themselves at me because they know I'm only looking for a quick lay. There is the exception of Michelle and Gabby. But I'm pretty sure they never would've talked to me had they not seen me hanging out with Carter and Alex.

"You never told me where we're going," she continues.

Shit. She has me so distracted that I still haven't come up with an idea. I open my mouth to say something, but then I hear a rumbling noise and see Aly put her hands on her stomach.

"Did your stomach just growl?"

"Maybe..." she responds.

"You're still hungry?" I notice Aly isn't shy when it comes to food. Which is another thing I like about her. I hate when women eat like birds.

"I was full from dinner, but I had been mentally preparing myself for all the food Gabby wanted me to try at The Local."

"You didn't eat anything there?"

"Uh, I was kinda preoccupied and then someone insisted I go with him...wherever." She waves her hand around in the air.

"Okay, fine. I know where I'll take you." I turn Carter's Jeep around. A quick two-minute drive later, we pull up to what looks like a little hole-in-the-wall. Aly reads the hand-painted wooden sign above the building that looks no bigger than a shack.

"Whips?" she asks with an amused tone to her voice.

"Gabby and Michelle haven't told you about this place?"

"Uh, no. I think I would remember a name like that." She jumps out of the Jeep, and her eyes immediately focus on the large menu attached to the outside walls. Whips is actually a place to get ice cream. They have your typical flavors, but their claim-to-fame is their flavored whipped cream, of which they give generous portions. You tend to get more whipped cream than ice cream. No one complains. It's delicious.

Their shack/hut/stand/whatever you want to call it sits right on the outskirts of the beach, making it a great place to grab some ice cream and take a walk on the sand or sit at one of their picnic tables nearby. It used to only be open during the summer, but a petition went around a few years ago to keep the place open year-round. Now, people just sit in their cars during the winter months and enjoy their frozen desserts with the heat running.

"My favorite is a scoop of coffee ice cream with salted caramel whipped cream," I offer and realize I've never freely given such random information about myself. I prefer to stay a closed book.

"That does sound good," she says, still reading the menu. "But I think I'd like to try the chocolate ice cream with peanut butter whipped cream."

I take out my wallet and head for the counter.

"Wait!" Aly calls. "I can pay."

"I got this." I shake my head. "After all, I did pull you away from the bar food." I look her up and down. "Didn't you have a purse?"

"It's probably back at The Local." She shrugs like it's no big deal. "I'm sure Gabby or Michelle will grab it. Besides, all my important stuff is in my pockets." She pats the sides of her denim skirt. I can't imagine anything fitting in there, but she proves me wrong as she starts pulling random things out of her pockets like she's Mary Poppins.

"How did you pack all of that in there?"

"Habit of a teacher," she answers nonchalantly. She takes a hair tie out of her back pocket and puts her hair up into some sort of bun.

We place our order, receive our ice cream, and decide to take a walk on the beach.

"Is this where Carter took you the other day to see the ocean?" I ask as we walk along the coast.

"Hmm, no. It must've been down farther because I definitely would've remembered seeing this place." She points her spoon towards the back of Whips. "How did you know he took me to see the ocean?"

"He mentioned it when you first moved in. It was before we met. Well, before I knew who you were. I should've put two and two together with you being the new girl and all."

"It's a big building. I could've been anyone." She takes a large spoonful of whipped cream and lets out a moan. "This is delicious! I'm going to yell at Gabby and Michelle for not telling me about this place." She does a little wiggle as she takes another spoonful. I'm grateful she looks towards the ocean because I take that moment to adjust myself. Shit, this girl has me all mixed up.

"So, when did you start swimming?" I ask, trying to think of a topic to distract me from her eating whipped cream.

Except now I'm thinking of her in a bathing suit with those long, lean legs of hers on display. Dammit. This cannot be happening.

"Hmm..." She taps her spoon to those perfectly pink lips of hers. "I think from about six months old? My parents had an inground pool and they didn't like the look of those security gates for kids, so they got me lessons."

"Wow!"

"Yeah, it was like the only good thing they did for me." Her eyes dart away from mine. "I didn't swim competitively until I got into middle school."

"Your middle school had a swim team?"

"Oh, no, my school didn't have a swim team. I swam for my county's recreational team. The school district I grew up in wasn't big on sports. I grew up in Norfolk. The majority of students were military kids, so they were always coming and going throughout the year. Kinda hard to maintain a team like that. What about you?"

"I started swimming around ten when an indoor pool was built in our town. I know it sounds cocky, but I was a natural. I fell in love with the sport and then joined my high school team."

Of course, my love for the water made me a perfect candidate for the Navy. When I enlisted, my recruiter told me I qualified for the construction battalion (better known as Seabees) or a rescue diver. While becoming a rescue diver sounded exciting, in the end, I chose to become a Seabee. If I couldn't become an architect, at least I could learn how to fix or create new structures.

"I swam on the rec team for about four years. I stopped the summer of junior year," she answers.

"Why did you stop?"

"The competition, the cattiness of some of the team members, and the coach was awful. It took a lot of enjoyment out of it for me."

I nod in understanding. Swimming is mainly an individual sport. Many times you end up competing against your own teammates.

"It all worked out for me in the end. I became a lifeguard and loved it."

"The beach?"

"Oh, no." She shakes her head with a look of disgust. "I only guarded pools. I may have grown up right near the ocean, but I don't swim in it."

"Wait, what?" I sputter. "What do you have against the ocean? We're literally standing next to it right now. Are you afraid of sharks or something?"

"No! I love this." She waves her hand out towards the water. "I mean, honestly, I could never live anywhere that's landlocked. Like if a university in the middle of nowhere contacted me, I would have turned down the position without a second thought. Being near the ocean makes me feel like I can breathe. I might not come out to see it every day, but I know it's there and that brings me comfort."

"But..." I smile. The more we talk, the more animated Aly becomes and it's very amusing.

"Fish poop in the ocean."

18

"You don't swim in the ocean because fish poop in it?" Jax howls with laughter. I think this is the first time I've heard him laugh. I have a feeling he doesn't do it often.

"It's not *just* the fish poop," I explain. "Think about it—there are boats that leak fuel, garbage people throw into it, shipwrecks, dead animals, and who knows what else. Yet people just run on in thinking nothing of it."

I think my aversion towards swimming in the ocean started when I went on a field trip in elementary school. We learned how fish unknowingly consume microplastics and other debris. It was supposed to be a lesson on how pollution affects wildlife, but, as usual, my brain took it a step further.

"I've never heard of that before." His voice is light and filled with amusement—a stark contrast to how Trent belittled me for my overthinking.

"I'm serious!" I point out towards the ocean. "You know damn well there are dead bodies out there, but people still go in it anyway. And don't get me started on eating seafood.

People who eat shellfish? They're bottom feeders... BOTTOM FEEDERS! I say I'm allergic to seafood to get out of eating it, but honestly, I'm not."

"What goes on in that head of yours?"

"You have no idea," I say softly. "So, why did you pull me out of The Local anyway?" I ask, wanting to move the focus away from my crazy ideas.

"Oh, umm." He shoves a spoonful of ice cream in his mouth and I know he's stalling. "The truth is... I don't know. You threw me off when you pulled that shit at the bar. No one has ever done anything like that to me. I felt the need to get out of there after that, but I felt like you needed to come with me."

"Well, once again, I wouldn't have done that if—"

"Yeah, I know," he says with a look of remorse. "I didn't get a good vibe off those guys. You...and Gabby don't seem like the type of girls to hook up with guys like that."

"Definity not!" I snort. "Trust me, Gabby and I had no interest in going home with those guys."

"You didn't?" Jax snaps his head to look at me.

"Of course not. I mean, they seemed nice enough and they did have sexy accents, but I'm not looking for anything and neither is Gabby." A few mornings ago, Gabby and I had a heart-to-heart conversation. We both discovered that neither one of us has a desire to be in a relationship right now...or maybe ever. I don't know. This whole swearing off men for eternity thing would be a lot easier if I wasn't currently standing next to Jax. There's something about him that draws me in. Yes, I'm physically attracted to him. I mean, who wouldn't be? But I feel like there's more to him than meets the eye.

"Wow! I didn't expect you to say that."

"What? That I'm not looking for a relationship? Well, I've been there done that." I'd like to say I moved on. I've tried to move on, but Trent is like a gag gift that keeps on giving.

"What does that mean?"

Oh, shit. Did I say that last part out loud? "Oh, umm...nothing." I brush him off.

"Well, you're not the only one who's been there done that."

"Care to elaborate?"

"Nope. You?"

"Nope." I purse my lips together to keep me from saying any more.

Jax's phone dings in his pocket. He pulls it out, reads a message, and rolls his eyes.

"Stand still for a minute. I need to take a picture of you."

"What? Why?"

"Everyone is home and the guys said they want to see proof of life." He holds up his phone for me to see and I burst out laughing when I read it.

"Did they really think you would do something to me?" I can see where Jax's size and chiseled looks may be daunting to some, but I have never once felt unsafe with him.

"I don't know. I usually keep to myself. They're probably just surprised at how I acted." He holds up his phone and snaps a picture of me.

"Well, I'm grateful that you did."

"You are?" He places his phone back in the pocket of his shorts.

"Absolutely! First, I wasn't enjoying my time with those guys, so thank you for getting rid of them. Second, I got to embarrass the crap out of you, which I find hilarious. Third, I have now learned that flavored whipped cream is ah-mazing, and fourth, I got to know a little more about you."

"You really try to see the silver lining in everything, don't you?"

"I try." I look up into his eyes. They remind me of dark, thunderous clouds rolling in off shore on a hot summer day. I wonder what happened to him to cause such turbulence.

19

Jax

It's three thirty in the afternoon, that weird time between lunch and dinner where you don't know whether to eat something light to hold you over until dinner or say screw it and eat something heavy and consider it both lunch and dinner. My sister likes to call it "dunch."

I don't usually have jobs near the university, but today I sold my latest flipped house and the title company's office happens to be a block from campus. I could live simply off my disability check from the Navy, but life can be expensive and I can't sit around all day anyway. After my last tour in Iraq, I realized I could no longer work for someone. The shit show that went down there—losing Taylor and Goodwin to an IED—nearly tore me apart. Working on houses keeps my mind off the negativity and gives me the physical outlet I need. I also get to work with my best friend Travis, who was also injured with me. We recently became partners, but I handle all the paperwork since he's not comfortable in most social situations.

Dealing with people isn't one of my favorite things to do either, but at least the title company's office is next to one of my favorite pizza places, Molly's. It doesn't look like it would be known for pizza; they have a little bit of everything, from pancakes to burgers, and it's set up like a typical fast-food joint where you place your order and they call your number when it's ready. I've had pizza all over the world and for some reason, Molly's is my favorite and the perfect place to celebrate another home sold.

I open the door and the chaos of smells that is signature to the restaurant immediately assaults me. The smell of coffee is always the first to hit my nose. Then comes a mixture of maple syrup, spaghetti sauce, meatloaf, and the crap cologne the frat boys are wearing these days. As I walk up to the counter to place my order, the back of my neck tightens and my heart starts to race. She's in here somewhere. I just know it. My body only reacts this way to her, and for some reason, I've developed a sixth sense that alerts me when she's nearby.

After our first real conversation on the beach, I realized that Aly is someone I could really enjoy having in my life…as a friend. Or at least that's what I keep telling myself. Deep down, I worry I want more than just a friendship, but I can't consume myself with those thoughts.

I place my order with the overly perky college student manning the register. She hands me my order number and drink. As I turn to look for an empty table, I spot Aly in the far-right corner. She is wearing jeans and a green polo with the university's crest of a lion in the upper-left corner. Her dirty-blond hair is pulled back into a messy bun. She is sitting cross-legged on her chair and concentrating on writing something in a notebook. I can't help myself and head towards her table. She must sense me too because she slowly looks in my direction. Her mouth turns into a friendly smile as soon as we lock eyes.

"Hey! What are you doing here?" Her tone is a mixture of surprise and curiosity. She nudges the chair across from her with her foot as if to tell me to sit down.

"I had some business to take care of nearby and missed lunch." I sit down and look at her tray. "Pineapple and pepperoni on your pizza, huh?"

"I know, I know. Some people don't believe pineapple belongs on pizza, but seriously, don't knock it until you try it."

"Perhaps I will," I say.

"Number eighty-four!" a kid yells, pushing a tray onto the counter.

"That's me." I hook my thumb over my shoulder. "Be right back." She nods and puts her notebook away in her bag.

A second later, I place my tray down next to hers and she looks up in disbelief.

"You can't be serious," she says, still staring at my plate.

"Well, you said I should try it."

"Bullshit! You ordered that before you saw what I had." She leans back into her chair, her eyes still on my tray. "Huh, I've never known anyone else to like pineapple and pepperoni on their pizza."

"What can I say? I guess great minds think alike."

Aly and I make small talk as we eat our meal together. She tells me that her schedule changed unexpectedly due to a water main break near the campus. Because of that, all college-level classes temporarily switched to an online format until further notice. She wasn't even supposed to be in Molly's when I came in.

"Okay, so now that we've established that we have the same favorite pizza toppings, what kind of business were you doing out this way?"

"Do you know what I do for a living?" I take a bite of my pizza.

"Apparently, that's a mystery among the girls." She takes a sip of her drink. "Michelle thinks you're some sort of hitman for hire and Gabby thinks you're a stripper."

Her words make me nearly choke on my food. "Carter works with me sometimes. Could you picture him as a hitman or a stripper?" I say after clearing my throat.

"Hmm..." She taps her chin. "I don't think Carter has the ability to hurt a fly, but he is a great dancer."

"Good point! Are you done for the day, or do you have to go back to work?"

"I'm actually done for the day."

"Great! How about you come with me and I'll show you what I do."

"Okay, but if you're a hitman and plan to kill me, just know that I *will* come back to haunt you."

"Fair enough, and if I'm a stripper?"

"We need to stop at an ATM 'cause I don't have any cash on me."

I throw my head back in laughter. We finish our meal amongst more small talk. It's funny how we can talk about nothing and it feels right, good even. With the exception of my family, I don't normally talk so freely with women. I don't know why, but I've decided to show her what I do for a living and I'm oddly excited to see what she thinks. "Come on, let's get out of here. I promise you won't need cash."

"Great! Haunting it is."

I grab onto her shoulders and lead her towards my truck. We drive for about fifteen minutes toward the rural section of town. The conversation flows easily as we talk about everything from our favorite movies to bands we like. I even notice she has a decent singing voice...when she gets the lyrics right.

"You do realize he's saying *tiny dancer* and not *Tony Danza*, right?"

"I do *now*. Jess broke the news to me a few years ago, but I still like my version better."

"Your version doesn't make sense."

"Yes, it does." She sits a little straighter in her seat and I know I'm about to get a little more insight on whatever goes on in that beautiful mind of hers.

"The original song became popular in the '70s," she continues. "And that's when Tony Danza's career began to take off. Coincidence? I think not."

"You've really thought about this, haven't you?"

She nods proudly as we pull curbside of my latest project.

"Whose house is this?" Aly asks as she stares out the window at the white ranch-style home with teal shutters. I can already tell that the wraparound porch is catching her eye. The house has been a bear to work on, but it's going to be my best flip yet. I'd move into it myself...if I had a family.

"Mine." I wink.

"Oh! Are you planning on moving out of your condo?" she asks, confused.

"Nope." I shake my head. "This one is only mine for another few months. As long as nothing crazy pops up, we'll have it done and on the market by early next year."

"So...you flip houses?"

"Yup. That's why I was near the college. I was at the title company signing papers for my last completed house."

I tell Aly to have a look around while I go hunt for Travis. His SUV is parked outside, so I know he's around here somewhere. I hope he is okay with me bringing Aly along. He's not usually up for meeting new people.

A short yelp takes me out of my thoughts and has me running down the hallway. I'm assuming Aly found Travis, and if she outwardly yelped about his appearance, I will instantly lose all the respect I have for her. I've seen the looks, stares, and comments Travis gets when he's in public. People are downright ruthless.

I follow inaudible sounds to a bedroom we have yet to work on and grab the doorframe. There in the middle of the room stands Travis with his arms around Aly's waist and they're...laughing?

"Parker! You gotta tell me when you're bringing someone over. I thought she was breaking into the house." Travis lets go of Aly, but they are still laughing wholeheartedly.

"We scared each other," Aly adds as she tries to catch her breath. "This room is like a funhouse. Please tell me this was here when you bought it because if this is what you do to flipped houses, my opinion of you is going to greatly change."

I rub my hand over the back of my neck and chuckle. "Yeah, we call this the Hotel California Room and it was most definitely here before we bought it."

"I can see where the name comes from," she says as she looks up at the mirrors lining the ceiling. "I wonder what the people who used to live here were like."

"We've wondered that too." Travis chuckles, seemingly at ease with our new visitor. We don't know who lived in the house beforehand. It had been foreclosed and abandoned for a few years prior to us purchasing it from the bank. That hasn't stopped us from making up crazy scenarios for the former owners.

The sound of panting has me turning around and grinning. "It's about time you showed up," I shame Gus, the laziest dog in the world. Gus pays me no attention; he rarely ever does unless I have food in my hand. "Hey, Aly! Are you okay with dogs?" I ask.

"Of course," she replies. A sunny smile crosses her face. I figured she was a dog person, but you never know. Gus won't hurt a fly, mainly because they move and would take too much energy to catch. I shift to the side, allowing Gus to pass through the doorway, and I witness love at first sight.

Gus takes one look at Aly and hops over to her as she kneels down on the floor with open arms for him.

"Oh! My! God! Who is this?" She plays with Gus's ears as he happily licks her cheek. A pang of jealousy hits me. Why am I becoming so jealous of the dog?

"This is my buddy, Gus." Travis bends over to give the mutt a scratch on the head. He happily accepts the affection but quickly turns his attention back to Aly.

"What is he? He looks like a beagle, but his hair is longer." Gus flips over onto his back for tummy rubs and Aly happily obliges. "Are you a hairy beagle, Mr. Floofy Bottom? Who's a good boy?"

"Aw, come on, Aly, that's emasculating," I whine.

"He doesn't seem to mind it at all. Do you, Mr. Floofy McFloofster?" Gus turns his head towards me and I swear he winks—WINKS—at me. Asshole.

"He's just a mutt I picked up at the shelter a few years ago. They were going to put him down since he only has three legs. It pissed me off because…" Travis lifts his pant leg a bit to reveal his own prosthetic. I hold my breath. Aly has already seen the scars marring Travis's face and arms, but the prosthetic might be the straw that breaks the camel's back.

Aly's eyes widen, but her face remains soft. "Looks like you two are a perfect match."

"That's what one of the volunteers at the shelter told me."

We hang out a little longer at the house. Travis and I give Aly a tour. We show her before and after pictures of houses we've previously renovated. Turns out, she's really into it. Apparently, some of her favorite television shows are the home renovation type. She asks a lot of questions, and Travis and I take turns answering her. I'm surprised at how comfortable

Travis is around Aly. It usually takes him a lot longer to warm up to people.

"This looks like the kitchen of my dreams," Aly gushes. "I've never seen cabinets like this." She gently brushes her hand over the door of the craftsman pantry.

"That's because they're one of a kind." Travis puffs out his chest with pride. "Custom-made by yours truly." I leave most of the woodworking to him; he's got one hell of a skill.

"You're very talented."

"Ah, it's not a big deal." Travis's cheeks pinken. He's not used to getting compliments and you can see that Aly is being genuine.

"It is a big deal!" She scrolls through the tablet that displays our before and after pictures. "You've taken something so broken and made it beautiful again. Well, except for that weird mirror room, but judging from the rooms already completed, I know it will be amazing."

We finish talking with Travis, and I lead Aly back to my truck. Remembering I needed to pick up some paperwork, I tell her I'll be right back and run back into the house where Travis is leaning against the refrigerator with a smug look on his face.

"What?"

"You've never brought a woman to a job site." Travis smirks.

"Yes, I have," I say in defense.

"Your mom and sister don't count, asshole." He walks around to give me a clap on the back. "I like her. I think she's good for you."

"Oh, no! That is *not* happening. We just happened to run into each other over at Molly's and I offered to show her what I do."

"That's it?" Travis cocks his head to the side and crosses his arms over his chest.

"That's it."

"Cool, so you're good if I ask her out?"

"No!" I snap and flinch at my harshness. I feel like a complete jackass. Travis hasn't been with a girl since we were injured. He's convinced that no woman will be able to look past his injuries. It's going to take a special woman to not only look past his physical injuries but emotional wounds as well. Travis acts like he's assimilated back into civilian life, but I know he still has demons that haunt him. "I'm sorry, man... I just... What I meant to say—"

The sound of laughter cuts me off. "I'm just messing with you! I figured that would get a rise out of you."

"I'm not interested in her!" I snap back.

"Uh-huh, keep telling yourself that."

I roll my eyes and head towards the door. Travis begins humming a tune that sounds very similar to "Here Comes the Bride." Without looking back at him, I raise one finger over my head and slam the front door shut.

"Everything okay? You look a little flustered," Aly says as I slide into the driver's seat.

"Yup, all good. Just Travis trying to mess with me." I fumble with my keys before I find the right one and start the ignition.

"Travis seems nice."

"He's one of the best people I know. Thank you for not saying anything about his scars or leg."

"Why would I say anything? That would be rude. I mean, I think it's human nature to wonder how something happened, but it's none of my business."

Her response makes me like her even more. "You'd be surprised what he has to deal with when he goes out in public."

"I can't even imagine." Her shoulders slump a bit. "He said he served with you."

"He did. That's how we met. We were the only two in our squadron from Oregon, so we kind of bonded over that."

Aly nods and looks out the window. "Thank you for showing me what you do."

"No problem." I can't believe I actually liked showing someone else what I do for a living.

"I have to admit..." Aly says with a playful smile on her lips. "I'm a little disappointed that you aren't a stripper."

"Let's get you back to your car." I laugh and realize this is the most I've laughed in I can't remember when.

20

Aly

Shit! Shit! Shit! Shit! Jax's last name is Parker? What are the odds? Seriously, what are the odds that out of all the names in the world I could have chosen to go by, I choose the last name of the guy who lives across the hall?

I never bothered to find out his last name. I know Carter's and Alex's last names because they were making fun of each other one day. I have to admit, living next door to Mr. Rogers does sound pretty funny. And Alejandro Jones? Priceless.

We drive in comfortable silence for a bit when I feel the need to say something. "So... I take it your last name is Parker?"

Jax nods without taking his eyes off the road.

A thought occurs to me. "Is Travis his last name or his first?"

"What?" He glances at me for a second.

"Travis. I know a lot of military people go by their last names, but that could be a first or last name—which is it?"

Jax only replies with a small grin.

"You're not going to tell me, are you?"

"Is it going to drive you crazy?"

"No." I slump my shoulders a bit. "Okay, yes."

He lets out a low chuckle.

"Well, I'm going to assume since he called you by your last name, that Travis is his last name."

"You know what happens when you assume."

"Don't start." I point a finger at him. "Since you're not going to tell me, can I try to guess?"

"Sure. I'll give you three guesses."

"Only three?"

"We're almost back to your car."

"Okay, fine. Hmm..." I chew on the inside of my cheek. "I think I will go with the classics. Is it John?"

"No."

"William?"

"Nope."

"Michael?"

"Wrong again! But here's your consolation prize—a drive home by yourself."

He pulls into the parking lot of Molly's. My little white Honda is easy to spot with the Georgia plates. I hop out of his truck and turn around to face him. "I guess I'll see you back at the condo."

"I have a few stops to make before I head home, but drive safely, okay?" He stays in the parking lot until I'm settled into my own car with my doors locked and engine started. It's a small gesture, but it means a lot to me, especially considering the last year and a half of my life. Thankfully, my paranoia of being watched has dissipated, but at one time that anxiety nearly crippled me.

One thing's for certain. Jax is not Trent and I need to remember that.

***

"Do you hear that?" Michelle asks, looking up from her coffee. I finished my swim about twenty minutes ago and was happy to discover that both of my roommates and Carter were home this morning to join me for coffee and homemade muffins with loganberry jam Michelle made from scratch. I didn't like the idea of living with roommates again, but waking up to the scent of freshly baked pastries nearly every day is quite the perk. I also hear the stomping sounds, which seem to be getting louder and closer to our door.

Our door flies open to reveal a very peeved Jax standing in nothing but his wet bathing suit. He makes eye contact with me but says nothing as he stomps over to my chair. In one smooth swoop, he lifts me from my seat and places me on the kitchen counter. He cages me in with his arms, his chest heaving up and down from his angry breathing. I become slightly mesmerized watching beads of water drop down his body. He's so chiseled that the droplets actually skip over the divots in his abs. Fascinating.

"Where is it, Aly?" he growls.

"Where's what?" I feign innocence.

"You know exactly what I'm talking about. You mess with my towel all the time and now you replace it with this?" He holds up a crumpled towel with Alex's face on it. That's funny. I didn't notice he was holding a towel when he walked in; then again, I wasn't looking at his hands.

About a year ago, Alex was asked to pose for one of those hot firefighter calendars. He was Mr. February, which upset him because even though February is the month Valentine's Day is in, it is also the shortest month of the year. No one could enjoy a full thirty or thirty-one days of Alejandro Jones. This, of course, did not stop him from having a towel with his Mr. February picture printed on it. He gave it to Gabby for her birthday about a month before I moved in. The towel is now part of our communal linen closet, and I was all too happy to borrow it today.

"Oops, must've taken the wrong one by mistake." I shrug my shoulders.

"The last thing I need in the morning is to wrap a picture of Alex around my junk! Why do you do this to me? I know you messed with the settings in my truck the other day too."

I may have played around with his air conditioning and radio while waiting for him to finish talking with Travis. I don't know why I have this innate urge to annoy the hell out of Jax. There's just something about him that intrigues me. It's like he's been lying dormant for years and something inside of him is starting to awaken. Basically, Jax is a hibernating bear and I really, *really* want to poke the bear.

"You were in Jax's truck?" Michelle asks, interrupting whatever this is.

"Yup!" I look over Jax's shoulder. "He took me to where he works!"

"Aw! You went to the strip club without us?" Gabby jokes. Carter chokes on his coffee. I've since learned that Carter does all the electrical work on Jax's houses, confirming our suspicions that the boys have always known what he does for a living.

"He wouldn't let me stop at the ATM ahead of time." I pout. I turn my attention back to Jax, who still has me caged in on the kitchen counter. I place both of my hands on each corner of his mouth and try to press his frown upward. "You know, your face could get permanently stuck like this with the way you frown so much."

He grabs my wrists and moves them back down off his face. "Where did you come from?" A contorted look washes over him.

"You mean like Georgia, or do I need to go back further like the sperm and egg thing? I can explain it if you want, but it might be a little awkward considering your age and all." He scowls at me. No surprise there. I continue, "If you give me some time, I can go to the daycare on campus and borrow some hand puppets if you need visualization." I make my hands look like they're talking to each other.

"You're crazy!" He takes a step back and pulls at the short tips of his hair.

"Maybe. But I'm not the one standing in the middle of the room half naked and dripping wet."

"Ahem." Carter clears his throat, holding Jax's green towel that I hung over our couch. He hands it to Jax. "I think you need this."

"What I *need* is for her to leave me alone." He wraps the towel around his waist, ignoring the water droplets that still cling to his chest.

"And what I *need* is for you to stop trying to drown me every morning! You can keep trying if you must, but let it be known, I'm unsinkable!" I cross my arms over my chest with that last remark. I thought the other day with Jax might've meant some sort of truce in the pool. I really enjoyed him showing me what he did for a living. We were definitely building a bond, or at the very least something was happening. But the very next morning he jumped in the pool and tried to drown me again. Okay, maybe it's not purposeful, but I want him to realize it's not appreciated.

"I'm not trying to sink you! I'm trying to get my frustrations out, which have only multiplied since you moved in."

"I frustrate you?"

He leans in closer to my face so only I can hear his response. "In more ways than one."

I try to hold back a grin. I get what he's saying and I'm not going to lie, I like it.

Sitting up a little straighter, I try to compose myself. "Swimming is my happy place. It's my form of relaxation and I can't relax when you keep trying to drown me. We only overlap by like fifteen minutes. Can't you wait to do that stroke until after I leave?" I wildly move my arms, mimicking the upper body movement of the butterfly stroke.

"Aly," Carter interrupts. "If Jax promises not to drown you every morning, will you stop annoying him?"

Jax crosses his arms over his broad chest. If he were a cartoon, he would have steam coming from his ears. I should say no. I will not stop annoying him because, quite frankly, it's a great source of entertainment. But I really would like to have more peaceful swims. Swimming every morning really helps keep my anxiety in check. It took a long time for me to figure out what works for me, and I don't want to regress.

"She's not answering." Jax looks over at Carter.

"Oh, fine. I'll stop, but the second those tree trunks you call arms start pounding the water, the deal is off!" Now, I'm the one who's frustrated and for a completely different reason. This man affects me in a way that could make me lose control.

"Fine." Jax pivots towards the door but stops and turns around. "And don't you even think about ever touching my goggles."

I gasp and put my hand over my heart. "I would never do something so sacrilege." For swimmers, finding the perfect pair of goggles is like finding the holy grail. I'm pretty sure I fell into a small depression when the straps on my favorite pair finally wore out. I might enjoy messing around with Jax, but that's a line I won't cross.

The corners of Jax's mouth begin to turn into a smile, but he quickly composes himself, lets out a huff, and stomps out the door.

"Thanks, Aly," Carter refills his coffee mug. "I'm going to be working with him later today and working with a pissed-off Jax is not fun."

I glance over at the girls, who are sharing looks of utter confusion. "This guy"—I point to Carter—"has been holding out on us. Not only does he know what Jax does for a living, but he works with him too."

"We're not strippers!" Carter holds up his hands in surrender. "And I really am an electrician. Jax flips houses, and I do the electrical work for him. It's just always been fun to make you girls guess. Now, if you don't mind, I have to warn Travis that Jax will be a ray of sunshine when he gets to work today."

Carter spins around when he gets to the door. "Don't forget that SummerFest is next weekend. I was asked to participate in a surfing expo."

"SummerFest?" I ask.

"Yeah, it's this big thing that Starboard Beach holds. It's typically on one of the hottest days of the year, so everyone comes to the beach to hang out. They set up food trucks, games, and rides near the pier. It's a lot of fun!"

"Sounds like it!" I look at Gabby and Michelle. "Are you two going?"

"Of course! Wouldn't miss it! Especially if Carter is going to show off his skills." Michelle winks at Carter; his grin stretches from ear to ear.

The moment Carter leaves, Gabby turns to me. "Okay, first, now I see why you get up at the ass crack of dawn to go swimming."

"I would be swimming whether Jax was there or not." I hop off the counter where he placed me. "But, I admit, I do enjoy the view." I've been swimming for pretty much all my life, so I've been around half-naked, muscular guys before, but something about Jax draws me in.

"And second..." Gabby's voice pulls me out of my thoughts of a shirtless Jax. "How in the world did you get our closed-off neighbor to show you what he does for a living?"

I sit back down at the table and tell the girls how we ran into each other at Molly's and how he offered to show me his current project. I also tell them about Travis and his adorable dog, Gus.

"Amazing!" Michelle says. "I have lived here for over a year, Gabby has been here for about five months, and in less than six weeks, you already know more about this guy than the two of us combined."

"I don't know *that* much," I try to justify. I do understand what the girls are trying to convey. Jax has apparently been closed off for a long time, yet he's shown me glimpses of his life. I wonder what makes me different.

21

Jax

It's been a few days since Aly and I had our little truce. She's stayed true to her word and has stopped messing around with my things. But now I have a new problem because I miss all my little interactions with her. So here I am, hanging out at the girls' place, waiting for a pizza delivery because apparently, that's my thing now. I've always had an open invitation, but I was never comfortable enough like Alex and Carter, who consider this their second home. Truth be told, I felt like an outsider until Aly came along.

Somehow, Michelle convinced me to play Uno with her and Carter while waiting for Aly and the pizza to show up. If someone had told me a few weeks ago that my life would be like this now, I would've thought they were completely insane.

My heart begins to race when I hear movement coming from the hallway. I focus on the door that is about to open just as Michelle hits me with a Draw 4 card.

"Hi, guys!" Aly places her keys on the hook near the door. She's wearing that green wrap dress she wore the first time I laid eyes on her. Well, not the first time, since that would be at the pool, but the first time we formally met.

Everyone gives a collective "hey," including me. I don't want to seem overly enthusiastic about her arrival. It would make it obvious that I might possibly be attracted to her. Hell, it's probably obvious anyway since I've increased my presence here by like ninety percent.

"Did a package or something arrive for me while I was gone?" she asks as she grabs a bottle of water from the fridge.

"Nope. Are you expecting something?" Michelle asks as she hits me with a reverse card.

"Yeah, it's kind of strange. Jess texted me and said I had to be home to receive a package at six thirty, but it might be late."

"You don't know what it is?" Gabby asks.

Aly shakes her head. "I can't even imagine. She said I would like the package better than she would. Weird, right?"

The pizza arrives a few minutes later and we all settle down at the table to eat. Everyone falls into conversations about their day, work, and other normal stuff. Aly seems quieter than usual. She keeps checking her phone and I'm sure it's because of Jess's text.

Shortly after six thirty, someone knocks on the door.

"I'll get it!" Alex jumps up. He's the closest to the door anyway.

"I guess this is my surprise." Aly shrugs at me, but when she turns to face the door, her eyes light up in pure amazement. She covers her mouth with her hand and I hear a muffled, "Oh my God!" She gets up and runs full speed towards the door.

I turn just in time to see a life-sized Ken doll slightly towering over Alex. He looks cocky as hell with his styled blond hair and expensive-looking clothes. His green eyes focus solely on Aly as he leans into the frame of the door and gives a "Hey, darlin'" in a heavy Southern drawl.

Aly squeals and leaps into this asshole's arms. He scoops her up, spins her around, and kisses her on her cheek.

"Jacob! Oh my God! What are you doing here?"

"I have a photo shoot in LA this weekend. I know it's kinda far, but I couldn't be on the same coast without checking up on you." He gives her a squeeze.

My jaw tightens and my hands clench into fists under the table. He is way too comfortable touching her.

"Everyone, this is Jacob," Aly gushes as she turns towards all of us sitting at the table. He keeps a hand casually wrapped around her waist and she has her hand on his chest.

"Jacob as in your friend Jess's brother?" Michelle asks.

"Yup!" Aly replies.

"We're twins actually, but I got all the good looks." He winks.

"Behave!" Aly playfully smacks him.

"Oh great, just what we need around here, another Alex." Michelle rolls her eyes.

"Easy, tiger," I hear Alex whisper and I honestly don't know if he's talking to me or trying to calm himself down.

"Jacob, there's something about you that looks familiar, and I can't place it," Gabby pipes up.

"You've probably seen my pictures around. I'm a model," he confirms.

"Of course he is," Alex mutters under his breath. It's so odd to see him agitated. Carter just sits quietly, picking at his pizza.

"What do you model?" one of the girls asks. I'm barely paying attention at this point because all I can hear is my heart beating in my ears.

"Underwear and swimwear mostly, basically anything with my shirt off." He shrugs likes it's no big deal. Like it's so normal to work shirtless. Okay, I may be known to take my shirt off while working in the heat, but it's not so people can admire me.

"Oh, wait! I know where you've seen him!" Aly leans into Jacob's ear and whispers something. He smiles smugly, turns to the side, and lifts his shirt.

"Fuck my life!" Alex throws his head back and groans. I know exactly what he's thinking. Alex, Carter, and I are all athletic. We all sport some muscle and six-packs, but this guy is ripped beyond compare. It's like we went to Walmart and got the standard six-pack while this guy went to Costco and got the economy size.

"Eeeeeekkk! You're on the cover of the book I've been reading!" Gabby starts jumping up and down like a freaking fangirl and then runs into her room to presumably get said book.

"Every now and then I get asked to pose for a romance novel," he says, though no one asked.

"It's hard to go out in public without him being recognized or have people hit on him. And when I say people, I mean men, women, old, young—you name it, he attracts it," Aly states matter-of-factly.

"Yeah, it's even harder to go out now that I lost my exterminator."

"Your exterminator?" Michelle asks. Gabby comes out with her book and asks Jacob to sign it.

"That would be me." Aly raises her hand.

"Yup, if I needed to get a girl off me at the club or I had a stage five clinger, Aly played the part of a crazy, jealous girlfriend." Jacob writes something in Gabby's book.

So that's why she had no problem getting that girl away from me at the bar. I wonder if she ever gave Jacob an itchy rash diagnosis or whatever it was.

"How long are you staying?" Aly asks.

"Gotta leave in the morning. I booked a hotel a few miles away. I know it's not much time, but I thought you could stay with me and we can recreate Orlando."

I have no idea what "recreate Orlando" means, but I already know I hate it.

"Yes! Perfect!" Aly claps her hands. "It won't be the same without Jess, of course."

"Yeah." Jacob snorts. "It will be better."

"Don't forget about SummerFest tomorrow! Carter is surfing in the expo!" Michelle chimes in.

"Of course! I wouldn't miss it!" Aly turns to Jacob. "Maybe I can just leave from the hotel and head there?"

"Parking gets pretty packed," Gabby says. "Maybe we can pick you up at the hotel?"

"I can drop you off on my way to the airport. That way no one has to go out of their way," Jacob offers. Oh, how polite of him.

"Perfect!" Michelle agrees. "We'll pack a bag with extra towels and stuff for you. Just take your bathing suit and wear it under your clothes so you can switch out when you meet up with us."

I leave soon after Aly and Jacob head out for whatever they're doing. I know I'm not going to be able to sleep tonight, so I decide to go to the gym to take my anger out on a punching bag. Alex heads down with me.

"Can you believe that guy?" Alex steadies the punching bag for me. "He just waltzes through the door like he's God's gift to Earth."

"Kind of like you do?" Carter appears from the doorway with an apple in his hand.

"That's different! I just do that for shits and giggles. The girls know that! They didn't even know him."

"He knew Aly." I throw a punch, nearly sending Alex backwards.

"And did you see his eyes? What's up with that? Those have to be contacts. No one's eyes are that green."

"Says the Latino with blue eyes," Carter chides.

"I am Mexicanadian! How many times have we been through this? I can't help that I got the best genes from my parents, and why are you here anyway?"

"I came down to watch you two clowns beat the shit out of each other." He takes a bite of his apple.

"We're not beating the shit out of each other! It's arm day and we both forgot." Alex takes a swing at the punching bag.

Carter barks out a laugh. "Yeah, sure, and it has nothing to do with the underwear model Gabby was drooling over and Aly went off with to a hotel."

"How would you feel if Michelle started acting all schoolgirlish like Gabby was?"

"Michelle and I are just friends." He tosses his apple in a nearby trash can.

"Yeah, sure you are." Alex rolls his eyes.

"We *are* just good friends. She can gush over whoever she wants. And you..." Carter turns his attention towards me. "Will you just admit that you like Aly?"

"What? No!" I trip over my own two feet trying to grab my water bottle. "I told you already, I'm not interested in her."

"So why did you look like you wanted to kill Jacob?"

"I don't trust that guy, and she just went bouncing off to spend the night at a hotel with him. I was thinking of her safety." My voice grows harsher with each word, but I'm proud of the excuse I just thought up.

"Ah, yes. You are always thinking of her safety. Like when you told that guy in the bar she was a lesbian? Jacob is her best friend's brother and they were all roommates at some point.

I'm pretty sure she wouldn't have willingly gone to a hotel with him if she didn't feel safe. Give her some credit."

I want to, but I can't. It kills me to think of what she's doing with that asshole right now.

22

Aly

"I am so loving this!" I say between mouthfuls of ice cream.

We're hanging out in Jacob's hotel suite, recreating a trip that he, Jess, and I all took to Orlando. It was after Jacob got his first big paycheck from a modeling job. He decided we should take a weekend trip to Disney World. Unfortunately, there was a tropical storm that weekend and the parks closed. We ended up ordering everything from the hotel's room service menu and binge-watching classic eighties movies. It was one of the best weekends ever.

"So, tell me how you're doing? You know I need a full report to turn in to my sister by the end of this trip."

"I'm good." I take a huge bite of a chocolate chip cookie. So far, we have pigged out on wings, potato skins, nachos, pot stickers, sliders, and some sort of macaroni and cheese dish. We are now getting into the dessert portion of our feast, which includes two different types of pie, brownies, and a cookie platter.

"You look good," Jacob agrees. "Last time I saw you, you were so stressed. Now you seem a lot more relaxed. Calmer."

"I am calmer. I never thought I'd like living on the West Coast, but it's really starting to grow on me. Plus, it's a lot more peaceful knowing I don't have to deal with Trent's bullshit every day."

"Look, about that." Jacob runs a hand through his hair. "I'm so sorry I couldn't help you more."

"Jacob, it wasn't your battle to fight! Besides, you opened up your home to me when I didn't feel safe in my own."

I stayed in Jacob's bachelor pad during my last few months in Beaute. I adored my little cottage, but after several incidents, I didn't feel safe there anymore. My home was a bit isolated as it was on a dead-end street. Jacob's apartment building always had people bustling in and out. Even though his place only had one bedroom, he was rarely ever home and he graciously took the couch whenever he was in town.

"Yeah, but I wish I had been around to support you more. Jess was already living in Maine and I was barely around with work. You were basically alone. I still want to kick that mother ducker's ass."

"And if you kicked his ass or even came anywhere near him, he would have had *your* ass thrown in jail with the snap of a finger. It would have ruined your life. Also, you're still on the *duck* kick?" I laugh. Jess and I like to joke that Jacob's phone has the personality of a nun; everything autocorrects, whether he likes it or not.

"He still deserves a good ass kicking." Jacob pounds his fist into his palm. "And yes, I've finally stopped fighting autocorrect and have chosen to embrace the *duck*."

"Well, I'm sure one day someone will see his true colors and he will get his ass kicked."

"I wish I could've seen his true colors earlier in your relationship," Jacob says; remorse fills his voice.

"You?" I snort. "I wish *I* had seen his true colors before I even started dating him!" Sadly, Trent was sweet and caring at first, though it didn't last much longer after we were engaged. I now realize that I was so desperate to find love that I went into the relationship with blinders on.

"Let's not bring this night down with talking about him. Tell me about your life here. Your roommates seem nice, but who was that G.I. Joe-looking guy who was shooting daggers at me?"

"That's Jax! He's harmless... I think. Apparently, he's supposed to be super growly and private, but he talks to me just fine...well, sometimes. Other times he just ignores me. It's complicated, and for the record, he was a sailor, not a soldier."

"Well, for the record, the guy wants to jump your bones."

"Jacob!" I smack his arm.

"I'm serious! I know that look. Hell, I've given that look. That is the look of a man who wants to do the horizontal tango, shake some sheets, go spelunking in the bat cave, slam the cla—"

"Are you googling euphemisms for sex?"

Jacob puts his phone down with a cheesy grin. "Figured I'd try to change things up a bit, but seriously, have you been out of the dating game for so long that you can't tell when a guy is interested in you? Does he know?"

"Does he know that I'm used goods? That I'm a runaway bride? No, I don't exactly advertise that." My heart begins to race. I hate talking about what happened with Trent. Who would want me after finding out that I couldn't go through with a commitment to get married? Granted, he pulled a complete one-eighty and wasn't the man I originally agreed to marry, but in some way, I still feel like I failed at life.

"You are not used goods and you are not a runaway bride! That's just Trent and his ducking fan club trying to break your spirit. You are stronger than that, Aly."

"You really believe that?" I say, starting to feel a bit choked up.

"I absolutely do. Now, come on." Jacob starts placing our food on the room service tray. "We both need to get our beauty sleep and I cannot keep eating like this. I have an early morning flight and you need to go to the beach tomorrow and show G.I. Joe what he's missing out on."

I jump up and throw my arms around Jacob's shoulders. "I love you, you know."

Jacob gives me a big squeeze back. "I know." He places a chaste kiss on my cheek. "I love you too and I know you're going to be just fine."

The next morning, Jacob drops me off as close as he can get to the pier. Carter was right. SummerFest is packed. There are sections for food trucks, kiddie rides, and craft vendors. I walk away from the large crowd and follow the signs for the surf exhibition that is taking place farther down the beach.

Up ahead, I spot Gabby and Michelle. They have quite the setup going with two large beach umbrellas, several blankets laid out on the sand, and coolers full of drinks and snacks. I smile as I approach them. It was so good to spend time with an old friend like Jacob, but I'm quickly warming up to my new friends as well.

"Hey, girl! How was your date with Jacob?" Gabby asks while waggling her eyebrows. She hands me a towel to lay out next to her.

"You know it was *not* a date. Jacob and I have been friends and *only* friends since we were eighteen."

"Yeah, well, the guys were all convinced it was a date," Michelle states while spraying sunblock on herself. "Jax looked like his head was about to explode."

"That's ridiculous." I shake my head. "First of all, Jacob and I are strictly platonic. I have always been immune to his playboy ways and he's respected that. Second, there is nothing going on between me and Jax, so why would he be upset?"

"I don't know, Aly." Gabby adjusts her sunglasses. "Jax has never acted so territorial around anyone until you came along. I think you might be the one to tame that growly beast."

I take off my shirt and shorts to reveal the bathing suit I have underneath. I'm so excited to finally get a chance to wear it.

"That's so cute!" Michelle compliments.

"Thanks! I bought it at an end-of-summer sale last year, not thinking I'd ever be out here." The summers in Georgia last a lot longer than the summers in Oregon. My bathing suit is a two-piece but nothing skimpy. It's a baby pink color and twisted in the front to give the illusion like I have decent-sized boobs.

Something behind me catches Michelle's attention. I follow her gaze and see Alex and Jax walking our way. Their tanned, sculpted bodies remind me of the posters of random guys Jess and I used to hang up in our shared room during our early years in college. My eyes focus solely on Jax. I find it funny that I lived with an underwear model and felt no attraction. Yet just the sight of Jax sets my body on fire.

Trying not to stare, I kneel in the sand to put my clothes in my bag when I hear Gabby let out a low whistle. "I'm shocked you haven't spontaneously combusted with the look Jax is giving you right now."

"What do you—"

"What the hell is that?" Jax cuts me off.

"What the hell is what?" I stand to face him, planting my hands on my hips.

"What are you wearing?"

"A bathing suit. You of all people should be able to recognize that. You see me in one every morning."

"That is *not* what you wear every morning. You shouldn't be wearing that." Jax moves his hands up and down at me like he's Vanna White revealing a puzzle on *Wheel of Fortune*.

"I, for one, do not see what you're complaining about," Alex cuts in, earning him a death glare from Jax. He puts his hands up in surrender and sits down on the sand next to Michelle.

"You're a professor. Shouldn't there be some sort of rule about what you can and cannot wear?"

"You think I walk around campus like this? I'm sure that would go over well with the frat boys. Look around, Jax. I'm not at work."

He lets out a frustrated huff as he bends down to grab what I assume is his bag and comes up with something in his hand. He takes a step towards me and puts something over my head.

"What are you dohrigng?" Fabric that smells distinctly like Jax muffles my voice—a mix of his bodywash and chlorine.

"There." He stands back to admire his handiwork. "Much better."

Here I am, standing in one of Jax's T-shirts, with the hem of the shirt just a bit above my knee. The satisfied smirk on his face makes me want to smack him. I cross my arms over my chest and let out an agitated huff.

"Dude, if looks could kill right now…" Alex grabs his stomach, howling with laughter, while the girls try to subdue their smiles.

Before I can open my mouth to say anything, Carter comes trotting up to our group. "Hey, guys! Ladies! Aly, nice uh...muumuu?"

The roar of laughter rises up from my friends. Carter plops down next to Alex, and now Jax and I are the only ones left standing in some sort of face-off. Why is it always us going head-to-head?

"You have no right to tell me what I can and cannot wear." I lift the shirt over my head and throw it at Jax's face.

He grabs the shirt and leans in close to my ear so only I can hear his voice. "You should not be walking around looking like that. Other guys could get the wrong idea."

"And if they do? You have no claim to me. I can do whatever I want," I hiss back. Alarm bells should be going off in my head because Trent always tried to control what I wore, but I know with Jax, this isn't the same thing. I'm happy to push back and get a rise out of him.

"You know, you're right. You can do whatever you want, but I suggest you put this shirt back on unless..." Jax throws his hands to his sides and then an up-to-no-good smile spreads across his face. I don't like where this is headed, but I'm not going to back down either.

"Unless what?" I challenge.

"Unless you go swimming with me." His grin reminds me of when the Grinch came up with his idea to steal Christmas.

"You wouldn't!" I gasp. I'm vaguely aware of our friends watching this ridiculous scene. I can't even imagine what they're thinking. The only person in the group who knows about my aversion to swimming in the ocean is Jax.

Jax steps closer so we are toe to toe. He lowers his head closer to mine, and for a moment, it almost looks like he is going to kiss me, until he says the two words I never want to hear: "Fish. Poop."

I scowl at him and turn my body away to sit down, but before I plop my butt in the sand, my feet are lifted into the air. I let out a yelp as Jax hurls me over his shoulder, carrying me fireman style towards the ocean.

"Don't you dare, Jaxon!" I scream and smack his lower back as I bob up and down with his steps. If this was under different circumstances, I would probably be enjoying the closeness to him right now. Instead, I'm freaking out about being thrown into a cesspool of fish poop, debris, and who knows what else.

Dear God, I hope no one released their loved one's ashes recently.

I remain hanging over Jax's back as my view turns from sand to tide.

"Let me go!" I yell.

"Are you going to put on the shirt?"

"Never!" I challenge back. I can feel Jax's body vibrating with laughter.

"Then I guess you're going for a swim."

We're getting deeper into the water. Soon my legs or head will start to get wet. I can't tell which end since he basically has me bent in half.

"Oh, no! If I go down, I'm taking you with me. I'm not going to be the only one exposed to some flesh-eating bacteria or Great Aunt Edna's ashes! Also, if I die from something related to this, I'm so coming back to haunt you!"

"Seriously, what goes on in that head of yours?"

"My mind is a library full of facts and theories you never want to know."

I work up enough energy to pull my upper body right side up. I wrap my arms around his neck and start to wriggle my legs out of his grip. Jax is strong, no doubt about it, but I know I'm catching him off guard. Plus, I know the sunscreen I applied earlier is making me a little slippery. I manage to get my right leg free and hook it around his waist. While Jax focuses on grabbing my rogue right leg, I position my left leg around the other side of his waist.

"What are you doing?" he barks. I smile in triumph as I am now face to face with Jax. Granted, I'm not in the most lady-like position. Okay, I'm straddling him, but at least I feel more in control than before.

"If you are going to throw me in this open septic tank, I'm not going to make it easy for you!" I yell as I inch my way up Jax's body like I'm climbing a tree.

"Get down here, you crazy little spider monkey!" He struggles. For every step he takes farther into the water, I climb up him inch by inch.

"Not going down without a fight!" I yell back, but I can feel myself starting to slip. *Damn sunscreen*. I hook my ankles around his back for a more secure grip. This makes me slide down his body ever so slowly. If I weren't fighting for my life—*okay, yes, I know I'm being dramatic*—I would actually consider this kind of intimate. Apparently, Jax is thinking the same thing because as I slide farther down, I hit something rather solid and it most certainly is not a fish.

"Shit!" I hear him mutter and he buries his head into my shoulder.

"Are we farther in the water than I thought? 'Cause I think I feel a sea creature."

"Dammit, Aly," he grumbles and tightens my body further around him, so nothing is visible to onlookers.

"Hmm...a swordfish, perhaps? Maybe a barracuda? Definitely not a guppy."

Jax's eyes narrow on me. "Not funny," he grits through his teeth.

"Not funny? This is hilarious! This totally backfired on you. I don't even care if you throw me in now. The water looks like it's cold; it might benefit you to take a little swim." I start laughing uncontrollably. "This is so worth it!"

"Keep it up, Aly." He looks down between us. "You're making it worse."

I can only assume the vibration from my laughter is causing some extra sensations. Maybe Jacob was right and Jax is into me.

23

Jax

I'm screwed. I was still upset about Aly's little date night with Jacob, the underwear model, and then I got pissed when I saw her in that tiny bikini for all the world to see. Now, here I am balls deep in the ocean with a hard-on that could hit a home run at the World Series. Aly is straddling me while laughing her ass off. There's no way I can walk back towards the beach the way I am. Karma really is a bitch.

"The more you laugh, the more you vibrate against me," I growl in her ear.

She begins to laugh harder, then everything stops. She stiffens for a moment and focuses on something over my shoulder. I feel her foot press off my hip and she dives into the water, heading deeper into the ocean.

I'm utterly confused. Aly hates swimming in the ocean; why would she be going in deeper? Then I see where she is headed. A blur of blond hair is bobbing in and out of the water. Shit! Someone's drowning!

I quickly follow the same path she took towards the blur of blond. I can't even see the victim anymore. I have no idea if it's a girl, boy, child, or adult. I trust Aly's instincts and continue towards her. Aly's head goes under a wave and comes up with an unresponsive blond little girl. She couldn't be more than five or six.

Aly throws the little girl over her shoulder. The kid is like a ragdoll and my heart drops at the sight; her coloring is not good. Aly starts firmly slapping the child's back. I hear a gurgling noise and the little girl throws up water over Aly's shoulder.

"It's okay. You're going to be okay." Aly rubs the little girl's back. The little girl starts gasping for air then begins to cry. Music to my freaking ears. She's alive!

A flash of orange comes up next to me and two lifeguards try to grab the little girl from Aly.

"No!" the little girl cries. She wraps her tiny arms tightly around Aly's neck. It's clear that she is petrified and does not want to let go of her rescuer.

"I can bring her in," Aly says to one of the guards. "Give me your buoy." The lifeguard looks like he's about to argue with her but then does as he's told.

We all swim back to shore where a crowd of onlookers has gathered. A frantic-looking woman comes running out of the crowd screaming. The little girl Aly is holding finally breaks the death grip she has around her neck and leaps into the screaming woman's arms. Aly turns to talk to the lifeguards. I stand in the background, soaking up the entire scene.

Gabby and Alex appear out of nowhere and begin examining the girl. "She needs to go to the hospital. I've never seen someone throw up that much water," Alex says.

An ambulance comes screeching to a halt near the pier and two EMTs jump out and head towards the crowd. Alex,

Gabby, and presumably the girl's mom, stay with the little girl until they load her into the back of the ambulance. The crowd begins to dissipate, and I feel a warm hand touch my bicep.

"Hey!" Aly says, looking completely relaxed as if she didn't just save someone's life. I have no doubt the lifeguards who showed up after us would've been too late.

"Hey!" I swing my arm around her shoulders. "You okay?"

"I'm great! Although I'm dying to take a shower right now."

"Were the lifeguards mad that you took over?"

"Not at all." She chuckles. "They actually offered me a job."

"Oh, I can only imagine how that conversation went!"

"I just politely declined. I didn't want to tell them about my fish poop theory and have them quit too."

"Was that the girl's mother?"

Aly's shoulders drop. "Yup. It's your typical story. The mom got distracted and the girl wandered off and went too far."

"Is she going to be okay?"

"Yeah, but she was taken to the hospital for observation. She took in a lot of water."

"I can't believe that happened! I didn't even know someone was drowning behind me!"

"I just happened to be in the right place at the right time. I have no doubt you would've done the same thing if you saw her first."

"Soooo...it was a good thing that I brought you into the water?" I grin.

"Maybe. But my threat still stands. If I die from some sort of crazy disease that was floating around in there, I'm coming back to haunt your ass."

"Fair enough! Come on, let's get you home so you can wash the fish poop away, and, Aly?"

"Hmm?"

I place my hand under her chin to make sure those large sapphire eyes of hers meet mine. "That was amazing."

24

Aly

It's just about 4:00 p.m. when I finish up my last class of the day with my heart full and a smile on my face. While I didn't plan on falling in love with my job, that is just what is happening. Maybe Jess was right; this was exactly what I needed.

I give Jess a call since she likes to keep me company on my rides home. We're still talking by the time I get back to the condos and into the main lobby. I hit the button for the elevator, but nothing happens.

"Hey," I say to Jess. "The elevator isn't moving. I have to take the stairwell, so I may lose you." For some reason, my phone works great in the elevator, but it's hit or miss in the stairwell.

"Put me on video right now!" Jess yells. She has a fear of being attacked in a stairwell. It stems from watching too many horror movies when she was younger.

"I highly doubt anyone is waiting for me in the stairwell, Jess."

"You can never be too careful and if someone attacks you, I will be able to call for help. I'm literally saving your life here!"

"Pretty sure nothing will happen to me up the two flights of stairs."

"Don't care. Switch to video now." I roll my eyes but oblige. Jess's fiery red locks and green eyes pop up on the screen. It never ceases to amaze me how different she looks from her twin. Besides sharing the same eye color, Jess and Jacob look nothing alike. Jess is a younger version of her mom while Jacob takes more after their dad.

"Did you do something different with your makeup?"

"Yup! Trying a different mascara. You like?" She moves her phone to zoom in on her eyes.

"I do!" I begin my ascent up the measly two flights of stairs.

"Aly!" Jess stiffens. "I think someone's behind you! I knew you should've waited for the elevator."

I stop on the landing, look behind me, and smile. "Like the elevator is any safer? What if it got stuck and I got trapped with some psychopath?"

"Are you calling me a psychopath?" Jax's deep voice teases.

"Well, I wouldn't mind getting stuck in an elevator with that guy." Jess shrugs.

I bust out laughing and pull Jax closer into view of my phone. "Jax, meet Jess. Jess, meet Jax." They both give each other a small wave.

"I guess the elevator wasn't working for you either?" Jax asks as we continue up the stairs.

"Nope, and my bestie who is three thousand miles away thinks she can protect me from some creeper in a stairwell."

Jess ignores my comment as she studies Jax further. "Hey, Jax, are you single?"

"Umm, yes?"

"Jess, don't even think about it," I warn.

"Oh, please, what are you going to do to me? I'm three thousand miles away."

"And I'm hanging up now."

"No, wait! Aly's a real catch. She's a little broken right now, but I'm working on it."

"Goodbye, Jess." I hit a button on my phone and shove it in my purse. I look up at Jax, who has an amused look on his face.

"Sorry about that, I—"

"She thinks no one will want her because—" Jess's voice booms from my purse.

"Oh my God!" I fumble with my purse, grab my phone, cover the speaker with my finger, and shut down my phone completely. I know my face must be fifty shades of crimson right now.

"That was entertaining," Jax says as we reach our floor and stand near our respective doors.

"Yeah...umm...I gotta go and uh...th-threaten someone's life right now," I stammer and practically throw myself into the condo, thankful that the door is unlocked.

Fortunately, no more embarrassing situations took place with Jax, and the next few days went by as usual.

This morning I was craving Nonna Grace's infamous oatmeal walnut chocolate chip cookies and decided to throw a batch together. While Nonna Grace taught me several of her recipes, these cookies are by far my favorites. As I take a few and place them on a plate for later, I hear Alex's voice.

"Mmm, Peanut, these are probably the best cookies you've ever made," he moans.

"Gee, thanks!" Michelle responds sarcastically.

"Uh-oh! What did I do now?"

"I made them," I inform him. "And thank you for the compliment. I know my baking can't hold a candle to Michelle's."

Michelle may be the resident baker of our place, but I had to have Nonna Grace's cookies. Jess and I used to both crave them during our menstrual cycles and would devour a few batches at a time. Jacob eventually learned to make himself scarce whenever he smelled them baking.

I made extra because I knew the guys were coming over for dinner. Well, Alex and Carter, at least. Jax is still a wild card.

"Did I say these were the best cookies you've ever made? I meant to say the worst! Absolutely disgusting, horrid! Bleh! Please don't stop baking for me," Alex pleads.

"First of all, I bake for everyone, and second of all, I tried the cookies and they are pretty scrumptious, so I will give you a pass on this one, Alex." Michelle gives him a little side hug. "Now, quit eating them before you have your dinner."

"Yes, ma'am."

"Did you make dinner also, Aly?" Carter asks as I wipe my hands on a kitchen towel.

"No, just the cookies. I spent the rest of the afternoon grading papers. Gabby handled dinner today." I look over to see Alex doing a little dance.

"It's not empanadas, Alex. Just some baked chicken and veggies," Gabby says as she puts a large platter down on the table.

"Baby girl, I will happily eat whatever you're willing to make for me." I know Gabby is about to give him some sarcastic remark, but before she can open her mouth, the door creaks open and in walks Jax.

"Well, well, well, look what the cat dragged in," Alex chides. "I'm telling you right now, I am claiming any leftovers and I'm taking the cookies with me too."

"Did I miss something?" Jax asks, taking his usual seat.

"Just Alex fawning over Gabby's cooking and Aly's baking," Michelle teases.

"Seriously, guys, how lucky are we to live next to three beautiful ladies who all know how to cook and are willing to share their talents with our sorry asses."

"Wow, you're really laying it on thick today," Gabby remarks.

"You know what's also th—" Carter smacks the back of Alex's head, preventing Alex from saying something about the size of his penis.

"Thank you, Carter," Michelle says.

Dinner goes smoothly. The guys clean up as usual and head back to their homes. I walk into the kitchen to grab a cookie or two but only discover crumbs.

"Umm...what happened to the cookies?"

"What do you mean? They're where you left them, on the plate next to the toaster," Michelle answers.

"Not anymore!" I hold up the empty plate.

"Freaking Alex!" Gabby tsks. "I saw him eating a few while he was doing the dishes. He either ate them all or stole them."

25

Jax

Sitting on my couch, I shove another one of Aly's oatmeal walnut chocolate chip cookies into my mouth. I stole the rest. I couldn't help it; they are my favorite type of cookie. Not that she knew that, of course.

From the moment I took a bite of a cookie, I was transported back in time to when I was seven again, running up the porch steps of Gram and Pop's house following the delectable smell of Gram's baking.

Emma and I visited Gram and Pop often, and without fail, Gram would have warm batches of our favorite cookies waiting for us in her kitchen. Gram always made Emma oatmeal raisin because that was her favorite. Seriously, who would want an oatmeal raisin cookie when you can have an oatmeal walnut chocolate chip cookie? And let me tell you, there's nothing but disappointment thinking you're about to eat an oatmeal chocolate chip cookie, only to discover it's an oatmeal raisin one instead. Thankfully, Gram always made plenty to go around. After all, I was her favorite.

I'm so grateful it was a little chilly today because I wore my hoodie with the large pocket in the front. I was grabbing two at a time and shoving them in my pocket while Alex, Carter, and I cleaned up from dinner. Alex kept eating some while he worked, so I'm hoping the girls will blame him for it. Now, here I am staring at my loot and wondering if I should savor these over the next few days or get rid of the evidence as fast as possible.

Screw it, I'm eating them all now.

At some point, I fall asleep on my couch, overly full from my pilfered dessert, and wake up to a commotion outside my door.

"What's going on?" I peer out into the hallway. The door to the girls' condo is wide open and I walk in to see Carter moving the living room furniture around while Michelle and Gabby have boxes in their hands.

"Oh, Jax," Carter says. "I didn't realize you were home. Quick—grab something from Gabby's or Aly's room and bring it out here."

"What happened?" I ask.

"The place above us flooded. The ceiling above my room, Aly's room, and our shared bathroom is totally destroyed," Gabby answers.

I walk in and holy crap is this a mess! What were the people upstairs doing? Trying to create their own Roman bath? I know I can offer to fix the place, but I'm not on the list of approved contractors from our condo association. As a licensed contractor, I could've requested my name to be put on the list, but I much prefer working on empty houses and not dealing with insurance companies. Judging from the damage I can see, this will definitely need to be assessed by an insurance adjuster.

"It's going to take at least a few days to get this repaired," Michelle states. "Everything needs to be removed and thoroughly dried before we can replace it."

"We can't stay in our rooms until everything is fixed. Alex is at the firehouse for the next few days, so I'm going to stay in his room," Gabby says.

"Okay." I nod. "That works out. Wait—what about Aly?"

The girls look at each other and then back at me.

"Gabby, Michelle," I say slowly. "Where is Aly going to stay?"

"Well, about that," Michelle starts. "We were hoping you would..."

"Hey, roomie," I hear from behind me.

"Oh, no! No! No! No!" I shake my head.

"Oh, come on, Jax! You're the only one who has a spare bedroom. Otherwise, she'll have to sleep with one of us, in our bed. Or are you going to make her go pay for a hotel room for a few days?" Michelle whines.

No way will I have Aly go to some sleazy hotel until her room is fixed. I can't bear the thought of her being far away. Out of the group, I am the one with a spare room. It's rarely ever used, but I keep it in case my family stops by. Occasionally, my dad and I take fishing trips and he stays with me instead of making the drive home after a long day.

"Told you he wouldn't go for it," Aly says as she brushes past me to grab more stuff from her room. It's not that I don't want Aly to stay with me. I'm afraid of what could happen if she does. I don't have much self-control when it comes to her as it is.

"Aly! You can't go to a hotel. It will get too expensive. You can sleep in Alex's bed with me. It's a king size, so there will be enough room. Although, I'm not sure what you will do when

Alex comes back from the firehouse. We'll be on opposite shifts, but you work normal days," Gabby says.

Oh, no! There is no way Aly is going to share a bed with Alex.

Michelle shakes her head in disgust. "I can't believe you, Jax. She needs help."

"Hello! Right here. Don't need help. I can take care of myself, and, Gabby, I can sleep on the couch, no problem-o," Aly yells from her room. I look over at the couch that is now littered with items from the girls' bedrooms. It's awfully small.

I let out a breath. How will I handle her sleeping in the room next to me? Then again, the thought of her alone in a hotel room or in Alex's bed makes my skin crawl.

"Aly, it's fine. You can stay with me. I was just caught off guard by everything." God, I feel like a selfish ass, but the girls can't know what my real problem is; I'd never live it down.

"Seriously, Jax, I don't need your pity. I'm a big girl; I can take care of myself. I'll find a hotel. No big deal. The one Jacob and I stayed in was pretty nice. Granted, he had a suite, but I'm sure the other rooms will be fine," she says, carrying a lamp out of her room.

I grab the lamp from her hand and lower my head towards her. "It's fine. The room is just sitting there not being used."

"I don't know." She bounces back and forth on her feet.

"Aly, please just stay with Jax. It would make me feel better knowing that you're right across the hall instead of at some hotel on the other side of town," Michelle says.

"Ugh, fine," she huffs. "But who's to say that Jax's place is any better than a sleazy hotel?"

"You're going to drive me insane, aren't you?" I groan.

A mischievous smile slowly spreads across her face. Yup, I'm screwed.

26

Aly

"Okay, so this is basically it." Jax waves his hand nonchalantly around his condo. "The kitchen and living room are obviously where we are standing."

"Huh, for some reason, I pictured something different," I say, looking around. Jax's place is an open concept, similar to Michelle's with a bar-height island that separates the kitchen from the living room. It's masculine but not as caveman-ish as I expected. It's clean with a hint of fresh bleach or cleaner. It's a bit impersonal, with no pictures or decorations on the plain white walls. There is a black leather sectional in his living room and a matching overstuffed leather chair near a large picture window. The sun has already set and I'm curious about what the view from his side of the building looks like in the morning.

"What were you expecting?" he asks while I continue to scan my temporary new home.

"I always figured you lived in some sort of dark cave." I place my hand on the back of the sectional. "It's not made of concrete. I'm impressed."

He rolls his eyes then grabs my hand to lead me down the short hallway. "This is my guest room," he says, opening the door to a small room that holds one dark wooden nightstand, a roll-top desk, and a full-sized bed with a plain blue comforter on it. It's simplistic, much like the rest of his place, but I like it. It makes me feel safe.

"Technically, my place is only a one-bedroom, one-bath deal," Jax says, bringing me out of my thoughts. "This room is supposed to be an office, but I keep a bed in here for when my family comes to visit."

Still holding my hand, he leads me towards the next door. "Here is the bathroom. Since I only have one, we will have to share it."

"Not a problem." I shrug. "I'm used to sharing a bathroom with Gabby. I will have to run back over to my place to grab my bodywash and hair stuff."

"You can use my stuff; that's not a big deal."

I pick up his shampoo and pretend to read the bottle. "Hmm...all-in-one bodywash, face wash, shampoo, furniture polish, and oven degreaser. That's not gonna cut it for me."

"Smart-ass." He smirks. "Go ahead and grab your coconut-vanilla stuff."

"How do you know what I use?" I cross my arms over my chest and raise an eyebrow. Does he really pay that much attention to me?

"Lucky guess." He drops my hand and heads towards what presumably is his bedroom. I try to look over his shoulder to get a glimpse, but his large frame blocks any view. I wonder if it's similar to the rest of his place. "Go get your stuff. I'm going to bed." He closes the door without another word.

"Good night!" I say to the closed door, utterly confused that he just dismissed me like that. But I shake it off and go back across the hall to grab some items I'll need from Michelle's.

The next morning, I wake up before Jax and quietly walk to the kitchen to make myself a cup of coffee. I slept great last night. The bed in his guest room is much more comfortable than my own and I feel so much more refreshed. I take my coffee and place it on the small side table next to the overstuffed chair near the large picture window. Behind the chair is a built-in bookshelf that I didn't notice last night. I scan the books to see what he likes to read. It's mainly architecture and military history books. It's easy to see that his books are organized by subject. I decide to take a book from each genre and switch them with each other. I wonder how long it will take him to notice.

I sit down in the chair with my coffee and become entranced by the view. The condos on Jax's side overlook a forested area, whereas Michelle, Gabby, and I have a view of the courtyard. I could easily wake up to this scene every morning. I get lost in my thoughts, watching a doe and young fawn walking amongst the trees, when I hear a noise from the hallway. Jax walks out and heads straight to the coffee maker, oblivious to my presence and also completely naked.

Speechless and not quite sure how to handle the situation, I choose to watch him as he opens the fridge and grabs some milk while waiting for his coffee to brew. I try to open my mouth to say something, but the view makes me temporarily speechless. I see Jax in his bathing suit every day but seeing the rest of him entirely bare is a whole different experience.

"Umm...good morning?" I finally squeak. He turns to look at me, giving me a full-frontal view of, well, everything. I try not to show interest, but I have the worst poker face on the planet.

"Shit!" he yells, looks down at himself, and hustles back to his bedroom. He comes back a minute later shirtless but wearing basketball shorts. "I thought you'd be at the pool by now."

I look at the time and realize that I have been sitting here much longer than I thought.

"I was enjoying the view," I say innocently and then my eyes go wide at the realization of what I just said. "I meant that view." I point to the window. "Not that view." I point to him. "Not that there's anything wrong with that view. Seriously, it's impressive. Good job!" *Will the Earth please just open and swallow me whole?*

Silence.

"Sooooo...I take it you sleep naked?" *God, why do I have to be so awkward?*

"Is that a problem?" He lifts his freshly brewed coffee to his lips, now looking pleased with himself.

"To each their own." I shake my head. "I would never sleep naked, though."

"Why do I have a feeling that your reasoning is going to sound like your fish-poop-in-the-ocean logic?"

"First of all, fish *do* poop in the ocean, so I'm not saying anything untrue. Second, the reason why I would never sleep naked is because if, God forbid, there was a fire, I would probably die putting on clothes before trying to get out of wherever I was."

"Here we go." Jax leans his head back.

"I'm serious! With my luck, the day I decide to sleep naked will be the day there is some sort of evacuation for whatever. I will probably have to climb out a window, which would put my naked ass out on display for the world to see. Then the news stations would come and shine their bright lights on me in all my embarrassing glory, and I'll end up as the next viral video or as a meme or something."

More silence.

He puts his coffee cup down, walks over, and kneels in front of me so his face is level with mine. He places both hands on each side of my face; they're extra warm from the hot coffee he's been holding. For a moment, we are frozen, just looking into each other's eyes. His gray eyes seem lighter compared to the storm clouds they usually mimic.

"What goes on in your mind absolutely fascinates me and scares me at the same time."

"Glad I can entertain you." I swallow.

"It's more than entertaining, but I don't know how to describe what it does to me." He shakes his head. I realize there's more to that statement, and I only wish I were brave enough to find out what it is.

The alarm on my phone sounds, warning me that I have about fifteen minutes to get ready for work. *Saved by the bell.*

"Looks like you get the lane to yourself this morning. I have to get ready for work," I say, acting like this is a normal morning and the heat building between the two of us has nothing to do with the simple fact we're attracted to each other…a lot.

His hands remain on my face, but he breaks his gaze for a moment. "Have a good day at work, Aly." He places a gentle kiss on my forehead that sends a fluttering sensation right down to my toes. He rises and walks away into his bedroom.

I get up and rinse out my mug, trying to decipher these feelings that only happen when Jax is around. I don't think I've ever felt this way about anyone, and of course, I pick the guy who doesn't do relationships.

After I get dressed and head to my car, I dial up my bestie and put her on Bluetooth. I tell her this morning's story and am so glad my love life is entertaining to her.

"You said 'good job'?" Jess howls through the speakers.

"I'm going to have to move to another state...again!" I groan as I turn out of the condo's parking lot and head towards work. I can still feel the heat in my cheeks from this morning and I know I will be replaying that faux pas in my head for years to come.

"But then he kissed you?"

"It was a super quick forehead kiss, so it was probably nothing."

"Well, you did compliment his manhood." She is laughing so hard, she's practically gasping for air. "I mean, you're like a dream come true. What guy wouldn't want to wake up and have his junk complimented?"

"You are terrible! And I didn't specifically refer to that part of his anatomy. I was kind of complimenting the whole package."

"Oh, God, I'm gonna pee my pants if you keep this up! Although that's not that hard to do these days; I mean, who would think a baby the size of a raspberry would put so much pressure on my bladder?"

Jess recently found out that she and her husband are expecting a baby early next year. I'm happy for her, but part of me is also jealous. I have always wanted a large family and at this point in my life, it looks like I might have no family at all. I know I have options; I'm still young enough to go to a sperm bank or maybe even adopt, but it won't be the same as having someone go through the journey with you. A pit forms in my stomach; instead of checking off the boxes of my life plan, I'm scratching them out and moving backwards.

"It's probably just your hormones working on overdrive. Plus, are you still drinking like a gallon of sweet tea a day?"

"Uh, I'm trying to cut back. My OB was horrified when I told her what I usually drink. Can you believe she'd never heard of sweet tea before? She thought I was talking about that iced tea crap that comes in a bottle. Damn Northerners!"

"Man, I miss your sweet tea." Jess makes the best. It's probably a good thing we no longer live close to each other. While it's one of my favorite drinks, it's also loaded with caffeine and sugar, something that doesn't sit as well with me now that I have crossed the threshold over to thirty.

"I will make you some when you come out to visit the baby for the christening. Remember, you and Jacob are going to be the godparents!"

"How could I forget? Unfortunately, I don't think I will be able to follow through with my promise." My heart drops. Years ago, Jess and I promised each other that when we had children, we would be the godmothers to each other's kids. We thought it would be a great way to connect our families a little more.

"Don't go there, Aly! Stop acting like you're all washed up!"

"Yeah, yeah, okay. Hey, I'm pulling into the parking lot now," I lie. Hot tears pierce the back of my eyes. "I'll call you later, okay?"

"Yeah, okay," Jess says. I know she knows I'm lying. We've only been on the phone for a few minutes, and it takes at least twenty to get to the university.

I hang up with Jess and drive the rest of the way to work, wiping tears from my eyes. Once I arrive at work, I pull down my visor to check my makeup in the mirror. I can't show up to class looking like the mess that I feel inside. I reapply some foundation over my tear-stained cheeks while reminding myself over and over again that I really am happy for my best friend. With the evidence of my sadness covered up, I get out of my car and head towards work to do what I do best: pretend that I'm okay.

27

Jax

"Dude, what happened?" Carter points to my wrapped hand as we ride the elevator up to our floor. I was hoping not to run into anyone on the way home, but at least it's Carter and not Alex. Alex would be having a field day with this.

"Accident with a nail gun."

"What?! That's not like you. You're always so careful about everything." Carter knows how meticulous I am about my work and the safety precautions I take.

"Got distracted." I shrug.

"This wouldn't have anything to do with a certain new roommate of yours, would it?"

I throw my head back against the wall of the elevator and let out a groan. It has everything to do with my new roommate. It's been a few days since Aly moved in with me. I woke up this morning and remembered to put on shorts before heading out to the kitchen. I wasn't prepared to see Aly in tiny pajama shorts and a thin tank top. I know she said she will never sleep naked, but those clothes left little to the imagination. She was bending over near the trash can. When she stood up, she was carrying a spider on a piece of paper. I watched as she walked past me, opened up the window, and let the spider outside on the windowsill.

"You're afraid of fish poop, but you touch spiders?" I asked her.

"I know. I'm a conundrum." She turned around to look at me. Ugh...that look paired with the little shrug she gave. Why does she affect me this way? I go to bed thinking of her; I wake up thinking of her. I wonder about how her day was and what she had for lunch. She's not only moved into my home, but she's moved into my mind as well.

I also can't help but think about Gram's last words. I don't believe in destiny or fate or whatever you call it, but Aly did show up soon after Gram passed and she's the only new person in my life. The draw I feel towards her is undeniable, but how would she be connected to Gram?

"Dude! You've got it bad!" Carter says, pulling me out of my Aly-induced haze.

"Hmm...what?"

"You were so lost in thought that you didn't get off on our floor." He points to the floor numbers above the elevator doors. *How the hell did we get to the eighth floor?*

"Why didn't you tell me?"

"It was kinda fun to watch you all starry-eyed and stuff. Never thought it would happen to you."

"Starry-eyed? Dude, how insulting—that's something teenage girls do."

"I call it like I see it." Carter shrugs. "Gabby and Alex shouldn't be home right now. Come on over to my place for a distraction and a free beer."

We finally get off the elevator on the right floor and walk into Carter's place. He hands me a beer and I relax on the couch.

"So how is it with *your* new roommate?" I ask.

"Gabby is great! We don't see each other too much with her working those twelve-hour shifts. Alex will be back tomorrow, but with the way their schedules work out, they will both be able to sleep at different times."

"They're hot racking."

"Hmm?"

"Hot racking. It happens in the military. It's when there aren't enough beds to go around, so people who work different shifts have to share a bed. The bed always stays warm since someone's always in it."

"Hmm...interesting. I don't think either of them mind."

"I don't either. Do you think those two will ever get together?" There is no question about Alex's feelings towards Gabby. Alex would give up everything he has for a chance to be with her. Gabby acts like she's not interested, but you can tell she has feelings for him just by their interactions. I think she's worried that Alex is too much of a playboy, but I have no doubt he would be faithful to her.

"I hope so," Carter says. "Gabby is a great girl and Alex would put her on a pedestal. But let's talk about why you had an accident with a nail gun and forgot to get off the elevator."

"I don't know, man." I lean forward and rest my arms on my knees. "It's like she's invading my thoughts all the time. She caught me walking around in the buff the first morning she stayed over. She felt bad about it, so she made me dinner that night."

"She saw you naked and then made you dinner?"

"When you put it like that, it sounds kind of weird, but it was fantastic." Aly had made a pork chop dish that was one of the best things I've had in a long time. When I was little, I would only eat the pork chops my gram made. It frustrated the hell out of my mother. She would try to recreate what Gram did, but since Gram kept her recipes locked up better than Fort Knox, they never came out just right. The meal Aly made? Perfection.

"Then this morning she was walking around in these skimpy little pajamas..." My mind begins to wander again to the memory of her in those scraps of fabric. She insisted they covered her body entirely and even showed me that her shorts had pockets...like anything would actually fit in there.

"Dude! You're doing it again!" Carter waves his hand in front of my face.

"Doing what again?" Wow, I really need to make more of an effort to school my features or admit that I'm feeling something for Aly. Travis's eyes nearly bugged out of his head when he found out Aly was staying at my place. Then I nailed my hand—literally. Damn, I'm a mess.

"You drifted off into la-la land...or Aly Land."

"Shit! I did? God, Carter, what am I going to do?" I rub my non-bandaged hand over my face, hoping the sensation will somehow wake me out of this fog I've been in.

"I don't know. Aly is a really sweet girl. She's the kind of girl who does committed relationships, and no offense, but you're..."

"Not that kind of guy. Yeah, I know."

"Though lately"—he holds up his beer like he's about to say something profound—"I've noticed you and Alex have been slowing down. When's the last time you guys hooked up with anyone?"

"A while." I lean my head back, trying to remember my last one-night stand. "Not since Aly's been here."

Truthfully, I haven't had the desire to be with anyone...well, anyone but Aly. I know what Carter is thinking. Aly is not a fling sort of gal and he knows I only do one-night stands. I've never brought a woman back to my place. I've never had a woman in my own bed, and yet here I am with Aly sleeping in the bedroom next to mine. She's been invading my personal space, but instead of being turned off by it, I actually love it.

"Huh." Carter rubs his chin as if he's deep in thought. "Do you think you could handle being in a committed relationship? I mean, with Aly, if she wanted more?"

"Damn, Carter. If you asked me this a few months ago, my answer would've been a solid no. But now..." My mind begins to wander. But now what? Nothing's changed. The scars from Maranda's actions are still deeply engrained within me. That's what I get for being so naïve. Can I put my trust in Aly? I feel like I can, but maybe that's just the physical attraction talking.

"A leggy girl from Georgia is making you rethink everything." Carter takes a sip of his beer.

I nod in agreement. After everything that happened with Maranda, I swore to myself I would never get into another relationship again. Now, I don't know what to think.

"You've changed, you know," Carter continues.

"I have?"

"In a good way, man. Since Aly moved in, you smile a lot more. You've definitely become friendlier. I mean, look at us. You've never come over here to have a beer and shoot the shit, yet here you are." He waves his hand around the room.

"I've been here before!"

"You've been here before to meet up with us to go to the bar or gym, but you've never actually sat down and had a conversation like this. And how many times did you use to go to Gabby and Michelle's for dinner—maybe once a month, once every other month? Now, you're over there all the time, and trust me, I'm not complaining. I like this new you. You're a lot less of an asshole to work with now too."

"You think I'm an asshole at work?"

"I *know* you're an asshole at work. If it weren't for Travis, I would've bailed on you a long time ago. I probably shouldn't tell you this, but Travis and I have plotted your death a few times."

I open my mouth to say something, but it would be a lie. I know I'm not the easiest to work with. I'm demanding of my employees. I expect them to come in early and stay late. After all, if I don't have much of a life, why should they? I bark out orders rather than asking nicely. I know I've let the resentment of my past fester into anger and I know I need to work on my shitty attitude.

I think back to how I've changed since Aly popped into my life. I've cut my hours to match hers. I even bought my crew lunch two times this week. Aly suggested it would be a good morale booster. You should've seen their faces when I put out a spread of various sandwiches and sides. I swear they worked harder than ever before.

I was irritated during the first few weeks of meeting Aly. I didn't know why, but then somewhere along the way, I've recognized that foreign feeling I get when I'm around her. Peace. Something about this woman brings me a type of calm and peace I've never felt before in my life.

"There is one thing, though," Carter says, turning serious. "Have you talked to Aly about her past?"

"Like her childhood, or her friendship with Jess and Jacob?"

"No, like past relationships."

I shake my head. "That hasn't come up. Why? What do you know?"

"It's not what I know; it's just a feeling that I get. I don't think she left Georgia just for the new job, especially since this is only for a year. I think there's more to her story. I think someone may have hurt her."

I stiffen in my seat, my hands balling into fists. If someone so much as laid an unwanted finger on Aly, I will make sure they regret it.

Carter holds up his hand. "I don't think anyone's physically hurt her. I know what a woman who's been physically abused acts like and that's not it. I do think someone messed with her, mentally or emotionally."

"What makes you think that?" I'm still angry. Maybe no one physically harmed her, but mental and emotional abuse is still abuse.

"I can't really explain it." He shakes his head. "It's more of a feeling. You probably wouldn't notice because she's less reserved with you."

I stare at Carter's face for a minute. "Yeah, you lost me."

"When you're around, she's bubbly, happy, funny. She jokes a lot. She's a lot quieter and subdued when you're not there."

"I don't think I've ever seen her quiet or subdued." From the moment we met, she's been doing and saying little things to tease me or egg me on. She's always trying to get a rise out of me and she never seems fearful of my reaction. Not that I would ever do anything to hurt her.

"Exactly! Which is why you wouldn't see that other side of her that the rest of us see when you're not around. I don't think she's purposely being two different versions of herself. No matter what, she's still Aly. But with you around, I think she feels free to be one hundred percent herself."

"Interesting...but why?"

"I think she feels safe with you." He takes a sip of his beer.

Pride swells in my chest. I want her to feel safe with me.

"If you want my advice, go slow and get to know her better. Ask her out on a date. I know she's claimed to have sworn off men, but I think it's just a defensive thing. If anyone has a chance with her, it's you."

A date. I haven't been on one of those since high school. I wouldn't even know how to ask her, and what if she says no? I have a lot to think about.

***

Much to my dislike, I ended up taking today off to allow my hand to heal from yesterday's mishap with the nail gun. I didn't injure my dominant hand, but it's still a pain in the ass to lay down flooring with one hand that looks like an oven mitt.

I thought a lot about what Carter said yesterday. His words really resonated with me. There's something about Aly that draws me in and I need to find out what it is for both our sakes. So, I decided to ask her out on a date. Okay, I didn't exactly ask her out. That just kind of fell into place.

Aly got home early and said she was hungry. I mentioned that I was in the mood for tacos. She said she was picky about Mexican restaurants because she doesn't like cilantro. I also hate cilantro because to me, it tastes like soap. Apparently, the same goes for Aly. I don't know why I am surprised to find that she and I have yet another thing in common. It's like we are programmed to like and dislike the same things. Anyway, I may have strongly hinted that we should check out my favorite Mexican restaurant and here we are.

"So, you're telling me that you actually picked out your sister's husband? Aren't big brothers supposed to be like super protective of their sisters dating?" She scoops some salsa on her chip. As she bites into it, her eyes close in pure enjoyment, which sets off a stirring in my pants. I can't believe my body's acting like I'm twelve years old all over again.

I clear my throat to answer her. "Well, I didn't shove him in front of my sister's face and tell her to marry him. Grant and I met in basic training. We hit it off when we first met and I just knew he would be great for my sister." Yeah, I didn't like to think of her dating, but I figured I could at least give her an example of the type of guy she should date. Grant is an all-around stand-up guy.

"How did you introduce them?"

"After basic training, we both went our separate ways for our specific training. We kept in touch and both ended up stationed in San Diego a few years later. I took him home on leave with me, and the rest is history. They dated for a while—a lot of it had to be long distance—but they've been happily married for two years and are expecting twins in February."

"That's awesome. He's not a Seabee like you?" she asks. Since moving in, Aly has asked me random questions about my time in the Navy. I was surprised when she knew that a Seabee meant construction battalion, but it turns out that she's pretty well versed in military lingo.

"Nah, he's an M.A. I, uh, mean a—"

"Master-at-arms, like military police."

"I keep forgetting you know this stuff."

"Growing up, our school always hosted a career day where parents could come in and talk about their jobs. Since like ninety percent of the kids I went to school with were from military families, I picked up a thing or two."

"What about your parents? Did they ever come to career day?"

"Oh, no, my parents wouldn't have been caught dead at one of those things. That would've forced them to admit they actually had a child." Her statement catches me off guard. My family has always been tight. I was the one who drifted, but even then, I still knew my family, especially Gram, was always there for me.

"What do they do for a living?"

"They're both realtors—commercial and residential. They get a lot of business with military families coming and going all the time. They love their jobs, probably a little too much." A brief wave of sadness crosses over her face.

"I take it you're not close to them?"

"No." She shakes her head. "I haven't talked to them in years."

Now, it's my turn to feel a surge of sadness. How can anyone not adore this girl sitting across from me? She's intelligent, funny, bubbly, and as sweet as can be.

She notices my change in demeanor. "Don't go feeling bad for me. I didn't have a horrible life. All my basic needs were taken care of. I grew up in a safe neighborhood and never had to wonder where my next meal was coming from."

"Still doesn't sound like a happy childhood."

"It might not sound wonderful, but compared to what some kids go through, I had it pretty good. While I was in college, I had to intern at a school in a not-so-great area. These kids would come to school in dirty clothes that didn't fit them, with no school supplies or backpacks. Their only reliable source of food was the crappy breakfasts and lunches the cafeteria supplied. I saw kids who were abused or ones who bounced around from foster home to foster home. My parents may not have won any parenting awards, but my life was nothing like the kids I worked with."

"Did you always want to be a teacher?"

"No, not always. The idea kind of found me. I worked as a lifeguard at an indoor pool in the winter. My boss noticed I was good with kids and asked if I would be interested in getting my Water Safety Instructor Certification. I couldn't afford it, but she made me a deal; if I stayed and worked for her for a year, she would pay for my certification. I eventually became an instructor. I really enjoyed working with the younger kids, and then one day it hit me—if I liked it so much, why not go into education? What about you? Did you always plan on joining the military?"

"No!" I choke on the word. "Joining the military was a kind of a...rash decision. I always thought I'd be an architect."

"Really?" Aly cocks her head to the side. I know I surprised her with my answer.

"Oh yeah, from the time I was little I loved building and creating. I was obsessed with Legos, but I didn't like to build the stuff from the kits. I liked to design my own. When I got older, I started drawing blueprints for all different types of builds—houses, stores, offices, everything."

"So, why didn't you become an architect?" she asks. Yeah, I should've known that question was coming, but I'm not ready to air out that dirty laundry just yet.

"Life didn't work out that way for me," I say, hoping my answer is good enough. Aly nods and doesn't press any more. Apparently, we both have our secrets to hide...

28

The waitress comes over to leave the check, but Jax scoops it up before I can reach for it.

"I got this," he says while pulling out his wallet.

"I can at least pay for my half," I offer. We're not on a date, at least I don't think we are. But even if we were, I'd still offer to pay. I always offer to pay. I don't ever want a man to think I need to depend on them.

The waitress comes back to take Jax's credit card and I swear she gives us a weird look. Now that I think of it, I think she's been giving us weird looks the entire time.

"Is it me, or has the waitress been looking at us strangely?" I ask in a hushed voice while leaning over the table.

The corners of Jax's lips turn up. "You *just* noticed?"

"Wait! So, she has?" I sit up a little straighter. "It's not just me? I thought I was being paranoid! What do you think that's all about?"

Jax sits back in the booth and studies me. "You really don't see it, do you?"

"See what? What do you mean? Oh, God! Is there something on my face? Do I have a boob hanging out or something? Dammit! I knew I should've gone with the other bra, but I hate straps showing, you know?"

Jax throws his head back in laughter. "Aly, you look beautiful."

"Oh." My cheeks flush.

"The waitress is probably looking at us weird because we look like total opposites."

"We do?" I scrunch up my nose. Now, it's my turn to study him, and yeah, I don't see it.

"Look at me." He waves his hand near his face. "I have dark hair and eyes. I'm in a black shirt and dark pants, with my tattoos visible, and I'm literally sitting across the table from the sun."

"I'll have you know this is buttercup yellow!" I say, referring to my spaghetti strap sundress. I love sundresses and practically lived in them year-round in Georgia, but the weather is getting cooler out here in Oregon. The extra warm days are hit or miss. Soon it will be time for warmer clothes. While I love sundresses, I also love the feel of a good hoodie, so I'm not too upset about switching out my wardrobe.

"Yellow is yellow. But do you see my point now?"

"I guess. But I still don't know what the big deal is."

"It's clearly not a big deal to you, but some people have issues with my look—my tattoos, specifically. There's usually a negative stigma attached to them."

"Huh." I sit back and think. "I've never thought about tattoos one way or another."

"Well, trust me, you are rare. Most people have an opinion on them."

"My opinion of someone else's tattoos shouldn't matter." A thought occurs to me and I jump in my seat. "Oh! Wait!

No! I'm lying!" Jax gives me a quizzical look and I continue, "I probably would judge you if you had a tattoo on your face."

"So, you're saying you wouldn't be sitting across from me right now if I had a gigantic scorpion on my face?"

"Exactly! Also, I don't condone anything violent, like a polar bear eating a puppy."

"That's oddly specific."

"Oh! One more! You don't have anything that's misspelled, right? Like 'no regerts' or something?"

Jax belts out a laugh. "No, I most certainly do not have any misspelled tattoos. Besides, you should know that. You've seen them all." He winks and I know he's not referring to our time spent in the pool, but rather the other morning when I saw him naked.

"Well, we're good then." I smile. A tingling sensation flows throughout my body. I have never been attracted to anyone as much as I am to Jax. Sure, I thought Trent was good-looking, but this is on a whole other level. I know our lunch is done, but I'm not ready to end whatever this is.

"Why did you choose those designs?" I ask. I may not have any tattoos, but I've been around enough tattooed people to know that designs are very individual and often have personal meanings behind them.

"I was injured a few years ago. My arm got the brunt of it. I have a lot of scarring and a few burn marks that cover my entire arm. I hated looking at them and what they represented. So, once I healed, I found a tattoo artist to help me cover them up. It's not easy tattooing over scar tissue, so we chose a design that was forgiving. Now, the emblem on my chest..."

"That's a given." I smile. "Will you tell me? About how you were injured?"

The more I learn about Jax, the more I realize how much I enjoy getting to know him. He may have a hard exterior, but I feel like I'm slowly breaking through those tough outer layers of his. He's intelligent, caring, and handsome as hell.

Crap, I'm falling for him.

29

Jax

I normally don't talk about what happened to me. My family knows most of the details since they were an integral part of my recovery. I don't like to talk about it because I don't like the pity that often comes along with it. I'm okay. I recovered. Some, like Travis, went through a lot more than me and some gave their all.

Something about Aly, though, makes me feel comfortable. I'm okay with telling her because I know she won't treat me differently afterward. Plus, I know in order for her to open up to me, I have to open up to her. I may not be ready to tell her why I joined the Navy, but I can tell her about what happened during my time in.

"Yeah." I nod. "I'll tell you about it, but not here. Come on, let's go for a walk."

I take Aly to one of my favorite places, Portside Beach. We watch as the waves crash against the large rocks that jet out into the ocean. It's a stark contrast to the sandy beach we were at during SummerFest.

"This is gorgeous!" She beams and steps out on a flat rock to get closer to the ocean. She closes her eyes, stretches out her arms, and takes in a deep breath of salty air. I love how genuine she is. She's not putting on a show for anyone; she's just enjoying the moment.

I take a step back to fully admire her while she's preoccupied taking in the view I've seen so many times before.

"Is it safe to walk out farther?" Her voice brings me out of the daydream I should not be having at this moment.

"Yeah, I've walked all the way out to the end before. There's a large flat space near the end that's perfect to sit on. Just follow my lead. I know which places to step."

She follows behind me as I make my way out to the end of the rock formation. The only sound I can hear are the waves that slap up against the sides of the rocks. A large wave crashes, leaving us in a mist of salt water. I turn to see if Aly is okay. "Everything okay back there?"

"Yup!" she replies with a lightness to her voice.

"Sorry about getting a little wet. It's kind of inevitable walking out here." I hope she doesn't consider the bit of moisture hitting us contaminated.

"That's okay. I've been through worse." She smirks and I know she's talking about the full-on dive into the ocean at SummerFest.

We make our way to the end and I point to a section of flat rocks. It dawns on me that I should've brought a blanket or something for her to sit on, but she happily plops right down on the rock. I sit beside her and look out to the water. The sun is still high in the sky. Its rays reflect off the ripples of water, making the ocean look like it's sparkling. Aly once said she would feel as though she were suffocating if she didn't live near an ocean, and I feel that in my soul.

"This view is breathtaking. Thank you for bringing me here."

"You're welcome," I say. "I discovered Portside Beach when I moved here a few years ago. It's always been a place of peace and solitude for me."

"When did you move out here?"

"About four years ago. I'm originally from a town an hour away from here. I stayed with my family for about a year after the incident, but once I healed, I knew I needed to move somewhere else. Travis has lived all over the U.S., but he considers Starboard Beach his home. I came to visit him and something about this place just felt right."

"I can see the draw to this place. It's pretty peaceful out here."

"It is." A small breeze kicks up and blows some of Aly's hair in her face. Before she can fix it, I sweep her dark golden locks behind her ear. My fingertips lightly graze her cheek. I pause to take in the beauty before me. Her features are soft; she can be outspoken and sarcastic, but there's a gentleness about her that draws me in. I also notice that she never shies away from my touch. Maybe Carter is on to something and she does feel safe with me. Her bright blue eyes meet mine and I realize I'm sitting here staring at her like an idiot.

"So…umm…you asked me about what happened," I continue.

"You don't have to explain if you don't want to. I don't want to make you uncomfortable. I'm just…curious, I guess."

"No, it's okay. It's just that no one has ever asked me before."

"What?" Aly scrunches up her nose. I love it when she does that.

"I'm serious. No one has ever asked me about my injuries. I mean, my family knows because that's why I came home, but that's about it. I don't really talk to many people."

"But you're okay with telling me?"

"Yeah, I am." I don't know why I feel comfortable telling Aly about one of the darkest times in my life. Something about her makes me want to spill all my secrets and that scares the hell out of me. "I can't tell you too much because I don't remember a lot. I was knocked out for the majority of it."

Aly nods in understanding, so I continue, "We were out in the desert; it was my second tour and Travis's first. We got word that there was a building collapse not too far outside from the base. We were told that women and children were trapped. We had to help, you know?

"Anyway, we rolled up to the scene and saw the building. It looked like a bomb went off and half of it was caved in. The thing was—" I pause and take a breath. I still remember the spine-tingling feeling that happened as we got closer to the building.

"It's okay if you can't finish," Aly says softly.

"No, it's okay. I can do this. Have you ever been to the scene of an accident when it first happens?"

"No accidents, only minor water rescues."

"Gotcha, there's generally some type of chaos. Even if it's controlled chaos, it looks like a crazy scene. People are running around trying to help others, yelling things at one another, and so on. But this. This was different. Everyone was calm. No one was running around trying to help. No one was yelling orders or crying for help."

She gives me a quizzical look.

"It was a setup." I hear Aly give a small gasp. "Before we knew it, we were ambushed. They knew if we heard women and children needed our help, we would come to the rescue.

We were like fucking fish in a barrel. The first IED threw us from our vehicle. I remember seeing a flash and I blacked out. I came to for only a minute. There was a body on top of mine that shielded me from the brunt of everything."

I point to my arm. "This was the only body part of mine that was fully exposed. All these marks are from the shrapnel. I have a few on my side, but they aren't as deep. You have to look really close to see any scarring from them. I woke up the next day in the hospital with a bad concussion and my arm bandaged. The doctors told me I had nerve damage and that I would never regain full use of my arm."

"I ne-never noticed," Aly stammers a bit. "I mean, at least when you swim, it doesn't look like there's anything wrong."

"I had some surgeries and did some rehab. It took a while and the VA tells me I only have about seventy percent mobility, but I'd say it's more like ninety percent."

"Does it hurt?"

"I feel pain every day, but I push through it. It's not a debilitating pain, more of a nuisance now. Considering what could've happened to me, I don't complain."

"Was Travis with you?"

"Remember when I said a body had fallen on top of me and blocked me from the brunt of everything?"

Aly's eyes turn into saucers. I watch her as she puts two and two together.

"I don't know what would've happened to me had it not been for Travis. Not that he covered me on purpose. That's just how we landed from the blast. He swears he was knocked unconscious too, but I have a feeling he saw more than me."

"That's...wow..." Aly shakes her head back and forth. "How did you handle that emotionally?"

"I dealt with survivor's guilt big time. We lost two members of our squadron, but knowing that I was spared because of

Travis? That was hard." Every time I look at Travis, I'm reminded of what could've happened to me and I think about Taylor and Goodwin more than I'd like to admit. They were both married with small children. Sometimes I wonder why I was spared and they weren't. After all, I had no one back home depending on me.

"Do you think what happened brought you two closer, or does seeing one another bring the memory back and make it more difficult?"

"Maybe a little bit of both," I answer honestly. "In a way, Travis represents the good and bad times. We have a bond. Our whole squadron was a brotherhood. To completely walk away from them and the military would've felt like I lost a part of me." Joining the Navy certainly wasn't in my plans when I was a teenager, but it did help shape me into who I am. I learned a lot about construction, which I use on a daily basis, and I did enjoy the camaraderie.

"It's hard to explain..." I trail off. Maybe one day, I will be able to put my feelings into words. Then I'll tell her. I don't know what surprises me more—that I'm talking about my feelings or that I'm considering talking to Aly about this again in the future.

"And now you're best friends and business partners."

"Yup." I smile. "Travis had a lot more recovery to do. I visited him every chance I had. He went through a deep depression for a while, but there's a reason we both survived. I don't know what it is, but it kept us both going."

"Thank you for telling me your story."

"Thank you for listening." I can't believe how much I've opened up to Aly...and I like it. We sit in comfortable silence as the sun begins to drop lower in the sky. I've seen some beautiful sunsets in my life, but nothing compares to the sunsets on the Pacific Coast. And the sweet girl sitting next to me? It just adds to the majesty of it all. Aly starts to shiver as the wind picks up. "Come on," I tell her. "Let's get back in the truck and get you warmed up. I think I have an extra hoodie in there."

I reach out my hand to help Aly off the large flat rock and lead her back towards my truck.

"I know I said it before, but thank you for taking me here."

"The pleasure was all mine." I grab my navy and gold hoodie and place it over her head. She pushes her arms through the sleeves but has to roll them up a bit as the size of my clothing swallows her body. I can barely see the hem of her dress and she now looks like she has nothing on but my hoodie.

"This is cozy," she says happily while shoving her hands in the front pocket. She jumps up into the passenger side of my truck while I slide into the driver's side. I pray I can keep my eyes on the road for the rest of the drive home.

***

"Parker! What the hell are you doing up there?" Travis yells up to me. I'm on the roof of our latest project house. There was a nasty windstorm last night and it looks like we lost a couple of shingles. I came up to inspect the damage. I know I should've waited for him to get here to spot me, but it was an impulse thing. I needed something to do to distract myself from Aly.

Yesterday was incredible. I've never opened myself up to anyone like that and it felt surprisingly good. I briefly considered telling her about Maranda and why I joined the military. I still feel rage within me just thinking about it. To find out everything I did was all for nothing, that Maranda had been cheating on me with her brother's best friend is a story I'm not eager to tell. I hate thinking about it. I don't regret the military, the guys I met. After all, I grew up there. But I hated that I couldn't follow my dream.

I wonder what Aly would think if I did tell her the rest of my story. Would she be turned off by the fact that I'm divorced? I shake my head. I can't even believe I'm thinking these things. I don't even know if Aly is interested in me. Maybe she's just nice to everyone and I'm seeing it in bigger doses because of our current living situation. Then again, I caught a glimpse of her headed to the bathroom last night and she was still wearing my hoodie.

Taking a deep breath, I look up towards the heavens as if all my questions will be revealed in the clouds. A dark spot appears in the sky, growing larger as it gets closer. I watch the black and white blur become clearer and then hear a honk. A large Canadian goose lands on the roof right in front of my ladder.

"Dude! Do you even hear me?" Travis yells to me again.

"Yeah, I hear you, but now I have company." I let out a groan. I like most wildlife, but these geese can be downright bastards. I take a cautionary step towards the goose. His beady little eyes are fixed on me.

"Shoo!" I wave my hands. "Get out of here!"

The goose responds with a hiss.

"Come on. Don't you guys usually fly in flocks?" I look around to see if there are more nearby. Nope, just this guy. "Did you get kicked out of your group or something?"

I take another step forward and the feathery asshole hisses at me again. He spreads out his wings and lifts one leg in what looks like some sort of attack stance.

"Look, you giant cobra chicken," I try to reason. "Neither one of us is supposed to be on this roof right now, so how about you move on and I'll do the same."

The goose lunges towards me with a honk. I jump back, losing my balance. For a moment, I'm weightless feeling zero Gs until I land with an "Oof!"

Rolling onto the ground, I immediately do an inventory of my situation. My ankle hurts like a bitch, so that means I have feeling in my legs; that's a good thing. I know I didn't lose consciousness. I try to push myself up, but I can't get much traction with my one ankle.

"Do not move! I have an ambulance on the way!" Travis yells with his phone up to his ear.

"I don't think I need an ambulance."

"The hell you do! You just fell off a roof! How did you even fall?"

"The cobra chicken pushed me!"

Travis's eyes widen and he whispers something to the 911 operator. I roll my head back and try to think of something that will distract me from my aching ankle. The vision of Aly walking around in my hoodie pops into my head. That takes my mind off the pain for a minute. Then I think of Aly wearing nothing but my hoodie. Yup, that does the trick.

"Dude, what the hell are you smiling at?" Travis's voice mixes in with the sound of sirens.

The ambulance comes quickly. The paramedics put a neck brace on me as a precaution, but as they wheel me towards the ambulance, I'm reminded of a promise Travis and I made to each other years ago.

"Hey, Travis?" I yell to my best friend.

"Yeah, man?"

"I'm pretty sure I'll be fine, but just in case, you remember our deal?"

"Yeah, yeah, if you die, I'll delete all your browser history."

"You're a good man, Trav!" I'd laugh, but the pain is back. The paramedics close the doors and I watch Travis jump in his

SUV through the small window of the ambulance. God, I hate hospitals.

30

"Oh good! You're here!" Gabby says as I walk through the door of Jax's place. She pushes me back out into the hallway but keeps the door wide open. Behind her, Jax sits on his couch with a bandaged foot propped up on the coffee table. It looks like he has bruises and bandages lining his arms.

"Oh my God! What happened?"

"He fell off a roof," Gabby says casually.

"He...what?" I try to look around her to see if Jax is okay.

"Fell off a roof. I take it you didn't run into Travis in the parking lot? You must've just missed him."

I shake my head, taking in the crazy sight before me.

"I ran into Jax and his friend Travis in the hallway," Gabby explains. "Travis saw him fall and called an ambulance. They spent a few hours in the ER. Travis had to go take care of his dog, so I offered to help until you got home."

"He...fell off a roof?"

"Yes, I've already said that." Gabby snaps her fingers in front of my face. "Get it together. He is extremely lucky his injuries are minor. He sprained his ankle and has a few deep cuts that need to be watched. He's all cleaned up for now. I have to go to work, but Alex and Carter are going to bring dinner for everyone. Alex will check Jax's wounds when he comes over; he's a certified paramedic, so he knows what he's doing. All you have to do is babysit him."

"Babysit him?"

"Yeah, I went over his discharge papers. It looks like the ER doctor misjudged his tolerance for pain meds."

"Meaning...?"

"Meaning he thought with Jax's history and injury in the military, he would need a higher dosage of pain meds compared to civilian patients. But apparently, he didn't and, well, he's really loopy."

"Loopy," I parrot back. I'm still trying to wrap my head around this whole thing. To me, Jax seems like an invincible giant. Okay, yes, he did have that incident with the nail gun the other day, but even with a bandaged hand, he was doing just fine.

"Yeah, it's kind of like he's drunk and high at the same time," Gabby says informatively then starts giggling.

"Gabby! This isn't funny!"

"It's freaking hilarious!" Her giggles turn into full-on belly laughter. "Mr. Tall, Dark, and Broody is as high as a kite right now." She grabs onto the doorframe, trying to compose herself.

"Gabby! You're supposed to be the professional here!" I hiss.

"This is not my hospital, and he is not my patient." She straightens. "I'm just helping a neighbor. The pain meds should wear off by tomorrow morning. He has ibuprofen to take for the pain and swelling. If he gets frisky with you, just kick him in the bad ankle. He'll go down like a sack of potatoes...or if he gets frisky and you like it, just go with it. I'm all about consent, but I'm pretty sure he won't mind. He's been staring at you like he just got out of a ten-year prison sentence and you're the first woman he's laid eyes on."

I look over at Jax, and yup, I've never seen a man who just came out of a ten-year prison sentence, but if I had to guess, it would look like the guy currently ogling me from the couch.

"Gabby, you can't leave me with him like this." I snap my head back to look at her.

"I have to go to work. Trust me, you'll be fine. It's not like you haven't been staying here with him anyway."

"Yeah, but..."

"Gotta go!" She pushes me back through the threshold and shuts the door. Hysterical laughter comes from the other side.

I walk over to Jax and sit on the coffee table across from him. "Hi," I say. What do I say in this situation? "So, you fell off a roof today?"

"Mm-hmm," he answers.

"Are you in any pain?"

"Nope," he says with an emphasis on the *P*.

"Do you...umm...need anything?"

"I can think of a few things." A devious smile spreads across his face. He leans forward so we are facing each other nose to nose. My heart accelerates. We continue to just stare at each other until he places his finger on my forehead with a "boop." Well, his hand-eye coordination leaves something to be desired, but at least he didn't poke me in the eye or stick a finger up my nose.

The sound of the door opening has me jumping to my feet. Alex and Carter barrel through the doorway carrying bags of what looks like takeout food.

"I thought you were coming over later," I say to both.

"We were supposed to, but when Gabby told me how drugged this guy was, I had to take advantage of it," Alex says with a mischievous grin.

"Alex! That's terrible!" I get up to help Carter in the kitchen. It looks like the guys picked up Chinese for dinner and I relax a bit knowing they are both here.

Alex sits on the coffee table in front of Jax, much like I was sitting just a few moments ago.

"Jax! Jax!" He gently pats him on the face a few times. "Don't fall asleep on me, man. We need to talk."

"Alex! Hey! When'd you get here?" Jax slurs.

"Dude! I gotta know if you were in Intelligence," Alex says.

"Mmm...no," he responds.

Alex mutters a "damn" under his breath.

"Alex! What are you doing?" I throw a packet of soy sauce at his head and miss.

"Come on, Aly, don't you want to know if this guy did some super-secret shit? Jax's guard is completely down right now. It's like he's been given truth serum. It would be such a wasted opportunity."

"Alex!" I reprimand. "That is so wrong. You can't take advantage of him like that." Am I curious? Sure, but I wouldn't be able to sleep knowing that I did something so morally wrong.

Everyone sits around Jax's coffee table to eat. Jax remains quiet but manages to eat a decent amount of orange chicken without spilling too much rice or sauce all over himself. In hindsight, it probably would've been better to order a pizza.

"Why do you even want to know if he was in Intelligence?" I ask, twirling some lo mein with my fork.

"Because I want to know if aliens are real."

"You can't be serious." My fork falls from my hand. These guys are even worse jokers than me.

"Oh, trust me, he is dead serious." Carter shakes his head. "He's convinced if there is ever an alien invasion, he will be on the first wave to get beamed up or whatever."

"Everyone knows they take the good-looking ones first!" Alex explains.

"Funny, I thought they always took the lone farmer in a cornfield."

"That's what I tell him," Carter says in agreement.

"Whatever. You don't have to worry about anything 'cause your ugly mug will be one of the last to get beamed up," Alex says to Carter, and I bust out laughing. I didn't plan on coming here to make friends, but that's exactly what's happening. I hate to think what life will be like when my contract is up and I have to say goodbye to them all.

Alex stands up and stretches. "Okay, time to be serious Alex now." He grabs a penlight out of the back pocket of his jeans and sits down in front of Jax to examine him. I watch as Alex goes from goofy to serious. It's a rare sight. He uses his light to check Jax's pupils and examines the scrapes and bruises. "So, is Aly doing a good job taking care of you?" he asks Jax and shoots me a wink.

"Mm-hmm...I like her. She smells pretty," he whisper-yells.

"She sure does, buddy, and I'll tell you what, if you take your medicine tonight and don't cause any trouble, I bet she will give you a sponge bath in the morning." Alex winks at me again.

I choke on my drink and mouth, "What the hell," to him.

"But if you don't behave tonight, Carter is going to give you that sponge bath and you don't want that, do you?" Alex continues. Now, it's Carter's time to choke and I slap him on the back to get him to stop coughing.

Alex lets out a low chuckle as he walks up beside me. "I think he's going to be just fine. He's going to hurt like hell in the morning and might feel a little hungover tomorrow thanks to the pain meds. Make sure he takes the ibuprofen every six hours. That will help a lot. Keep his ankle elevated as much as possible. Leave the door unlocked tonight so if you need us, we can run right over. If he starts to fall, just yell 'timber' so we know what to expect."

I roll my eyes and thank Alex and Carter for bringing dinner. Knowing that those two will be just a few steps away if needed helps me relax a bit.

I put on some TV for Jax to watch while I clean up from dinner, grateful that everything has been going smoothly. Jax hasn't been difficult to handle at all. He hasn't moved from the couch and has remained quiet for the most part. I'm putzing around with a game on my phone when I hear the click of a crutch on the hardwood floor.

"What are you doing?" I run over to Jax as he tries to use the crutch to stand.

"Gotta pee," he says so low I can barely hear him. I try to steady him as he stands. For a moment, I consider calling Carter or Alex. Jax is a big guy and if he takes a tumble, I'm going down with him. Thankfully, he steadies himself and with the help of me on one side and his crutch on the other, we slowly make it to the bathroom. I shut the door to give him privacy.

Several minutes tick by and I come back to the bathroom door to see if he needs help getting back to the couch. I don't hear anything, so I knock gently. "Umm, Jax? Is everything okay in there?" I say through the closed door.

"No," replies a muffled voice.

I slowly open the door, wary of what I'm going to find on the other side. Jax is standing in front of the toilet, his shorts are on the floor, but his black boxer briefs are still on. A mixture of sadness and distress plagues his face.

"What's wrong?" I ask.

"My penis," he cries. "It's gone!" He mindlessly pats the front of his underwear.

"Oh! Umm...it...it's still there." I bite my lower lip to hold back a laugh.

"No! It's not! It's gone! I loved that thing!" He hangs his head, looking like he just lost his childhood puppy.

I turn my head away from him. I don't want him to see me laughing; the poor guy truly believes his beloved appendage is gone. My phone buzzes in my pocket. I grab it and swipe to answer. "Now is not a good time," I whisper to Jess.

"Why? What's wrong?" I hear the panic in her voice. She always jumps to the worst conclusions. I can't fault her, though; I do the same thing.

"Nothing is wrong. Well, something is wrong, but...oh my God, you're not even going to believe me."

"Try me."

"Jax fell off a roof. He's okay-ish, but he's doped up on pain meds. I'm supposed to be babysitting him. He needed to use the bathroom and he's currently standing in front of me with his shorts down, claiming he lost his penis even though a weather satellite could probably detect that thing from space."

Silence.

"Jess?"

"Pics or it didn't happen."

"I am not taking pictures and it's currently happening in front of me."

"What am I gonna do?" Jax cries out.

"Listen to me. It's not gone. Your underwear is just covering it," I say as calmly as I can. The sound of hysterical laughter booms from my phone.

"Jess!" I hiss.

"Only you, Aly, only freaking you! How the hell do you get yourself into these situations?"

"I swear someone upstairs, a guardian angel, or whatever has the worst sense of humor when it comes to me. Oh, God, now he's half spinning like a dog trying to catch its tail."

"I lost my tail too?" Jax wails.

"This isn't happening," I groan into my hand. More wild laughter bursts through my phone. "Jess, I gotta go and... Oh, hell... I don't know what to do."

"Well, I know what you have to do. Go show the man his penis!"

"Why does this sound like you're giving me a pep talk?"

"I am! Now, go be the confident woman I know you can be and show that man his penis!"

"Ugh, how can I hate you and love you at the same time?"

"It's a gift," Jess says. "Good luck and give me all the details tomorrow."

I end the call and turn my attention towards a still distraught Jax.

"Jax, pull your underwear down." He gives me a look of total confusion and I know I'm going to have to physically help instead of just telling him. Okay, how do I do this? I could call Alex or Carter, but they probably wouldn't be happy to help with this kind of thing. Plus, they'd give Jax hell over it later.

I look at Jax standing there so vulnerable and half naked. "Come on, Aly," I say to myself. "It's not like you haven't seen a man naked before." Hell, I've even seen Jax naked before. With a bit more confidence, I move closer to him and look down at his very non-missing penis.

Okay. How should I do this? Do I just push his underwear down or do I pull it through the little hidey-hole thing guys have built into their underwear?

I make up my mind to just push his underwear down. That's much less invasive. Jax lets me do so without protest. As soon as he watches himself spring free, he pulls me in for a very awkward hug.

"It's back!" he rejoices. He thanks me profusely until I remind him that he still needs to pee. I walk out of the bathroom and close the door for privacy. Although, at this point, I'm not sure if privacy even matters. The toilet flushes a few minutes later and the sound of a crutch clicks on the tile floor.

"All better?" I ask when I hear the bathroom door open. "What happened to your clothes?" I yell. Jax appears in the doorway now completely naked. How did he get his shirt off so quickly with all the bandages on him? I don't even want to know what he did with his underwear. He probably flushed them down the toilet or something.

"I'm going to bed," he says nonchalantly. He fumbles with his one crutch and braces his other side against the wall as he makes his way to the guest room.

"Umm, that's uh...my...you know what? That's fine. I'll just sleep on the couch tonight." I'm not about to argue with him about sleeping arrangements in his own home. I follow him into the bedroom to make sure he gets to the bed safely.

"Aly?" Jax says once he reaches the foot of the bed.

"Yes?"

"I stole your cookies." And with that, Jax belly flops onto the bed and instantly begins to snore. I grab a blanket and cover his naked self...but not before I take a moment to appreciate the gorgeous body before me. With a nice mental image burned into my mind, I head for the couch to get some sleep.

31

Jax

I wake up feeling like I was hit by a truck. My head feels heavy and I groan in pain with every shift of my body. I slowly open my eyes and realize that I'm not in my bed. I'm in the guest room, the guest room that Aly should be in. I sit up and look around me. Everything seems normal, but Aly isn't in here. I grab the crutches that are propped next to the nightstand. I wonder if Aly left them here for me. I hobble to my bedroom, rest my crutches against my dresser, and shift to sit on my bed, which has a lump in the middle of it.

I pull back the blanket to reveal a sleeping Aly. She looks so peaceful and content. I wonder why she's in my bed and I was in hers. I chuckle to myself. I've never had a woman sleep in my bed and of course it would be Aly to break that rule of mine. She's broken several rules of mine already and for some reason, it doesn't bother me. I gently brush back a piece of hair that has fallen in front of her face. Her eyes flutter open and the sleeping beauty screams.

"What the hell are you doing?!" She springs to a sitting position.

"What am I doing? I came in here wondering what I was doing in the guest room and found you sleeping in my bed." I hold up my hands in defense.

She rubs her hands over her face, trying to wake herself up. "Look, I know I've seen you naked a few times now, but do you have to make this a habit?"

I look down at myself and yup, I don't know why I didn't notice a draft until now. Maybe I do need to reconsider the whole sleeping naked thing. I turn towards my dresser to grab some shorts, but my foot gets caught in a blanket on the floor. My arms start to make a windmill motion as I try to steady myself, and pain surges through my body. Aly lunges for me like there's actually a chance she can help. Together, we tumble onto the floor with my body breaking her fall.

"Is everything okay? We heard a scream," Alex's voice bellows from the doorway. Gabby is standing beside him in the scrubs she wore yesterday; she must've just gotten home from her overnight shift.

I take in the situation. I'm lying on the floor naked as the day I was born. Thankfully, I'm not exposing myself to anyone because Aly is doing a thorough job of covering me with her body. Her soft body in those thin scraps of fabric she calls pajamas. Her hair swept to the side brushes up against my shoulder, the smell of her shampoo fills my senses, and I begin to go into overload between her scent and our bodies touching.

And now it's like we're in the ocean all over again. I know the moment Aly can feel me because her eyes go wide and she mumbles a "Well, good morning to you too" under her breath. She makes no attempt to get off me, which makes me grateful for several reasons.

"We're fine!" Aly looks up at Alex and Gabby, who are still standing in the doorway. "Just a little mishap, but everything's fine."

"Do you need any help getting up?" Gabby asks.

Aly rests her head on her hand and her elbow into my chest like she's casually leaning on a table. "Nope, we're all good!" She gives me a look as if to say *say something*.

"Yup, all good!" I fake a smile.

"Aly, did you forget what I told you to yell if Jax fell?" Alex crosses his arms and looks at her as if he's a parent reprimanding a child.

"Ugh, Alex, now is really not the time."

"Oh, I think it's the perfect time." A shit-eating grin crosses his face. "Come on now, let me hear you say it."

Aly burrows her face in my chest and mumbles something inaudible.

"What was that?" Alex cuffs a hand to his ear.

"Timber!" Aly yells. "Now, can you please get out of here!"

"Okay then, if you don't need us, we'll be on our way," Gabby says and turns to leave. I may be looking at her upside down, but I can still see an amused look on her face. She grabs Alex, who has a shit-ass grin on his face, and pulls him with her. I hear Alex mumble something about her owing him twenty bucks. I'm sure they wagered some sort of bet on Aly and me.

Aly jumps off me as soon as the coast is clear. I grab the blanket that I tripped on earlier and use it to cover my lower regions. I know it's going to take a bit to stand, so I work my way to a sitting position with my back up against my bedframe.

"Are you okay?" Aly sits on the floor across from me with her back up against my dresser. "I'm so sorry about the blanket. I get hot when I sleep and must've kicked it to the floor in the middle of the night. God! You must be hurting so badly right now! How's your ankle? Do you need me to get anything?"

She's talking a mile a minute. I am hurting, but I don't even care about that right now.

"Why were you in my bed?" I blurt out.

"I tried to sleep on the couch, but I was so uncomfortable. I figured if you were sleeping in my bed, I could sleep in yours."

Fair enough. "How did I end up in your bed?"

"You went in there after the bathroom episode."

"The bathroom episode?"

"I take it you don't remember?" She raises an eyebrow.

"I don't remember much. I remember falling off the roof, going to the hospital, Gabby coming over, and talking to Travis. The rest is blurry from there. What happened?"

"I don't know if you want to know." She bites her lip.

"Just tell me." I sigh and place my head in my hands. I don't know what she's about to say, but I have a feeling I won't be able to look her in the eye when she's done. I wait for her to start, but I'm only met with silence. I look up to see Aly sitting on the floor across from me, shaking. "Are you crying?"

"No," she squeaks. I realize that she is in fact not crying but trying to hold back her laughter. She's trying so hard that tears are springing from her eyes.

"Oh, God! Is it that bad?"

"Umm..." She looks at me and tries to compose herself. "You...umm...you said you needed to pee, so I helped you to the bathroom. I left you alone to, you know, do your business, but you were in there a long time. I asked if you were okay and...and—" She loses it all over again.

"And? And what?"

"You were upset because you couldn't find your penis!" she cries out, holding her stomach as she literally rolls on the floor.

"Excuse me?" I've said and done a lot of dumb shit in my past; I am a sailor after all, but this is farfetched even for me.

"You...you really thought it was gone!" She swipes away the tears now falling freely down her face. "You were so upset! I tried to tell you that you still had your underwear on, but you didn't understand, so I had to...uh...help."

This cannot be happening. "How did you help?" I grit through my teeth.

"I just pushed your underwear down."

"That's it? You didn't like try to take advantage of me or anything, right?"

"Absolutely not! You should be thanking me! I could've called Alex or Carter to help, but I figured that would be too embarrassing. Once you discovered you were umm...back in business, I left you to take care of everything. A few minutes later, you came out buck naked and declared you were going to sleep." She waves her arm in the direction of the guest bedroom. "You walked directly to my room and lay down. I didn't think it would be helpful to argue."

"So, you decided to sleep in my bed." It makes sense, but I'm upset with how stupid I acted.

Aly's still recovering from her laughing fit and doesn't answer me, not that I need further explanation.

"It's...okay. I'm sorry I gave you some trouble last night. I don't know what they gave me in the hospital."

"You were definitely not yourself. Entertaining, though." A slow smile spreads across her face. "Can I help you up?" She begins to giggle. I know exactly where her mind is going and I'm headed right down the gutter with her. "I mean...umm...you really need your ankle elevated."

Aly helps steady me as I slowly lift myself back to a standing position and she hands me my crutches. I grab a pair of shorts and head towards the living room where I'll probably be spending the rest of the day.

She sets me up on the couch with a pillow and an icepack for my ankle then leaves to go do something in the kitchen. I feel bad that she is taking care of me. She didn't exactly volunteer for the job; it just defaulted to her. Of course, if I had to choose someone, it would be her.

"Let me know if I can help with something," I yell to her from the couch. I can't think of how I can help her, but it makes me feel better to say that.

"I'm good!" she yells over her shoulder from the kitchen.

"What are you doing in there anyway?"

"You'll see!" she says in a singsong voice.

A little while later, a delicious and familiar scent begins to waft from the kitchen over to the couch. "Are you making cookies?" My mouth waters at the thought of oatmeal walnut chocolate chip cookies. Yup, I can easily sit here for the rest of the day and eat nothing but those cookies. Maybe this whole falling off a roof thing wasn't so bad after all.

Aly comes over to the couch a short while later with a plate in her hand. I sit up a little straighter and try not to let my excitement show too much. She proudly presents me a plate with one tiny cookie on it.

"One cookie?" I look up at her with a frown.

"Yeah, I made the rest for everyone else."

"But I fell off a roof." I give her a sad look that she mirrors back.

"I know, and Gabby, Alex, and Carter were so sweet to come over and help. It's my way of thanking them."

I look back down at the one lonely cookie on the plate. "But I fell off a roof," I repeat, hoping she will take pity on me.

She sits down next to me, puts her arm around my shoulder, and gives it a little squeeze. "I know, so you just sit here, rest, and eat your cookie. I'm going to take a shower and bring the rest of the cookies over to everyone else."

As soon as I hear the bathroom door close, I poke my head up and over into the kitchen. There's a plastic container full of those delectable morsels sitting on the counter just waiting to be eaten.

I lower my bum leg to the floor and pull myself up. I don't want Aly to hear the sound of my crutches, so I decide to hop on one foot over to the kitchen. I steady myself on random pieces of furniture as I hobble over to the counter. "Come here, my precious," I say to the container of cookies. I stick a cookie in my mouth and decide to stuff as much as I can in the pockets of my basketball shorts.

"What are you doing?" Aly's voice scares the hell out of me.

I spin to see her staring at me with her hands on her hips.

"I ante e oogie," I say with my mouth stuffed to the brim.

"I told you they were for everyone who came to help you." She folds her arm across her chest. I feel like a student who's disappointed her.

"Wrorry."

She keeps her authoritative stance for a moment, then begins to laugh.

"So, you were the one who stole my cookies!" She points to me.

"You set me up!" I jump a little, making several cookies spill from my pockets and onto the floor.

"Oh! This is just pathetic!" She shakes her head.

"I'm not pathetic!" I say, trying to bend down in an awkward position to retrieve the fallen cookies. "They're just so good! I mean, it's kind of a compliment, right?"

"It's a compliment if you tell me you like them, not when you steal them. You let Alex take the blame, and don't you dare stick that cookie from the floor in your mouth!" She leaps forward to swat the cookie out of my hand.

"Five-second rule! It's still good!" I turn and vigorously hop away on one foot.

"Don't you dare fall over and make me yell 'timber'!"

I laugh and throw myself onto the couch. "I can't believe Alex got you to say that, and how did you know I stole your cookies?"

"You told me last night right before you passed out. Alex said the stuff they gave you acted like truth serum. He was trying to see if you had any government secrets, and oh!" She slaps her hand to her forehead. "I should've asked you about Travis's name!"

"You could've asked me anything at all and *that's* what you want to know?" I smile, thinking of how sweet Aly is. She really could've taken advantage of my mental state, but she didn't. Her honesty makes me even more attracted to her.

"It's a valid question... Is it Kevin?"

"No."

"Joe?"

"Nope."

"Nick?"

"Did you just list the Jonas brothers?"

"Maybe." She shifts her eyes and rocks on her heels a bit. "Wait! How do you know—"

"I have a little sister, remember?" I cut her off. "I even got stuck taking her and her friends to one of their concerts. Longest. Night. Ever."

"Huh." Aly grabs more ice for my ankle. "There is so much I have yet to learn about you."

You have no idea, sweetheart.

***

It's been a few weeks since my fall off the roof. Thankfully, I'm mostly healed and things have calmed down considerably. The girls' condo has still not been fixed. Michelle has been going round and round with the insurance company. Supposedly, the tenants don't want to take responsibility. I'm not complaining, though; this just means Aly and I get to spend more time together. Living with Aly is an experience, but an experience I'm very much enjoying.

"I can't believe you wash your dishes by hand when there's a perfectly capable dishwasher right here!" She points to my dishwasher that's never been used.

I hold up my hands. "I have two capable dishwashers right here."

"Well, I for one think the dishwasher was one of the greatest things ever invented. Back at home, everything goes into my dishwasher."

"What about the stuff that's not dishwasher safe?"

"Survival of the fittest! If you can't take the heat, you don't belong in my house."

"I like washing dishes. It reminds me of spending time at my gram and pop's place. They lived in an older home that didn't have one. I would wash and my sister would dry."

"Were you close to your grandparents?"

"Yeah." I smile. "They were the best. My sister and I spent a lot of time with them when we were little. Both my parents worked, so Gram and Pop would watch us. Pop was big on sports, so he was always outside throwing a ball to me. When I got older, he came to all my swim meets. Gram was the caregiver. She was always trying to feed us, saying we were too skinny. Did you know your grandparents?"

She shakes her head. "No, my dad's parents passed away before I was born and I guess my mom was estranged from hers or something." She takes the spatula she just dried and places it next to the ladle in my utensil holder.

"Umm...the spatula actually goes to the right of the potato masher."

"Does it now?" She gives me a coy smile. She knows exactly what she's doing.

"I like my things in a certain order, in case you haven't noticed, and while we're on the subject, stop messing with my books. I don't mind if you read them. Just put them back where they belong."

"Oh, I'm not reading them." A grin that could rival the Cheshire Cat spreads across her face.

"I didn't think you were. Why do you have to mess with my stuff?"

She takes the spatula in her hand and spins it around her fingers like she's twirling a lopsided baton. "You're very set in your ways, you know."

"I like order. Is that wrong?"

"No." She narrows her eyes. "But I don't think you've always been like this."

She's right. I used to be happy, but that was a long time ago before life got complicated. "Maybe I have Obsessive Compulsive Disorder," I suggest.

"If I truly thought you had a disorder like that, I would not mess with you. I've worked with people with OCD; it can be crippling for them. No, sir..." She points the spatula toward my chest. "You are just a grump who's become set in your ways."

I won't admit it to her, but she's right again. I figure if I make my life as predictable as possible, I stand less of a chance of getting hurt again. After all, I used to be more carefree and look where it got me. "Give me the spatula."

"No!" She curls her arm in towards her chest, cradling the metal utensil.

"Give it to me!" I take a step closer to her. She takes a step back. "Give it to me, Aly!" I lunge for her, but she predicts my move and ducks out of the way just in time for me to grab air.

"Ha!" she yells in victory and runs to the other side of the kitchen island.

"Aly, I'm not playing around. Give it to me!" I run around the island, which is stupid since she'll probably just take off in a different direction.

Whack!

"Oh! You did *not* just smack my ass with that!"

I dive for her again, barely getting a grip on the hem of her shirt. She lets out a squeal and breaks off towards the hallway. I catch up to her easily. Thanks to my height, the length of my strides is double the size of hers.

"Gotcha!" I cage her in up against the guest room door. She lets out a small squeak but doesn't try to break away. We lock eyes. The playful grin that was plastered on her face grows more serious by the second.

My hand cups the side of her face and I dip my head down closer to hers. "What are you doing to me?" The sound of my voice surprises me as it is lower than I intended. I lean in closer to her. There's no way for her to move away from me, but it doesn't look like she's trying to escape. My lips ever so lightly brush against hers, but the sound of a smoke alarm and a scream kills the moment and has us both running for the door.

"What's going on?" I huff as I run through the door of 312 and take in the scene. Carter is standing on a chair, trying to shut off the smoke alarm while Alex is kneeling on the kitchen counter, checking out the microwave above the stove. There's no visible fire, but there is a bit of smoke and an awful smell of something that has clearly burned.

"Michelle, are you okay?" Aly asks from somewhere behind me.

"Yeah. I just freaked out a bit." She nervously tugs on her hair. "I started heating up some leftovers in the microwave. I went into the bathroom to take off my makeup, but then I heard the smoke alarm. When I came out, I saw sparks and Alex on the counter."

Everyone shifts their gaze to Alex. "Lucky timing." He shrugs his shoulders. "I smelled food and decided to see if Peanut had any extra. I walked in and saw a small fire in the microwave. I unplugged it and it fizzled out on its own."

"I-I don't know what happened. I didn't put anything metal in it." Michelle wraps her arms around herself.

"I think it was a faulty wire within the microwave itself. I don't think you're in any danger." Carter comes up behind her and gives her a hug.

"But what if it's not? What if it's more than that? What if there's a fire behind the microwave, within the walls or something?" Michelle is obviously distraught and I'm glad the guys were here to help her.

"Peanut, there's no fire. The walls are cool to the touch. I do want to pull this thing out and get a better look at it, though." Alex looks at me for help. The microwave over the stove is a two-man job given the sheer size of it. I give him a nod back.

"If it makes you feel any better, I'll inspect the wiring in the rest of the place while Alex and Jax check out the microwave to make sure it was that and only that." Carter's suggestion seems to appease Michelle, though she still looks panicked.

"Do you want me to stay with you, Michelle? I can sleep on the couch if you don't want to be alone tonight," Aly suggests and I bite my tongue from yelling "No!"

I want her under my roof, not this one, I inwardly argue with myself. This is Aly's home and technically, we all live under the same roof since we are all in the same complex.

"I'll stay over," Carter offers before Michelle has a chance to respond. I breathe a sigh of relief.

"Thanks, everyone. Carter, it would be great if you could stay. Aly, that's really sweet of you, but you've already been put out of your room. I don't want... Why are you holding a spatula?"

All eyes swing over to Aly. Her cheeks begin to blush as she looks down at the spatula still in her hand. "Oh yeah...umm...I was just putting it back next to the ladle—"

"Potato masher," I cough.

"Potato masher, when I heard you scream. I guess if you don't need me, I'll just head back over to our place... I mean, Jax's place." Her cheeks redden and she quickly slinks out the door.

"Huh," Alex looks at the abandoned doorway. "Never thought Legs had a kinky side."

I smack Alex upside the head, but he gives me a grin, telling me his comment was worth it. "It wasn't like that, asshole. Nothing happened." But oh, how I wish something did, and I smile to myself thinking of how Aly referred to my condo as ours.

I look under the microwave to see what tools I'll need to get this beast of an appliance out. After a lot of inspecting, the guys and I determine that a faulty wire within the microwave caused the sparks and mini fire. Even though we assured Michelle she was safe, she still wanted Carter to stay the night.

It's late by the time I get back to my place. The door to Aly's room is shut and I know she's probably sleeping. We came so close to kissing; I wonder what would've happened if that alarm hadn't gone off. I stop and look at her closed door. Something between us is changing. We're growing closer and it feels like the most natural thing on Earth. For the first time in forever, I look forward to tomorrow and every day after.

32

Aly

I wake up in the morning with a heaviness in my heart. I know I should get up and get ready to swim, but almost kissing Jax last night triggered emotions in me. After Trent, I figured I would be on my own for the rest of my life, and now I'm falling for a guy who doesn't do relationships. I swipe away a few tears from my eyes. Maybe I am as messed up as Trent said.

"Aly?" Jax's voice sounds from the other side of my door. "Is everything okay? I know it's the weekend, but you're usually up by now."

"I'm fine," I say as I open the door.

Jax crosses his arms and leans against the doorframe. "It doesn't look like you're fine."

"I'm totally fine, just overslept a bit." I grab my goggles from the top of the dresser. I guess I'll forgo my morning coffee and head down to the pool.

"Wait!" Jax gently pulls on my arm. I spin around to face him. "Is this about yesterday?"

"It's nothing! Like I said, I'm fine." I turn to walk away.

"If there's one thing I know, no woman is ever fine when she says she's fine."

I turn back to scowl at him and begin to walk away again.

"Why did Jess say you didn't think anyone would want you?" he blurts out.

I freeze. I knew he'd bring up that day in the hallway eventually. I just wish it weren't right now.

"I have relationship issues, okay?" I say with an attitude.

"You think you have relationship issues?" He lets out a dark laugh. He places his hands on top of my shoulders and leans into my ear. "I'm sure whatever your story is, I can top it."

"Oh, I'm sure you can't."

"Try me."

"I'm a runaway bride."

"I was married and divorced at eighteen."

I suck in a breath. I was not expecting that. "You win."

"Not a competition." He looks me up and down. "Runaway bride, huh? Didn't peg you for that."

"I didn't peg myself for it either, but I couldn't go through with it." I wrap my arms around my middle. "Technically, I'm not a runaway bride because I didn't leave him at the altar. That's just what everyone called me after Trent and I broke up."

"You know I'm going to need more of an explanation than that."

"So, you were married and divorced at eighteen?"

"Don't deflect. You first," he says sternly. "I will tell you my story *after* you tell me yours."

"Promise?"

"Promise." Jax spins me around and walks me towards the living room. "Sit!" He points to the couch.

"Wow! You're really bossy all of a sudden." I cross my arms in defiance but quickly comply; I really want to hear his story.

Jax sits down across from me and waits for me to start.

"This might take a while." I fumble with my hands.

"How about you just start at the very beginning."

"So, you know I was born and raised in Virginia and then I moved to Georgia for college. I landed a teaching job there after I graduated, and life was going well. Then three years ago, I met Trent, the most eligible bachelor in Beaute." I roll my eyes and use air quotes at that last bit.

Jax doesn't say anything but nods at me to continue.

"I'm not overexaggerating when I say he was Beaute's most eligible bachelor. You know how in *Beauty and the Beast* the villagers swoon all over Gaston? Well, Trent was Beaute's Gaston, even down to the narcissistic personality, but I didn't see that in the very beginning. People literally would stop me and tell me how lucky I was to be with such an amazing man.

"It was exciting in the beginning and Trent *was* loving the first year. He proposed to me on our one-year anniversary and of course I said yes. Everything was great...until his true colors started to show."

I should've been walking on cloud nine during those first few days and weeks of being newly engaged. After all, everything in my life plan was going so smoothly. Then, one day, I woke up with a nagging feeling in the pit of my stomach. It was like the whole universe felt off. I think deep down I knew I couldn't go through with the engagement. I think that's also when I started to see Trent for who he really was.

"I have anxiety..." I pause and study Jax's face for a reaction, but he motions for me to continue. "I've suffered from it for pretty much my whole life, but it's been under control the last few years. Trent knew about my anxiety issues; he always seemed fine with it. Shortly after we got engaged, he started saying weird things about how I overthink or worry too much. At first, it was just little comments here and there.

"I tried to brush it off. He never said things like that before, but then things started spiraling. He wanted me to check in with him no matter where I went, which was mostly to and from work. Then he started going through my phone and computer like he was paranoid about something. The belittling got worse. Nothing I ever did seemed good enough. I questioned his behavior, but he turned it around on me and said I was the one being paranoid. Then, one day, I couldn't take it any longer and gave him the ring back."

"I have a feeling the story doesn't end there," Jax says with a tone of anger in his voice.

"Nope, but I wish it did. So, I gave him back the ring and he was devastated, like totally shocked that I would do such a thing. We split up for a few weeks, but then he started coming around again. He was on his best behavior. Things felt like old times, so we got back together. It was good for a few weeks...until it wasn't again. It was insanity. One minute he would be sending me flowers and saying that I was the love of his life, the next minute he would tell me what I should wear and who I could hang out with. We broke up and got back together three more times before I finally told him to stop contacting me."

"Did he stop? You know, contacting you?"

"He stopped contacting me directly for a while, but other things started happening."

Jax leans in closer, his full attention on me.

"Remember when I said the town loved him? Once word spread that we were finally finished, people started turning on me. I would walk into a store and hear people say stuff like 'Oh, there's the runaway bride' or 'I can't believe she thought she was too good for someone like Trent.' I even had a parent request their student be removed from my class because if I couldn't make good decisions about my future, how could I be trusted with the education of their child."

Jax turns his head and lets out a sharp breath. "You're not telling me everything, are you?"

I fidget with the hem of my shirt. Jax moves in closer to me. He gently puts two fingers under my chin and lifts it up so we are back looking at each other eye to eye.

"Hey, look at me," he says softly. "Tell me what else happened."

"At first, it was little things that started happening. I chalked it up to stress, my overactive imagination, my anxiety. Trent's dad is the chief of police and his brother is also a sheriff in town. Sometimes when I was driving, I would notice a police vehicle following me. The windows on their cars are heavily tinted so I could never tell who it was or if it was different people each time."

"Each time? How many times did it happen? You said you never got a ticket before you came here."

"I never got pulled over," I answer. "They never put their lights or sirens on. They would just follow me closely, like trying to mess with me. One time, I was stopped at a light and four of them boxed me in."

"Shit, Aly! That's harassment! What did you do?"

"I kept driving until I was out of town boundaries. I didn't know if they were on duty or not, but I figured if I could get out of their jurisdiction, I would be okay."

"You did the right thing."

For some reason, his reassurance soothes me. I give him a weak smile. "Thanks."

"There's more, isn't there?"

"Nothing could ever really be proven, you know? There was this one time I was working late and someone slashed all four of my tires at school."

"Aren't schools supposed to have surveillance cameras?"

"They weren't working that day."

"Convenient." Jax jumps up, clearly agitated. He starts pacing the room. "Keep going. I want to know everything."

"Sometimes, when I was at home or even out in town, I would feel like I was being watched but never saw anyone or anything. Then this one time, Jacob came home for a short visit. He keeps a small apartment back home for when he's not traveling. We went out to dinner and a movie. He mentioned to me that he felt like we were being watched. It kind of validated what I thought, you know? He told me he didn't feel comfortable leaving me at home alone, so he slept on the couch that night. Around three in the morning, we heard a crash; someone had thrown a rock through my living room window. There was a note tied to the rock."

"What did the note say?"

"Slut."

Jax mutters a curse under his breath.

"What was I supposed to do? I couldn't go to the police. His family *is* the police. Have you ever been to a small town in the South before? They are part of the Good Ol' Boys Club. You don't mess with them. After that, Jacob insisted that I live in his apartment. He wanted to take some time off work so I wouldn't be alone, but I knew they would just harass him too. It wasn't his battle to fight.

"I spent the last few months living in Jacob's bachelor pad instead of my own home that I worked hard for and loved so much. I tried to move back, but I jumped at every noise, every shadow that I thought I saw out of the corner of my eye. I started to feel like I really was losing my mind."

"So, that's why you came out here? Because of the harassment?"

"I had no intentions of leaving my home, but I didn't feel safe there either. I wasn't actively looking for an out, but then I was contacted by the university. One of the higher-ups read my dissertation, liked my ideas, and wanted me to take over a section of their Early Childhood Education Department."

"Just like that?"

"Just like that. Jess calls it divine intervention. Everything worked out so smoothly, like it was meant to be or something. I finished up my school year in Georgia and headed out here."

33

Jax

Anger courses through me as I pace back and forth in my living room. I'm pissed that Aly wasted so much time on this asshole and that he harassed her when she tried to break free. At the same time, I'm proud of her for finally cutting those ties.

Aly wants to see the good in people; I know that's why she let her ex back into her life so many times. Her ex mistook her kindness for weakness. Aly is no weakling, but I'm not sure she fully believes that. On top of it all, she had no support system with Jess moving out of state and Jacob traveling all the time. It kills me to think her parents don't even have ties with her. Thinking of how she handled that part of her life with little support makes me even more grateful for my family. They rallied around me not only through the divorce but my recovery as well.

"Umm... I believe you owe me a story."

In the heat of everything, I forgot that I promised her I would tell her about what happened to me. I sit back on the couch, close my eyes, and try to center myself. I have never opened myself up the way I'm about to right now.

"I met Maranda the summer I was sixteen. I was wrestling around with a friend and fell from his tree house. I broke my leg. It was the beginning of summer and I was super bummed that I couldn't swim or do all the typical summer stuff with my friends. My friends brought me to the movies to try to cheer me up. She was there with her friends. I had seen her around school before, but I was so caught up in swimming, I never really gave her the time of day."

"Until you had all the time in the world," Aly interjects.

"Exactly." I nod and continue, "We were together for all our junior and senior year. Life seemed good. I was accepted into my dream school for architecture. I got in on a swimming scholarship. I was on top of the world. Then Maranda got pregnant towards the end of our senior year."

Aly's eyebrows nearly shoot to the top of her head. I knew she wouldn't be expecting that.

"It came as a complete shock. I mean, yeah, we were teenagers and fooled around, but I always used a condom. I had so much going for me, I didn't want to mess it up. We told our parents. They were livid, of course. Her parents insisted we marry as soon as possible. I went along with everything because, well, it takes two, right? I wanted to do right by her. We married that May; we were both eighteen by then.

"Our parents started putting pressure on us to get our future in order," I continue. "My dreams for college were squashed because I needed to get a job to support her and our baby. My uncle suggested I join the military since I would have a steady paycheck and insurance to take care of our family."

"So that's why you joined?" Aly all but whispers.

"Yup, I went to a recruiting station and left for the Navy the day after high school graduation. Maranda stayed with her parents while I went off to basic training. The baby wasn't due until November, so I still had time to get my shit together. The plan was for me to get through basic training, receive my orders, and then have her come with me to my duty station once the baby was born."

"Sounds like you were highly prepared for being so young." Aly tucks her legs underneath her body.

"Yeah, that's the crazy part. I was scared shitless to be a young dad, but I was also kind of pumped too. I had a great childhood growing up and amazing role models. I was determined to be the best dad I could be."

"So, what happened?"

"Maranda had the baby—a little girl. We decided on the name Kinley. It took about two weeks before I was able to get paternity leave and fly out to be with them. She was able to send me pictures and videos, but something about the baby..." I shake my head. "Something wasn't right."

Aly cocks her head to the side in confusion.

"I felt no connection to this child. I thought maybe I would feel differently once I met her in person. I got home and the moment they put the baby in my arms, I felt...nothing."

"Nothing?"

"Nope." I take a long breath. "My dad and Pop had told me that the first time they held each of their children, something came over them. They described it as this astounding otherworldly feeling, this sense of wonderment that they had helped bring a child into this world, and I felt absolutely nothing."

I study Aly and watch her face as she begins to put the pieces together. She opens her mouth and shuts it several times before she says, "The baby wasn't yours, was it?"

"No." I shake my head.

"Did she know you weren't the father?"

"The truth came out when I asked her for a paternity test. Apparently, she and her brother's best friend weren't using any protection while she was cheating on me. She told me that she hoped I was the father since I was the responsible one."

"I'm so sorry." I can see the tears welling in those big blue eyes of hers.

"Don't feel sorry for me. You've been through shit too."

"Yeah, but nothing like what you've been through." Aly looks at me with concern. "What happened to the baby? To Kinley?" Of course this sweet woman would ask about the well-being of the child.

"She's fine, I guess. I don't think the father is in the picture. I know Maranda lived with her parents for a while so she would have support. She married some guy about a year ago. My parents saw it in the paper and told me."

That day, Travis and I celebrated with a steak dinner. While Kinley's last name was switched to her biological father's, Maranda refused to change her last name until she remarried. It killed me that this woman was walking around with my last name for so many years. It might not be a big deal to some people, but to me, it meant everything.

Many years ago, my pop and I started digging into our ancestry. The Parkers come from some impressive stock, including a decorated war hero, a doctor who opened a free clinic, and a distant relative who saved his entire village from a flood. It made me proud to know that I came from such a valorous lineage. But, heroism aside, my family represents love. Everyone has had happy, successful marriages, except me—the screw-up. Knowing Maranda was walking around with my last name for years was a constant reminder that I gave my name to someone who didn't take relationships as seriously as I did. I contemplate telling Aly about this, but I've already said more than I planned.

I jump to my feet with a sudden burst of anger. "So that's my story. The one good thing to come of it was that I did end up enjoying military life. Once my initial four years were up, I reenlisted for four more. I figured I'd do twenty and retire, but then I was injured."

I walk to the kitchen and grab two bottles of water from the fridge. "Put some sneakers on. We're going downstairs to the gym."

"The what? Why?" Aly scrunches up her nose.

"You have a crazy-ass ex out there, so I'm going to teach you some self-defense moves."

"Do you really think that's necessary?"

"I do."

Ever since I met Aly, I've had an overwhelming need to protect her. I know I can't watch out for her all the time, but at least I can put some power back into her hands.

34

Aly

Five days have passed since Jax and I told each other our secrets. Since then, I've felt like the weight of the world has come off my shoulders. Even though I feel lighter, the thought of Trent showing up is still a possibility. During my last few months in Beaute, his actions showed me that he was more unhinged than I thought. True to his word, Jax has been showing me some self-defense moves, and if I'm being honest, it's become my favorite part of the day.

Jax and I have fallen into a comfortable routine. We've been spending a lot of time with each other; we eat together and work out together. Our conversations are so natural and are never forced. It's like we've known each other our whole lives. But our time together is about to come to an end. Michelle messaged me this morning to let me know that my room is finally finished. I should be happy to be moving back in with my roommates, but instead I feel an overwhelming sadness that I'm leaving what feels like home.

"Hey!" Jax says, startling me. He grabs onto the top of the doorframe, putting his large biceps on display. "Ready for your next self-defense lesson?" He pauses for a moment when he takes notice of the items I'm packing. "What are you doing?"

"Michelle messaged me earlier and told me that my room is done." I zip up my duffel bag.

"You're leaving?"

"Well, yeah, I mean, I'll only be across the hall, but I don't need to stay here any longer."

"Yeah, yeah... I guess so." He frowns and looks away for a moment. "Do you still have time for another self-defense lesson? We can do it here instead of going down to the gym."

"Sure, that sounds good." I'm already in yoga pants and a T-shirt, so I don't have to change. I purposely dressed like I was ready for a lesson so he would ask. While I do appreciate the safety tips, I really enjoy the physical contact that comes along with it more.

Jax walks into his bedroom and comes out a moment later wearing only basketball shorts that sit low on his hips. I watch as he goes into the living room and pushes the coffee table up against the wall to give us a wide space to work. Thanks to our little self-defense lessons, I've gotten up close and personal views of Jax, and I will never not ogle him when his back muscles flex.

"Okay..." He turns to face me, and I hope he didn't catch me checking him out. "So, let's review. What is the most important part of self-defense?"

"Situational awareness," I answer like a good little student, although I will admit that I'm pretty terrible at paying attention to my surroundings. I no longer talk on the phone when I'm walking around outside, but the beautiful scenery around me often distracts me. Just the other day I walked right past my car because I was too busy watching a bald eagle flying overhead.

"Right. Now, we've already covered a few scenarios if Trent were to confront you face to face, but I don't think we've practiced what to do if he comes up to you from behind."

"Do you think he would, you know, do a sneak attack?"

"From what you've told me about him, he probably wouldn't, but you can never be too sure." He walks over to me and places his arms around my waist from back to front. I lean into him. The heat of his body goes right through my shirt and I wonder what it would feel like to have no barriers between us.

"Umm, Aly, you need to stand up straight for this," he says softly in my ear. The scent of his bodywash is faint.

"Oh, right, sorry about that." I straighten my body as my cheeks flush.

"No worries at all. So, as I was about to say, there are different moves you can do depending on where the attacker puts his arms." He slides his hands up my waist. The hem of my shirt lifts up slightly and his fingertips brush against the now exposed section of my stomach, causing a tingling sensation to flow through my body.

"So...umm...put your arms like this..." He removes his hands from my middle and I immediately feel cold without his touch. He moves my arms up slightly and pushes my back against his front. This time, not only do I feel the warmth of his body, but I sense his racing heartbeat as well.

"Are you okay?" My voice sounds breathier than expected.

"Yeah, yeah, I'm fine." But he sounds unsure of himself. He lets go of my arms and takes a few steps back. I spin around to face him and see his chest heaving, but we haven't done anything strenuous.

"Jax?"

"I can't do this." He rubs a hand over his face.

"Oh, umm, okay. I guess then I can get going," I say, confused and disappointed. He grabs hold of my arm before I can walk back to the bedroom to grab the rest of my stuff.

"No, I mean, I can't let you leave." The gray of his eyes seems to swirl with a sense of desperation behind them. He shakes his head back and forth as though he's trying to clear his mind. "Wait—that came out wrong. You are totally free to leave. It's just I don't *want* you to leave."

"You don't want me to leave," I repeat, making sure I heard right. He nods in confirmation and I take a step closer to him.

"These past few weeks with you here have been some of the best weeks of my life...even with the incidents of the nail gun and falling off the roof." He grabs my hand and brings it up to his lips. "I don't know what is going on between us, but tell me you feel it too."

"I do," I say as my heart begins to flutter. I take another step forward and place my hand on his chest. He wraps his arms around my waist and places a gentle kiss on my neck. The sensation makes me want to melt on the spot. I've never felt so drawn to another man the way I am with Jax.

"You make me want to become a better person," he says into my neck with another kiss. "I wake up every morning excited for a new day because I know you will be in it."

I want this. I want this so badly. His hands on me, his lips on me, but something holds me back. "I thought you didn't do relationships."

He pulls back a bit to look me in the eyes. His hand comes up to cup my face, his thumb brushing against my cheek. "This is different, Aly. I can't change how I handled my past, but if you give me a chance, I promise I will treat you right."

I believe him. I know he's opening his heart to me at this very moment. I want to tell him that I know he's being sincere, but all I can manage to say is, "Kiss me."

He pauses, taken aback for a moment by my boldness, but presses his lips to mine. He pulls me in closer and I wrap my arms around his broad shoulders. The sensation of his body up against mine sends electric pulses throughout my entire body. I part my lips and allow him to deepen the kiss. He lets out a groan when his tongue begins to explore my mouth.

"Aly," he says, pulling his head back for a moment and kissing a spot behind my ear that makes my knees go weak. "I will do whatever you want to do, but please tell me you want more."

"Yes," I shout as he lightly thrusts his hips, allowing the bulge in his shorts to press up against my stomach. "God, yes, I want this."

With that, Jax's lips crash against mine, and his arms reach under my thighs. I wrap my legs around him as he effortlessly lifts me up. Without breaking the kiss, he carries me towards his bedroom. He places me gently down on the bed and reaches for the hem of my shirt. I lift my arms up so he can easily pull it off. He reaches behind my back and with a snap, my bra loosens; I quickly shrug it off.

I grab him and pull him down on top of me, needing to feel his bare chest against mine. He lets out a groan as our bodies press so tightly together, but there's still some fabric hindering us from complete vulnerability. Jax kisses a trail from my chest down towards my waist. When he reaches the top of my waistband, he looks up at me as if asking for permission.

"Yes," I say affirmatively. I want him to know that I want this as much as he does. He hooks his fingers under my waistband and begins to pull my yoga pants off. I lift my legs to speed up the process. With my pants gone, I'm only left in my pink lacy underwear. Jax places a kiss on the top and ever so slowly works his way down. I let out a moan when he reaches my core.

"You're soaked through, sweetheart," he says in a husky voice and presses his lips to my inner thighs.

"You...next," I pant. The buildup and anticipation are more than I can handle. Jax stands and I get up on my knees to help push his shorts down.

"Not the first time you've done this to me," he says with amusement in his voice as I push both his shorts and underwear down together.

"Nope." I run my hand up the length of his rock-hard cock as soon as it springs free. He closes his eyes with a moan. "But this time is so much more fun."

He chuckles, grabs the side of my panties, and with a flick, they fall off.

"Hey! I liked those!" I pout.

"I will buy you a dozen more of those in every color." He moves back and I realize that for the first time, he is seeing me completely exposed. A wave of shyness comes over me, but Jax leans forward and places his hand under my chin. He lifts my face so my eyes meet his. "You are so beautiful," he says firmly, then presses his lips against mine. He breaks away only for a moment to put on a condom but quickly hurries back.

Together, we kiss, touch, and explore. Being with Jax comes second nature. Somehow, I already know how he likes to be touched. Jax handles me gently. I've never been super sexual, but I could easily get addicted to how he makes my body feel. And when he pushes himself inside of me? Sheer and complete ecstasy.

35

Jax

It's been a few weeks since Aly and I dove headfirst into this relationship of ours, and I have never been happier. Since the first night we were together, Aly has fallen asleep and woken up in my arms. She's kept most of her things in her room at Michelle's, stating that she feels it would be too soon to move in with me. I've reminded her that she did live with me (though not in my room), but I understand what she means and I don't want to push it. I'll take what I can get, and right now, I'm loving life.

No one was surprised when we told our 3rd East group that we were together, though I'm sure it tipped Michelle and Gabby off when Aly didn't return to her room that night. Alex high-fived me for hooking up with Legs and Carter warned me to take good care of her. Travis, of course, said *I told you so*. I think he was the happiest of everyone. It still amazes me how quickly he's warmed up to Aly.

"I wish you could come for Thanksgiving," I say as we lie in bed together. Her head rests on my chest and her hand lazily traces the lines of the tattoos on my arm. Our nightly talks have become something I look forward to the most. No matter what the day has in store for me, I know that when I get home, Aly will be there.

"I know, but I already made a commitment to Michelle and that was way before anything happened between us."

Michelle asked Aly to go to her family's Thanksgiving dinner just about a month after she moved in and about four months before the actual event. Michelle had explained that being around her family for more than five minutes stressed her out. I don't know much about her, but I know she comes from a family of bigwig lawyers in Northern California and they love their high-status lifestyle.

"Our flight is already booked," Aly continues. "She even bought me a whole new wardrobe, which is insane. I mean, the shoes alone cost more than my car payment. We'll only be gone for three days, but she insists I need to look the part."

"That's kind of a lot. Are you sure you'll be able to handle it?"

"Oh yeah. I mean, it won't be my first time thrown into a room of people who think they're better than everyone else. Michelle has been such a great roommate and she insists having me there will help keep her calm. I'm basically going as her emotional support person."

"I still don't know why she couldn't bring Carter," I mumble. I know Michelle and Aly have become good friends, but Carter would seem like the logical choice. Plus, I really want Aly to meet my family. I haven't told them about her yet. It's not something I wanted to discuss over the phone, and since my family has an open-door policy when it comes to the holidays, I figured I would surprise them.

"Carter goes back to his hometown to help his mom with the cooking. Plus, he has younger siblings that I know he misses," Aly reminds me, and I grimace. I've known Carter for about three years now and he is like a big kid from Thanksgiving through Christmas. The moment the clock strikes midnight on Thanksgiving, he transforms from regular surfer dude to festive surfer dude complete with a Santa hat and reindeer decorations for his Jeep.

"And you'll be back on Saturday?"

"Flight leaves first thing in the morning." She looks up at me and smiles. "I'll be back before you know it."

"Perfect. I don't want to go the whole weekend without you." Now that Aly is in my life, I can't imagine life without her. Truth is, I'm falling in love with her.

***

Tonight, our 3rd East crew decides to meet up at The Local for dinner. Everyone had a busy day today and no one is in the mood to cook. We pile into a large booth with Aly by my side. I put my arm around her shoulders and lean in to whisper in her ear. "Is something wrong, sweetheart? You look a little stressed."

"I don't know. It's been a long day." She shrugs. "The end of the semester is coming up, finals have uprooted the normal routine at work, and I'm worried about Michelle. She was really quiet on the ride over. I don't think she did well on one of her exams, and I'm pretty sure she started drinking before we left."

Aly and I drove separately since we both volunteered to be the designated drivers. I didn't get a chance to see Michelle until now. She does look a bit worse for wear, but I feel like there's something else that's bothering Aly.

"You sure that's it?" I ask.

"It's probably nothing." She picks up her menu.

I place my hand under her chin and tilt it towards me. "Tell me."

She holds my gaze for a moment then lets out a hefty sigh. "Remember when I told you that when I was living in Georgia, I felt like I was being watched?" I suck in a breath and silently start scanning the room as she continues, "I had a weird feeling when I was walking towards the faculty parking lot this afternoon and then again when we walked in here. It's probably just my nerves overreacting. Like I said, midterms have been stressful, and my anxiety is probably getting the best of me and making me overthink everything."

"But it wasn't your imagination. You *were* being followed."

"I have no tangible proof."

"Until someone threw a rock through your window."

She winces. "Okay, yeah. You're right, but I haven't seen anyone watching me. It's just a gut feeling right now."

I motion for her to slide out of the booth and I do as well. I tell her to wait for me as I find Alex and tell him to be on the lookout for anyone who seems suspicious. I head over to the jukebox, select a few slow songs, and pull Aly onto the dance floor.

"I didn't think you danced." She wraps her arms around my neck.

"I don't normally, but from here, we'll be able to see if anyone is watching. Worst-case scenario, we find someone watching you and I'll take care of it. Best-case scenario, no one is watching you and I get to keep you all to myself for a bit." I pull her in towards my chest. Although I saw her this morning, it feels like a lifetime ago.

We sway to the music, and I subtly turn us every now and then to get a better look at our surroundings.

"Thank you," she whispers and places her head on my chest. I pull her in as close as humanly possible. If someone told me a few months ago that I would be dancing in the middle of a bar holding the sweetest and most beautiful girl in the world, I would've thought they were nuts. Yet, here I am, reveling in her closeness. All my worries, my burdens, the anger I have held onto for so long disappear when I'm with Aly. I've never known such a peace.

Travis has started giving me shit about my "upcoming wedding." The dude already has us walking down the aisle, complete with Gus as the ring bearer. It should bother me, but it doesn't. Aly has easily accepted me and my life, including my past and our future. We talk about having a family and how my current project house would be the perfect place to start one. I can see it—birthdays, holidays, random Tuesdays spent with the family Aly and I can create. It will be the life I always wanted but never thought I'd have.

I dip my chin to look down at her. She should be looking around the bar to see if Trent is lurking anywhere in the shadows, but instead she's in her own little world, undoubtedly savoring the tranquility shared between us. She looks up at me and smiles. She knows she's safe with me. I don't know whether this guy is here or not, but she knows, no matter the scenario, I will keep her safe physically and mentally.

"I love you, Aly." The words tumble out of me like I've been saying them all my life. It's the most natural thing in the world to tell her I love her. Before she can respond, I place a quick kiss on her lips, but she pushes against me to deepen the kiss. The music, the people, the noise—everything fades to the background as we kiss in the middle of the dance floor.

"Hey! Lovebirds!" Alex interrupts, making Aly jump with surprise. He comes dancing up beside us with... Michelle? I look between them questioningly and Alex shrugs. "She was the closest one to me and I needed to talk to you."

The music turns to something faster and Michelle begins dancing circles around Alex. "Come on, Jones! Move those hips!" she demands. She's definitely been drinking and not paying attention to anything that's been going on.

"Listen," he says, trying not to let Michelle distract him. "I asked the bartender if there have been any unfamiliar faces in here and he said he didn't notice anyone. But one of the waitresses overheard me and told me that one of her customers doesn't seem to be from around here *and* he has a thick Southern accent."

"Where?" A cold sensation travels up my spine and Aly stiffens in my arms.

"The high top, back corner by the pool tables."

I swing Aly around to get a better look and see a guy in a dark green coat slip out the side door.

"Jax!" Aly warns, her expression fearful.

I stop her. "It's okay. Just let me check things out. Go back to the table with Carter and Gabby. I just want to make sure everything is okay." I give Alex a knowing look and he nods in agreement. I don't need backup, but I may need a witness.

As I head for the side door, I hear Alex try to get Michelle off the dance floor. "Come on, Peanut, I think you need to get something to eat," he coaxes.

"No! I want to stay!" she protests.

"I know you love to dance, but Jax and I have to go take care of something. I'll go get—Ow! Mother of pearl!" I look back to see Alex hopping on one foot. I quickly study Michelle in her five-inch heels and determine that she must've stomped on it. "Carter!" Alex yells. "Come get your girl!"

I exit the building; the crisp fall air hits me full blast, but the adrenaline surging through me keeps me warm. I scan the parking lot but don't see anything out of the ordinary. I decide to check the back parking lot where Aly and I both parked our cars. I know Trent has messed with her car before and I need to make sure it hasn't been tampered with again.

Rounding the corner, I see movement near Aly's sedan. A guy wearing a dark green coat appears to be looking inside the windows of her car.

"She's mine, you know," he says as I approach him, not bothering to remove his focus from the car. "You might act all cute and cuddly on the dance floor now, but she'll come to her senses and come back to me."

"She's not a possession, and she's not going back to you," I spit out. I study the asshole who made Aly miserable. His light brown hair is heavily styled, and his clothes are perfectly tailored to his lean frame. He looks like he's never had to work hard a day in his whole life.

"She did all those other times." He looks up at me with a devious grin. We may be standing a few feet apart, but I can tell that I have at least four inches of height on him.

"Except for the last time you broke up. She even moved across the country to get away from you. Why did you even come here?"

"To get her back!" His voice is venomous. "I'm the one who calls the shots. No one says 'no' to me."

I watch his face turn stone-cold. His dark brown eyes look nearly feral and an uneasy feeling stirs in my gut. This guy is a loose cannon.

"Well, it looks like someone finally did." I smirk, thinking that Aly was the first person to stand up to this jackass who clearly has had everything handed to him on a silver platter.

"Do you know how much work I put into her? You see, I had it all figured out. The most popular guy in town meets the wholesome little teacher. He brings her home to Mama, who loves her, of course, they get married, have a couple of kids, and do that happily-ever-after shit. We were gonna have this perfect little life together, you know? I had her just the way I wanted and then she started overthinking everything. I'm not starting over; I'm taking her back."

For a moment, I feel like I've had the wind knocked out of me as I realize just how sick this guy is. "You thought you could manipulate her? She's worked hard to better herself, and you thought you could convince her to give up everything she's worked for so you could get a perfect little wife who did everything you said?"

"I was trying to show her that if she just listened to me—"

"You took her weakness, her willingness to please everyone, and tried to use it against her," I cut him off. "She's not a fucking Stepford Wife."

A sinister sneer spreads across Trent's face and I know I pegged him perfectly. Aly is a strong woman. She has to be to have accomplished so much on her own. But Trent was determined to break her spirit for his own power. He wanted to make her weak so he could control her. My stomach sinks thinking how Aly's life might've been if she didn't muster up the courage to leave when she did. "You stalked her," I continue.

"Can't prove it was me." He shrugs his shoulders.

"You made her feel unsafe in her own home. Why?"

"I was just tryin' to send a message. She shoulda just moved in with me when I told her to, but she loved that piece of shit little house."

My hands begin to shake with anger. While I've never seen her house in person, she's shown me pictures. Aly took pride in her home; it was special to her, and he ruined her sense of security.

"Let me get this straight." I try to push down the rage rising within me. "You thought you'd scare her out of her own home, so she would come running back to you?"

"She had nowhere else to go...or so I thought. I never figured she'd pack up and move."

"What choice did she have?!" At that moment, a strange feeling of gratitude comes over me. Aly told me that had it not been for Trent's harassment, she wouldn't have taken the job out here. In a weird way, I'm grateful that this asshole drove her straight out of Georgia and right to me.

"There you are!" Alex appears from around the corner with a slight limp. "Peanut is crazy tonight!" He shakes his head then freezes when he sees I'm not alone. "Shit—is this...?"

"Yup," I reply, not taking my eyes off Trent.

"Who are you?" Trent spits.

"A credible witness," Alex replies as he moves to stand beside me.

Trent is quiet as he sizes up both Alex and me. I try to fight back a smile. It's easy to see he's had other people do his fighting for him. But out here, with no support, he's silently shitting his pants trying to figure out his next move.

The sound of footsteps has us all turning our heads as Gabby and Aly round the corner. Aly stops and stiffens; the color drains from her face. Trent's posture changes as soon as he spots his ex-fiancée, and I fight a primal urge inside of me to not kill this fucker right on the spot.

36

Aly

Only a few minutes passed, but it felt like hours since Jax went outside to check on everything. Alex followed a little bit later and Carter was too preoccupied with calming down Michelle. I had to see what was going on, so Gabby offered to come with me. I didn't expect to see Jax and Trent squaring off in the parking lot. I knew there was a possibility Trent could be here, but my self-doubt told me I was overreacting.

"Aly," Trent breathily calls my name. He gives me his signature puppy dog eyes. "I missed you so much, Aly Cat. Please come home."

I look between both men. Trent, the one who has manipulated me so many times by pulling on my heartstrings, and Jax, the stoic one who has never once questioned me for who I am. Without saying a word, I run towards Jax's side and he pulls me into the safety of his arms.

"So, is this the rebound?" Trent spits.

"Rebound? Trent, we spent six months on and off and then you spent a year tormenting me. Add in the time I've been here and that's nearly two years since we were together. I don't know what qualifies as a rebound, but I think the statute of limitations is over."

"Come on, Aly Cat," Trent says, completely ignoring my words. "I know you got cold feet and all, but enough is enough. You've had your fun. Now, it's time to come home."

"Aly Cat?" Alex asks.

"He said I was a stray when he found me." I roll my eyes and Jax grinds his teeth. I conveniently met Trent soon after Jess moved away and while Jacob was traveling the world. I still had other friends and acquaintances, but I realize now that without my core support system, I was much more willing to accept Trent into my life. Later on, I learned that isolation is a major red flag of controlling relationships.

"Didn't think you had it in you to move across the country," Trent continues. "I was searching up north. Figured you moved in with Jess. Good thing you got that speeding ticket. It helped me narrow down the search."

"I see your brother is still helping you with your dirty work." I cross my arms over my chest.

"Bros before hoes." Trent shrugs, and with that, Jax moves away from me and jumps off the curb with a fist aiming for Trent.

"He's not worth it!" Alex yells and pulls him back just in the nick of time.

"He's right, Jax," I say, gaining a little more confidence. "I don't want you to hurt him."

"See, it's 'cause she still has feelings for me." Trent gives an arrogant smile pointed at Jax.

"No, I don't want Jax to go to jail for assault. I don't think I could survive on conjugal visits." I can't help it. I look over at Jax and give him a wink.

Alex lets out a whoop. Trent stands in shock with his mouth gaping. He's never heard me this outspoken. Even when I broke up with him, I was still meek because I was afraid to hurt *his* feelings. Now that I've removed myself from the situation, I realize how much of a manipulator Trent really was. He may have tried to break me down, but Jax has built me up. I'm stronger than I've ever been before.

Trent takes a long look at the now widened space between Jax and me. The hair on the back of my neck begins to prickle. Situational awareness—this is what Jax has been preaching to me for weeks.

"Look, Aly Cat." Trent makes a small movement towards me. "I don't know what has gotten into you or what lies this guy has been feeding you, but you know your place is with me."

"Trent, you have no control over me anymore," I say assertively. I square my shoulders and widen my stance a bit.

"I was never trying to control you." He takes a baby step forward. I look over at Jax and Alex, who are standing at the ready. They're giving me the power in this situation, but I know they have my back if something goes wrong.

"Oh yeah, right, 'cause going through my phone and telling me who I can or cannot talk to isn't controlling." I cross my arms over my chest.

"I know what's best for you!" Fiery anger burns behind Trent's eyes. His fists ball up at his sides. This is what I would be seeing on a daily basis if I hadn't given in and pushed back.

"No, you don't," I say with a cocky smile.

With that, Trent makes a lunge for me, and in that moment, everything Jax has taught me flies out the window. I do, however, raise my leg up at just the perfect time. My knee makes contact with Trent's most prized possession.

"Son of a bitch!" Trent crumbles to the ground in the fetal position.

In the background, I hear the guys give a collective, "Ooof!"

"Sweetheart." Jax comes over to me, still wincing. He pulls me tight into his chest. "I'm so proud of you, but that's not one of the moves I showed you."

"Yeah, I kinda panicked and improvised." I look up when I hear the sound of a siren in the distance. "Did you call the police?"

"I did!" Alex says proudly while standing over Trent, who is still writhing in pain. Funny how he looks so small and weak to me now.

"She attacked me!" Trent cries as the siren gets louder.

"Self-defense, bro," Alex says. "We witnessed the whole thing."

"Too bad you're not within your family's jurisdiction this time," Jax calls out and gives me a kiss on the top of my head. "Maybe now you'll be able to get a restraining order."

"That sounds like a great idea." I wrap my arms around his waist and give him a squeeze. "Jax?"

"Hmm?"

"I love you, too."

37

Aly

The sun has already begun to set as I pull into the condo's parking lot. I grab my items from work and feel my phone vibrate with an incoming message.

> **Amelia:** Saw Trent today while getting groceries. He looked like he was walking with a little limp. You wouldn't happen to know anything about that, would you?" <winky face emoji>

Once the ink on the restraining order was dry, I called Amelia to tell her everything. Like Trent, she thought I moved near Jess and not clear across the country. It was so good to catch up with her, and she told me she would let me know as soon as there was a Trent sighting. We wanted to make sure he was back in Georgia and not lingering around somewhere.

The last time I saw Trent, he was handcuffed in the back seat of a patrol car. It is an image I will never forget. Seriously,

I'll never forget it because Alex took a picture to commemorate the moment. So far, I haven't heard a peep from him, and I don't expect to either. It is such a freeing feeling to know that Trent is officially out of my life.

I type a quick reply to Amelia.

> **Me:** Glad to know he's back where he belongs. And that limp? <shrugging emoji>

My phone vibrates with another text, but I ignore it and place it back in my purse. I will catch up with Amelia later. I have something important to do and I keep putting it off.

Today is the day that I'm going to tell Jax that I go by Dr. Parker at work. I probably should've told him from the very beginning, but my nerves got the best of me. I realize now it's foolish to worry. My choosing his last name is completely by chance. Besides, I chose it before I even knew him. I do wonder about his reaction. Maybe he will find it funny? I hope.

I give myself a pep talk on the elevator ride up to our floor. I don't know why I'm so nervous about this. It's just a name. A common name at that, and my reasons for changing my professional name are valid.

Still, there's a nagging feeling in the pit of my stomach. Jax hasn't been in a relationship in over a decade because Maranda broke his trust. I've been aware of his last name for a few months and still haven't mentioned the coincidence. I hope he doesn't interpret my silence as something sinister. I'm sure I'm overthinking this, but that's what being with someone like Trent does to you. It boosts your paranoia like it's on triple steroids.

I enter Jax's place and find him angrily pacing back and forth with his phone in his hand. He spins on his heels when he hears me come in. His face is hard, his jaw is tense, and his nostrils are flaring. I take a step back, feeling like I just stepped into a bullpen.

He waves his hand as if to tell me to walk past him. He must've picked up on my hesitant body language. I make my way towards the bedroom and start to change out of my work clothes. I guess I'll hold off on telling him until after he calms down from whatever he's doing on the phone.

I take my time undressing. I don't want to go back out into the living room and interrupt him. I can't imagine who he is talking to. His voice is muffled through the closed door, making it hard to decipher any clear words. Maybe it has to do with the house he's currently working on? I know he received the wrong shipment of tiles.

A few minutes later, Jax comes into the room still looking upset but not as hardened as earlier. "Hey, sweetheart." He pulls me into his chest, rests his head on mine, and takes a deep breath. I feel his body relax against mine.

"Everything okay?" I say into his chest since he won't release me. He often tells me I bring him peace, so I know whatever happened, staying close to him will help.

"Yeah, it's okay now." He kisses the top of my head. He loosens his hold a bit, so I'm able to shift myself to look up at him.

"What happened?" I ask. "Who was on the phone?"

"It was a credit card company." He sighs. "I got a letter in the mail addressed to—" His grip tightens on me once more.

"Addressed to whom?"

"To my ex, Mrs. Maranda Parker." He abruptly lets go of me and starts pacing again.

"I don't understand."

"Even though we were married for less than a year, Maranda still kept my last name until she remarried about a year ago. It drove me insane. It still drives me insane. I know I have a common last name, but I'm the only male left in my family to carry on our name."

Jax's eyes seem to wander off towards a distant memory. "My gram and pop meant so much to me." He shakes his head. "I stupidly gave it to her and she took it and ran."

"What do you mean by she took it and ran?" My body stiffens, but I try to act normal even though my anxiety begins to multiply. I don't want to disappoint Jax. I'm a people pleaser and now I'm feeling like I did something wrong when I didn't. Oh. My. God. *Don't freak out, Aly.*

"I didn't tell you this before, but soon after we divorced, she opened a bank account and a few credit cards under my last name. It fucked with my credit for a while. I had to hire an attorney to get things straightened out. Eventually, things calmed down, and now that she's remarried, she finally took her new husband's last name. But today I got a letter from a credit card company and it was addressed to her."

"Did she take another credit card out in your name?"

"No, I called the company. It was just an advertisement. They said things like name changes take time to switch over, but it just set me off, you know? I guess it just brought up shitty memories." He walks over to me and pulls me back into a hug. "Enough about that. How was your day?"

"Oh, it was fine, just the usual." I hug him back and smile.

Well, I know one thing for sure. Today is not the day I tell Jax my little secret.

38

Jax

I pull into the driveway of my childhood home; I haven't been back since Gram's funeral. It's going to be different this year without her. Back when the grandkids were younger, Gram and Pop would split the holidays between our family and Uncle Chris's. That all stopped once Uncle Chris and his family moved to Japan. The travel was too extensive for my aging grandparents. By the time my uncle and his family moved back to the States, everyone was in college and doing their own thing. My cousins now live all over the United States. The only family member who lives in Oregon is my cousin Claire. Uncle Chris and Aunt Maria are not too far away in Washington. Sophia lives in Florida, Mia is in Texas, and I'm not sure where Lyndsey is; she and her husband are both active-duty Navy.

The front door opens before I can even reach for the handle, and my sister Emma pops out. I take a step back in shock.

"Whoa! Did you eat the entire turkey, Ems?" It's so weird to see her pregnant.

"Very funny." She gives me a hug. "I've missed you."

"I've missed you too." I hug her back. "I can't believe you have two babies cooking in there! How are you feeling?"

"Pretty good despite the fact that I look like a whale," she says as we head towards the kitchen. The smell of a roasting turkey and my mother's homemade biscuits fills the air.

"You look great!" I throw my arm around her shoulder and give her a squeeze.

"Emma! You stop that right now! You are positively radiant!" My mother wipes her hands on her apron and heads towards me to give me a hug.

"Hey, Ma," I say as I hug her.

"Oh! It's so great to have both of my babies back under one roof." She glows as she tries to squeeze the air out of me. Her dark brown hair brushes up against my chin and I know she's standing on her toes, trying to make herself as tall as possible. It never ceases to amaze me how much my sister and I take after my mom's side of the family when it comes to looks. Besides my height and overall stature, I look nothing like the Parker side of the family.

"Nice to see you too. Could you give me some air?" I dramatically choke. Mom steps back and swats my head. Behind her, I hear the distinct low laughter of my father.

"Be nice to your mother, son. Remember, she brought you into this world—"

"And she can take us right out too," my sister and I say in unison.

"Don't you forget it!" Mom winks and goes back to her baking.

"How's it going, Dad?" I ask as I try to steal a biscuit. Mom smacks my hand away, then smiles and hands me a biscuit anyway.

"Can't complain. I'm going to cut back some of my hours once my grandbabies are here." My dad emanates excitement and my heart clenches in happiness for him. I know he's been patiently waiting for grandkids and now he's getting a two-for-one deal.

Unfortunately, the whole thing with Maranda did a number on my parents too. Sure, they were disappointed to think their teenage son was about to become a father, but I know they warmed up to the idea of having a grandchild. They also felt the loss when we realized Kinley wasn't mine. After everything happened, I vowed to never get involved with anyone else again, and I certainly never thought about having kids. Now, with Aly in my life, the once squashed dream of having a little family of my own might actually come true.

My phone vibrates and I look down to see a text from Aly, saying she and Michelle arrived safely in California.

"Uh-oh, what's that about?" My mom puts her hands on her hips.

"What's what about?"

"You're smiling." She glares at me. "You never smile."

"I smile!" I shove the biscuit in my mouth. I wasn't aware that I was smiling, and now I'm going to be grilled for it. I haven't told them about Aly yet for the simple fact that they will drive me nuts. I was hoping to at least make it to dessert before the interrogation started.

"Who was that text from?" Emma asks.

"What is this? The Spanish Inquisition? It's none of your business!"

"Ohhhhhh!" all three of them coo in unison, and my face turns red.

"Was that a text from a girrrrllll?" Emma sings.

"And you wonder why I like to keep my life private." I sigh.

"Jaxon, are you seeing someone?" My mother's excitement radiates off her. I'm sure she's visualizing a wedding and babies.

"Slow down, it's not a big deal." I try to act casual.

"It is a big deal when I see my big brother smiling for the first time in over a decade! Who is she?" Then Emma gasps. "Oh my God! Is this the one Gram was telling you about?"

"Did you really have to go there, Ems?" I rake my hand over my face. I fully intended to tell my family about Aly during this trip, but I would've preferred it not to be in the first five minutes of my arrival.

"What's this about Gram? She knew a girl? Is she local? She really didn't get out much after her stroke last year. Did she set you up with someone?" Yup, my mother can barely contain herself.

Something cold brushes my hand. "Looks like you're going to need this." Dad places a beer in my hand and starts to walk away.

"What? You're not going to stay for the show?" I yell to him over my shoulder.

"Oh, trust me, I'll hear all about it later." He laughs and heads towards the den, presumably to watch a game.

"I think I'm gonna go hang with Dad in the den." I turn to walk away.

"Not so fast, big bro!" Emma calls out. "You're not getting away without telling us about this mystery girl. Sit!"

"Fine. I'll answer three questions," I sigh and plop onto a kitchen chair. Between Mom and Ems, I know I'm not getting out of this.

"Eeeeeeek!" Emma squeals and claps her hands. "This is so exciting! Okay, okay, three questions. What's her name?"

"Alyssa, but everyone calls her Aly."

"Where did you meet?"

"Technically, I guess we met at the pool in our condo, but she moved across the hall from me."

"Oh! She's a swimmer like you?"

"Yes." I stand. "And that was your third question."

"Jaaaaaaaxxxx! You can't do this to me! I need to know more!" Emma whines.

"How does Gram fit into all of this?" my mom asks.

"Oh, I can answer this!" Emma bounces in her chair. "You know how Gram told me that I was going to have twin girls? Well, she told Jax that she was going to send him a woman of his own." Emma waggles her eyebrows.

"It wasn't like that."

"Close enough." Emma shrugs.

"I'm sure it's just a coincidence."

"Oh! This is so exciting!" Mom clasps her hands together. "Why didn't you invite her over for Thanksgiving? You know we have an open-door policy."

"She made plans months ago that she couldn't break."

"So, is it serious?" Mom asks.

"Kind of? It's still new." It's damn serious, but I don't want to get their hopes up just yet.

Mom glares at me like she's trying to subliminally press for more information. I avert my eyes; I know that look all too well. Ten seconds more and I'll be spilling everything.

"Look, I really don't want to talk about it. It's probably nothing." I shrug. Okay, I know it's more. I feel it's more, but I don't need my mother and sister prying into my love life. My mom and dad have been married for over thirty-five years. They have the kind of marriage people dream about, and they have certainly set a high bar for my sister and me. Of course, I feel like I failed them thirteen years ago after my lightning-fast marriage and divorce. How can someone recover from that?

"Doesn't look like nothing to me," Emma says as she holds up my phone.

I feel the blood drain from my face. There plastered for my mom and sister to see is a picture of Aly and me at the beach. Alex took it the day we were arguing in the water at

SummerFest. There we are in our bathing suits, Aly with her legs wrapped around my waist, my arms holding her up underneath. Her arms are wrapped around my neck and our faces are merely centimeters apart. I thought Alex was an ass for taking the picture, but honestly, I look at it all the time.

"Give me back my phone, Ems," I grit through my teeth.

"Nope! And unless you recently went on some tropical vacation, I'd say this picture was taken this summer, which means you've been holding out on us! Also, stop using your birthday as your passcode."

"We weren't together when that picture was taken, and noted about the passcode." I try to grab the phone from her hands. If she weren't pregnant with my nieces, I'd tackle her like when we were kids.

"Give the phone back to your brother." My mom laughs, looking at Emma. "We'll try to get more out of him later."

Emma reluctantly complies and they both give me a small reprieve as we settle in for Thanksgiving dinner.

"Well, this certainly is a quieter Thanksgiving." Mom sighs as we gather around the table. It's just the four of us this year. Next year, we will have Grant home and the twins will be here too. Hopefully, I will have Aly by my side as well.

"I miss her." Emma sorrowfully looks at the empty chair next to me.

"I miss her too, baby." Dad reaches his hand over the table and gives Emma's hand a squeeze.

"It's definitely not the same without her." Mom sighs. For being in-laws, my mom and Gram had a very close relationship. My mom lost her parents early in life; Gram and Pop were more than happy to welcome her into our family.

"I could really go for some of Gram's sweet potato casserole right now," Emma states, and with that, all eyes turn to me.

"I swear! She never gave me the recipes!" I put my hands up in the air. Gram was an amazing cook, but she wasn't one to share her recipes. Whenever anyone asked if she would share a recipe, she would just look at me and wink like we had some sort of secret. For years, my family has been convinced that I am the keeper of these recipes. I am not.

Dad breaks the silence. "I started going through some of Gram's items from the nursing home. I have a box of some of her things that she wanted you to have."

"What's in it?" I ask.

"I didn't look. She had boxes labeled for every grandchild."

"Wow, sounds like she was prepared."

"I think she knew her time was coming," Dad says, looking down at his plate.

"Did you look in your box, Ems?"

"I'm not ready yet." Emma shakes her head. I don't think I'm ready either, but I'll take the box off my parents' hands and open it when I am.

Gram lived on her own until her last year of life. She had a stroke that changed the course of everything. Her mind was as sharp as a tack up until the last few weeks, but her body became very weak. We couldn't take care of her full-time, so she went into a nursing home. My family took her out a lot and she even stayed at my parents' place on the weekends when someone was around to keep an eye on her.

My family doesn't know, but I used to make the hour-long drive home every Wednesday for weekly dates. I'd bust her out of the nursing home and take her to lunch. That was our little secret, not the recipes.

"So, what does Aly do for a living?" Mom changes the subject. The mood lightens and I'm then quizzed on anything and everything that is Alyssa Winters for the rest of the night.

I may not enjoy answering all of their questions, but at least it's on my favorite topic.

39

Aly

"I think this is the first time I've actually been hungry after a Thanksgiving dinner," I say to Michelle as I grab some chips out of my luggage. I've had some amazing Thanksgivings and some disastrous ones. My favorite Thanksgiving would be the first one I ever spent with the Parkers. Before they arrived, I was complacent about eating a bowl of mac and cheese while my parents were off vacationing on some tropical island.

Michelle had warned me ahead of time to pack some food because Thanksgiving at the Buchanans is more for show than anything else. I'm glad I took her seriously.

"Yeah, sorry about that." Michelle winces and bites into a cereal bar. "We can make it up when we get home."

We are currently sitting in what was once Michelle's old bedroom, although there is no evidence of a child or teenager ever living in this place. Michelle told me that as soon as she and her siblings moved out of the house, her parents quickly redecorated their rooms. Once I left for college, I never came back home. I'm sure my parents did the same thing to my childhood bedroom as well.

"Oh, don't bother! Now, I won't have to worry about fitting into my bathing suit when we get back! I am worried about you, though. Things were tense at dinner. How are you feeling?" Just as I suspected, Michelle and I grew up in opposite worlds. Both of our parents sought out money and prestige. But where my parents would rather pretend I didn't exist, her parents mapped out every detail of her life and are still trying to.

"As good as I can be when I'm back home." She gives a sad smile. "Honestly, this was probably the best visit back home I've ever had and I know it's because I had my emotional support person with me. I'm sorry I had to take you away from Jax, though."

"Well, if my presence helped you get through spending time with your family, then this was all worth it, and do *not* be sorry! I mean, yeah, I miss Jax, but I was kind of happy that I had a solid excuse not to spend Thanksgiving with him."

Michelle whips her head up from her focus on her cereal bar. "You didn't want to spend Thanksgiving with him? Is everything okay?"

"Yes. No. I don't know." I sigh. "It's just that, things are moving so fast and everything's been wonderful. It scares me with how well things are going. Plus, this would've required me to meet his parents and sister. I don't know if I'm ready."

"Aw, hon, I'm sure they would love you! Hell! My parents loved you and they hate everyone!"

"Yeah, but Jax has never been in a relationship like this. I know his family was beginning to think that he would be alone for the rest of his life. That's a lot of pressure. Plus, there's something else that keeps nagging me, and I don't know what to do."

"What's wrong?" Michelle cocks her head to the side.

"Remember the conversation we had before I moved here? About how I was trying to keep a low profile because of my ex?" I proceed to tell Michelle about how I was able to change my name at work and how out of all the last names in the world, I unknowingly picked Jax's. I tell her how I planned to tell Jax, but then he told me how his ex used his last name. I leave out the fact that they were married and just that they were exes.

"Wow! That's...wow!" Michelle sits up and leans forward, deep in thought.

"You should've seen him when he got that mail addressed to her. He was shaking with anger. How could I have told him after that?"

"Yeah, that's a tough one." Michelle sucks on her lower lip. "I don't know what I would've done in that situation. On the one hand, you've done nothing wrong, but on the other hand, you can trigger some rough memories again."

"Exactly."

"I think, for now, I wouldn't say anything. Just keep everything the same." A smile spreads across her face. "And if you eventually get married, it will be one less thing to change."

"Thanks." I laugh. "God, I can't even think about getting married. I mean, I honestly thought that after everything that happened with Trent, I would be on my own for the rest of my life."

"And now?"

"Now, I feel like I'm getting a second chance at everything I ever wanted."

40

Jax

For the first time in over a decade, I am looking forward to the holidays. Aly is planning on coming home with me to meet my family. I know they will all fall in love with her the way I have. She has officially and single-handedly broken down my walls. My mom was right at Thanksgiving; I never smiled anymore, but that changed once Aly came into my life. I feel lighter than I have in forever.

Tonight, we are going on a date. I made reservations at a fancy French restaurant in town. We will get dressed up, eat amazing food, and then take a stroll downtown where all the little shops are lit up for Christmas. The streetlights are wrapped up to look like candy canes, and all the trees are lit up in little white lights. It will look like we just stepped into the scene of a Christmas card. Cheesy, I know, but my girl will love it.

"Hey, sweetheart." I smile and kiss her as soon as she walks out of the bedroom. "You look beautiful as always." I step back to appreciate her form-fitting little black dress with hot-as-hell fire-engine-red heels and wonder how I got so damn lucky.

"Thank you. You clean up pretty nice too," she says, looking me up and down. I switched out my usual jeans and T-shirt for black slacks and a dark green button-down shirt.

"Are you almost ready to go?"

"Yup, I just need to drop off a pair of earrings Gabby wanted to borrow." She heads towards the door but turns around. "Oh! I switched out my purse to match my dress. I left it on the bed. Can you get it for me?"

"Sure," I say and head towards the bedroom. There are two purses on the bed, a small black one and the larger blue one that she carries most days. I grab the small black one but accidentally knock into the blue one, spilling the contents onto the floor. Muttering a curse under my breath, I bend down to retrieve the fallen items, which consist of a small planner, ChapStick, a pen, and a lanyard with her faculty ID attached to it. I stare in disbelief at the ID in my hand; surely, I must be reading it wrong.

"Jax?" I hear Aly call from outside the bedroom door. "Did you get my purse?" She rounds the doorframe and goes wide-eyed when she sees me holding the lanyard.

"What is this?" I grit through my teeth. I can hear the sound of my heartbeat in my own ears.

"Jax, I can exp—"

"Why does this say Dr. Alyssa Parker?"

"Well, I—"

"Your last name is Winters, is it not?"

"It is but—"

"Why are you using my last name?"

"There's a—"

"I can't believe you!" I run my hands through my hair. "Why the hell are you using my last name?"

"I'm not, well, I guess I am, kinda, but it wasn't—"

"I fucking trusted you!" I raise my voice, making her jump back a little.

"You still can!" She puts her hands up in defense. "I just need to—"

"I let my guard down," I cut her off. "For thirteen years, I've been guarded because I didn't want to get hurt again. I fell for you. I let you into my home, my bed, my life—something hardly anyone ever sees, and this is what you do? Did you think that maybe we'd get married so you'd just skip everything and take my name?"

"What? No!" She takes a step towards me. "Jax, I—"

"Get out!"

"Jax, please, I can explain everything," she says with a shaky voice, but there's too much going on in my head to fully comprehend her plea.

"I said GET OUT," I roar, surprising myself with the anger and force behind my voice. Aly makes a small gasping sound then disappears from my sight. A moment later, I hear the front door click shut.

And now I'm back where I started...alone.

41

Aly

I close the door to Jax's condo and stand in stunned silence as the reality of what just happened begins to sink in. We had an amazing night planned and in a mere five seconds, everything went to hell. It's all my fault. I know I should've told him about why I changed my name and how it was purely a coincidence, but in the end, my nerves won and I did nothing. Part of me wants to march right back through the door and demand that he listens to me, but I know it won't work. He's too angry to listen.

As I stand in the hallway of 3rd East, I realize I'm in limbo. I can easily walk back through the door of 312. While I've been staying with Jax for several weeks, I never fully moved out of the condo with Michelle and Gabby. I know they would accept me back with open arms, but if I go back with them, if I walk through that door, then Jax and I are officially over. I realize it's over anyway, but it feels more final going back to where I started.

I decide I can't go back—not yet. Instead, I run down the stairs and outside towards the parking lot. I sit down on the curb with my head on my knees, hoping the wintry air will bring me out of my shock. Hot tears pool behind my eyes.

In the distance, I hear the sound of a car door shut and feel someone come up beside me.

"Aly?" the familiar voice says hesitantly. I raise my head to see the warm blue-green eyes of Carter looking at me with concern. He kneels down to my level. "Are you okay?"

I open my mouth to speak, but nothing comes out. I look down to see my hands trembling, but I can't tell if it's from the cold or my nerves.

"Look, it's freezing out here and you're certainly not dressed for this weather. How about we go for a ride? Okay?" It occurs to me that I'm still in my little black dress and heels. I didn't think to grab my coat when Jax told me to get out.

I nod in agreement. Carter reaches out his hand to help me up and he guides me to his lime green Jeep. As soon as I am in the warmth of his Jeep, I grab him by his coat and start sobbing uncontrollably into his chest.

"Jesus, Aly, what happened?" He wraps his arms around me. The gesture gives me some comfort, but it's not the same as when Jax holds me. He doesn't feel the same, doesn't smell the same.

"I-I-can't. I-I n-need a minute," I cry breathlessly.

"Okay, umm...how about we take a drive around for a bit and when you're ready, you can tell me what happened."

I nod and wipe the tears with the back of my hand.

Carter hands me a beach towel. "Sorry, I don't have any tissues, but I always keep towels in my car." The towel smells like the beach and of better days. I desperately want to go back to better days.

We drive around for a good half hour before I am able to speak coherently. I tell him everything, starting with the story of how I made it out to Oregon and ending with how Jax kicked me out of his place. As expected, Carter listens with an open heart and mind.

"Damn, he's an asshole." He smacks the top of his steering wheel. "If he had just listened to your explanation, none of this would be happening."

"Thank you for listening to me, Carter." I sniff.

"Of course! Are you ready to head home?"

Home. I know he means Michelle and Gabby's place. While I didn't mind staying with them, I never truly felt at home until I was with Jax. Oh, God... Jax. I don't want to risk running into him. I also don't want to have to relive the last few hours over again, and I know that's exactly what will happen when Michelle and Gabby see me walking through the door. All I want is to go to my room, lock the door, and cry into my pillow.

"I don't want to explain it all over again."

Carter is quiet for a moment then nods. "Okay, I get it. How about you just let me handle everything, okay?"

We discuss what I will do and what he will say to my roommates.

"Okay," I finally whisper in agreement. We have a game plan that will hopefully go as gentle as possible for me.

My heart begins to race as soon as we pull into the parking lot. I don't want anyone to see me. I know I look like hell. I can feel the swollenness of my face from all the tears I have already cried. I know I will cry even more once I get to my bedroom.

As if Carter can read my mind, he pulls me into his side. "Lay your head on me and put your head down a bit," he whispers. "Don't worry about where you're walking. I'll guide you through the hall and won't let anyone talk to you."

I do as I am told, grateful for such an empathetic friend. Luckily, we do not run into anyone, but I choke up again the moment we reach 3rd East. My bags—all my items from Jax's place—have been placed outside his door. Thankfully, I chose to keep most of my stuff at Michelle's, so it's not much.

"I'll handle that," Carter whispers in my ear, casually tilting his head towards my belongings. "Let's just go inside, okay?"

Michelle and Gabby run to me as soon as we step inside.

"Oh my God! Aly! What happened?" Gabby gasps and throws her arms around me.

"Why are you with Carter? Where's Jax?" Michelle asks, concerned.

The floodgates flow open once more and I begin to sob uncontrollably. I was hoping to make it to the privacy of my own room before I started again.

Carter clears his throat. "Aly had a very rough night and is going to head to her room. She knows you both mean well, but she really just wants to be alone right now. She's given me permission to tell you everything because she doesn't have the strength to explain it again."

I give Carter a small hug and retreat to the solitude of my bedroom. I don't even look at Gabby or Michelle as I walk past them. I take off my dress and slip into pajamas. I then turn off my phone, crawl into bed, and cry into my pillow for the rest of the night and well into the next morning. Once again, I'm all alone in this world.

42

Jax

The thumping in my head becomes in sync with the sound of someone pounding on my door. I try to open my eyes but end up squinting as there's too much sunlight coming in through my windows. Groaning, I move to a sitting position on my couch. I haven't been able to sleep in my bed; it's not the same without Aly in it. The knocking becomes incessantly louder. I need to get rid of this headache and whoever is playing drums in the hallway.

"Your truck is in the lot, so I know you're in there." The distinct sound of Travis's voice travels through the door. I stagger forward to open it. I don't want to deal with him, but I've ignored him enough these past few days.

"What do you want, Trav?" I open the door and begrudgingly move to the side to let my best friend and his furry sidekick in. Gus immediately jumps up on my couch and curls up for what is probably his fifth nap of the day.

"What do you think I'm doing here? You texted me the other day to say you weren't coming in. Then you don't show up or answer my calls for days."

"I've been sick."

"Yeah, lovesick." He walks around and studies my kitchen. "Carter told me you and Aly broke up."

"What did Carter say?" I snap my head up. I wonder how much he knows.

"Not much. He was pretty tight-lipped about it all. He just said you broke Aly's heart."

"*I* broke her heart?" Annoyance bubbles inside of me.

"That's all he said." Travis holds his hands up. "He refused to tell me anything else. Maybe he doesn't know much more. But, come on, this is Aly we're talking about. What could she have possibly done to cause all this?" He waves his hand around my dirty kitchen and living room.

For the first time in days, I take a good look around my condo. It's trashed. The kitchen counter is littered with liquor bottles and various takeout containers. There are blankets and a pillow sloppily thrown onto my couch. I haven't vacuumed or swept. I can't remember the last time I did laundry or took out the trash, which I now see is overflowing and leaking with God-knows-what.

"I've been living in hell." I run a hand over my face and notice that my normal stubble feels more like a full-grown beard...complete with crumbs in it. When was the last time I took a shower?

"You smell like a dumpster fire," Travis says, reading my mind.

"I feel like one too."

"Man, what the hell happened?"

I proceed to tell him the story of how Aly completely duped me into thinking I was in some sort of amazing relationship.

How she built up my trust and broke it down. How could she wake up in my bed as Alyssa Winters and go to work as Alyssa Parker? If she lied about her name, what else did she lie about?

"I don't know, man," Travis says once I finish my story. "I just can't shake the feeling that there's a reasonable explanation. She only used the last name at work? Nowhere else? No credit cards or loans taken out in the name?"

"No, I ran my credit and did a few searches. Nothing has been touched. It looks like she only uses the name at work."

"Well, that makes sense."

"It makes sense that she goes by a different name at work?" I look at my best friend like he sprouted an extra head.

"Ah, you're too emotional to think straight." Travis seems to brush me off. "It makes sense, though. For years you've buried your emotions under lock and key. Then Aly came along and set them free. Now, you don't know how to control them."

I scoff at the statement. How did I turn into an emotional human being? I never should've strayed from being closed off; it was easier then. Okay, I wasn't happy being like that, but the hole in my heart Aly left proves that I should've kept everything buried.

"You really didn't think this through, did you?" Travis looks at me. "She came out here to get away from her crazy-ass ex. He would've found her a lot faster if she used her real name. Plus, it's not uncommon for professors to go by different last names. Don't you remember a few years ago a student at some community college in California failed a class, so he looked up his professor's info, went to his house, and beat the crap out of him?"

"I get the need for privacy, especially because she was trying to hide from her ex, but why out of a billion last names did she choose mine?" That's the million-dollar question.

"Did you ask her why?"

I lower my head. I'm sure Aly was going to explain everything to me, but I was in too much of a rage to listen. "No. I think she was going to tell me, but all I could think of was Maranda walking around pretending like we were happily married while I was off deployed."

"Aly is not Maranda," Travis says sternly. "And I really don't think she has a malicious bone in her body. I think you need to talk to her."

"Yeah, maybe…" I contemplate. Perhaps there really is a reasonable explanation and these last few days of hell were all for nothing.

"Good. Go across the hall and talk to her, but please, for the love of all things holy, take a shower first. You cannot go over there looking and smelling like that. Your clothes look like they're about to grow legs and walk right off of you."

I want to protest, but I know I can't let Aly see me the way I am. I'm surprised Travis lasted this long standing in such close proximity.

"While you take a shower, I'll start cleaning up this mess." He opens the window near my bookshelf and an icy breeze blows past. "Hopefully the cold air will get the smell out faster."

Travis begins cleanup duty while I head to the bathroom to shave and shower. While I'm washing the last few days away, I rehearse how I will approach Aly and what I will ask her. Will she even want to talk to me again?

I'm coming to my senses now and am realizing Travis was right. I'm an asshole. Parker is as common a name as Smith or Jones, and she most likely changed it so her douchebag of an ex wouldn't find her. Suddenly, I have a sense of urgency to go see my girl and grovel. I really fucked up this time. *Why do I do shit like this?*

Stepping out of the shower, I hear Travis clamoring in the kitchen. "Everything okay out there?" I peek into the hallway.

"Yup," Travis calls back. "Got it all under control. Do you have dishtowels anywhere?"

"Yeah, I'll grab some." I head to the closet in the hallway. It's basically a catch-all for random things. As I reach up to grab a dishtowel, I take notice of the box I've had on the shelf since Thanksgiving. Gram's box. I pull it down and run my hand over the smooth white top. A squiggly handwritten "J" in black ink is all that's written on the outside. Gram struggled with handwriting after her stroke. I'm sure it took a lot of effort to just write that letter. I run back to my room and place the box on my nightstand, thinking that maybe today will be a good day to open it.

I walk back towards the kitchen to the sight of a sparkling clean countertop and two large trash bags propped up against my door. Travis is in the living room folding the blankets I've been using.

"I have no problem scrubbing the kitchen or straightening things around here, but I draw the line at laundry. Like hell will I wash your nasty underwear."

"Thanks for all your help, man." I fold the clean kitchen towel over the handle of the oven. I don't know what I'd do without Travis in my life. We've gotten so used to picking up the slack for each other when times get tough.

"No problem." He folds the last blanket. "I don't mind helping and it gets Gus out of the house for a bit." We both turn towards Gus, who is now sleeping on his back with all three paws in the air.

"So, are you gonna go talk to her?" Travis asks, turning his attention back to me.

"Yeah, I thought about it and you're probably right, but I still need answers."

"And if you're okay with those answers, do you think you two will get back together?"

"I don't know. I mean, yes. I feel like I can't breathe without her. But what if it's an answer I don't want to hear, or what if I accept the answer, but she's so upset with me that she doesn't feel the same way anymore? Maybe the damage is done."

"It's been four days. I'm pretty sure she hasn't fallen out of love with you, dickface."

It's been four days since everything happened? I completely lost track of time. God, I've been so messed up.

"I need to do this. Fix this. I need to listen to her side," I say.

"Good, now let me get out of the way. When you two get back together, you'll be all over each other and I don't need to see that shit." He grabs the two garbage bags and steps out into the hallway. "Come on, Gus!"

Gus ever so dramatically slides off the couch, stretches, and reluctantly follows behind Travis. For a moment, I feel bad that his nap has been interrupted, but I toss that thought aside because I need to get my head on straight if I'm going to have a talk with Aly.

My heart pumps rapidly as I knock on the door of 312. The door opens to the sight of a sleepy-looking Michelle, who is still in her pajamas and holding a cup of coffee. She freezes mid-yawn when her eyes meet mine.

"Jax! Oh…umm…were you looking for Aly?"

"Of course I'm here for Aly," I snap and then realize how I sound. "I'm sorry, Michelle. I'm just a little nervous right now. Is Aly around?" I look over her shoulder but don't see anyone else in the condo.

Michelle lightly bounces from foot to foot and bites down on her bottom lip, suddenly seeming nervous.

"Does she not want to see me?" I frown and my heart sinks, thinking that maybe what we had can't be repaired.

"Umm...no, that's not it," she says, still bouncing from foot to foot. "Well, I mean, I'm not sure how she feels. She's not here."

"She's...what?" I swear my heart stops for a second.

"I don't know how much she would want you to know right now, you know, considering everything."

"Where is she?" I thought this whole time she was sleeping in the condo across from me. Has she bailed on me completely? Left her roommates? Her job?

"I don't know much." Michelle's eyes dart everywhere and I know she isn't being fully honest with me. "The other night, Aly received a call from Jacob. He told her that Jess had some sort of accident and is in the hospital. Aly took an Uber to the airport and was able to get a last-minute flight out."

"So, you're saying she's in... Maine?" I wipe my hand over my face. Jess is her best friend in the entire world, her support through everything. It makes total sense for Aly to drop everything and be with her, especially with Jess being pregnant.

"Do you know when she will be back?" I ask.

Michelle shakes her head. "She doesn't have a return flight booked yet, but her next semester doesn't start until mid-January, so I guess it will be sometime before then."

I blow out a breath. At least I know she is planning on coming back—hopefully.

Feeling defeated, I go back to my place and wonder if I should contact Aly or give her some space. Unsure of my next move, I flop on my bed and let out an audible sigh. The box Gram left me still sits on my nightstand. I pick it up and place it in my lap. I guess there's no time like the present to open it.

The smell of Gram's old floral perfume hits me as soon as I lift the lid. For a moment, I feel as if she's sitting right beside me. Man, I wish she were. What I wouldn't do to have just one more conversation with her. I wonder what advice she would give me. I smile thinking how much she would love Aly.

Thinking of Aly sends a ping of guilt right to my gut. Travis was right; I was too emotional to think rationally and I probably overreacted. Still, I need answers. I just hope I didn't scare her off.

Looking through the contents of the box transports me back to a simpler time in my life. I pick up something that looks like a blue rock but realize it's a clay elephant I made for her in kindergarten. I remember Gram was so excited to receive that hideous thing. I flip through a stack of old photographs and pause at one of Gram holding me on my first birthday. I had blue icing all over my face and was smiling from ear to ear. I continue to dig through the memories, which are mostly photos and some homemade birthday cards I made her.

Below the cards, I spot a small velvet pouch stuffed in an envelope. In the envelope is a picture of my cousins. They had to have been teenagers when the picture was taken. I don't know why Gram would want me to have a picture of my cousins, but she was becoming more confused and forgetful towards the end. Perhaps it was meant to go in someone else's box. I turn the photo over; "Mia's and Lyndsey's 14th Birthday" is written on the back. I guess I'll give it to Claire the next time I see her.

I put the picture off to the side to give to Claire at a later date, but as my hand goes to release the photo, I notice something. There are five girls in the picture, not four. All five girls are dressed alike in denim shorts and various colored tank tops. The girls are sitting on a bench with their arms around each other with bright smiles. My cousins look extremely similar to each other with their black hair and olive skin color. The girl sitting between Sophia and Mia has lighter features and I'd know those light blue eyes anywhere. It's Aly.

The room begins to swirl around me as a million questions hit me at once. Why is Aly in a picture with my cousins? How does she know them? Why would Gram put this picture in my box? Unless...no...it can't be possible.

I grab my phone out of my pocket and hit the icon for Uncle Chris. He answers immediately.

"Jaxon? Is everything okay?" The worry in his voice is palpable. I realize it's the first time I've ever called him. I rarely call anyone—they call me.

"Yes, everything's okay, but there's a girl and I think you know her. And a picture too and I need to know how you know her. Or maybe you don't know her, but you would have to know her because she's in the picture and Gram knew her and—"

"Jaxon!" Uncle Chris's voice is firm. "What is going on?"

I take a deep breath and try again. "Gram left me a box and in it was a picture of Mia's and Lyndsey's birthday. The girls are all sitting on a bench, and you know what? I'll just take a picture of it and send it to you." Why didn't I think to do that ahead of time?

"Stop!" Uncle Chris says before I can snap the picture. "All the girls have different colored tank tops on and there's a blond girl sitting between Sophia and Mia. Is that the picture you're talking about?"

"How did you know?"

"Because I'm the one who took that picture and I'm looking right at it. We have it framed in our living room."

Yeah, I would know that if I ever visited my aunt and uncle. They've invited me to their place in Washington, and while it's not too far away, I've never taken them up on the invite.

"Why do you want to know about the girl in the picture?" Suddenly, my uncle sounds like an overprotective dad questioning his daughter's date.

"Well, you're not going to believe this..."

I proceed to tell Uncle Chris everything, from how I met Aly at the pool, to how we fell in love (I leave certain parts out), to how we were basically living together and how everything ended.

"My God, I can't believe it." My uncle's voice is shaky. "Are you sitting down? I need to tell you everything."

"Yes, I am," I respond and listen in awe as my uncle fills in the gaps of Aly's life story. Aly was always so open about everything, except aspects of her childhood. I never wanted to pry or make her upset. But after listening to my uncle Chris, I get it now. I understand everything.

I end the call with my uncle and take the picture back in my hands. I stare at it for I don't know how long, then I start to do the math. Mia and Lyndsey are two years younger than Aly and me, which means Aly is sixteen in this picture. This was the year I broke my leg. The year we canceled our trip to visit Uncle Chris and his family.

This was the girl Gram wanted me to meet.

Anger runs through me. If I hadn't broken my leg, I would have met the girl of my dreams at six-fucking-teen years old. That's fifteen years of happiness that I missed out on. That we missed out on.

I take my water bottle, which is the closest thing to me, and hurl it against the wall. It's not enough. I need to expel more energy. I throw on some gym shorts, planning to head down to the gym, so I can punch something there. As I turn to leave, I remember the velvet pouch that accompanied the picture. I go back to the pouch and pull out the familiar silver chain with Gram's and Pop's wedding bands still attached.

I've got to find Aly now!

43

Aly

Thump. Thump. Thump. The heartbeat of Jess's baby holds strong on the monitor.

"You two gave us quite the scare," I say as I hug my best friend. It feels so good to be in her presence again, even though it's not under the best circumstances. Jess's husband, Brady, had come home to find her on the floor and unresponsive. In true Jess-like fashion, she was doing too much, and her blood pressure got too high. She passed out and hit her head on the side of the coffee table, leaving her with a mild concussion, some nasty bruising, and a couple of staples in her head.

"The doctor is telling me I have to be on bed rest for the next few weeks. What the hell am I going to do?" Jess whines.

"Catch up on Netflix? You could always do some reading. Maybe read one of those books with Jacob on the cover." I wink.

"Oh, hell no!" she yells, and I burst into laughter. Jess and I both like to read the occasional romance novel, but we draw the line at reading anything with Jacob on the cover.

"I can't believe I'll be spending Christmas in the hospital," she groans.

"I can't believe I'll be spending Christmas with you!" It's not that I'm not happy about that; it's just that I never expected to be back on the East Coast this soon.

"You look like hell."

"Gee, thanks." I sit down next to her bedside and pull at the waist of my leggings that keep riding down.

"You've lost weight," she states.

"Haven't had much of an appetite lately." Truth be told, I haven't had the energy to do much of anything. If Jacob hadn't called to tell me about Jess, I would still be in my bed, drowning in my own self-pity.

"The circles around your eyes are so dark. They're worse than when we used to pull all-nighters during finals."

I tried my best to cover up the circles under my eyes with makeup, but my eyes have been so swollen from all the tears I have shed.

"I'm fine, Jess," I say, a little annoyed since I'm supposed to be here for her, yet she's concerned about me. "I'm just jet-lagged."

"You know you can't pull that with me, Aly. It might work with your roommates because they don't know you as well, but I know you're beating yourself up inside."

"I should've told him. I was the one woman outside of his family who he trusted and I blew it. I broke him. I broke us." My eyes burn with fresh tears brewing. Jess and I rehash everything over again, but talking about it doesn't make me feel any better. I thought the breakup with Trent was bad, but it's nothing compared to the enormity of losing Jax. I don't think I can recover from this.

"You really love him, don't you?" Jess says softly.

"It doesn't matter anymore." I stare out the window at the gray sky and snow-covered trees. "It's over."

"I don't think it is."

I snap my head back to look at my best friend. She must've bumped her head harder than expected.

"Aly." She starts to giggle. "I know you think I'm crazy right now, but I really don't think this is over."

"Oh, it's over all right. You didn't see how angry he was." I shake my head, thinking of the twisted look on his face when he told me to get out.

"I don't think he was angry; I think he was hurt. Think of it from his point of view. He had been burned so badly by his ex, he finally let his guard down, and then his world got turned upside down again. He was probably experiencing some really shitty déjà vu."

"Why do I feel like you're taking his side?"

"Because for the first time in years, I got my best friend back." Jess's eyes begin to swell. "You don't realize it, Aly, but all that bullshit with Trent? It changed you. You became like this scared little hermit crab hiding in your shell. I lost my happy, bubbly friend. Then one day, something in your voice changed. You told me the guy across the hall was driving you crazy, but you weren't mad about it; you were...amused."

"He wasn't really driving me crazy." I smile.

"I know." Jess returns my smile.

"I'm scared." I fumble with the drawstring of my hoodie.

"I know that too."

"Why do I feel so out of control?"

"Because this isn't in your control. Not everything. Remember what I told you when you were offered the job at the university?"

"Divine intervention," I reply.

"Exactly! I always felt that there was a bigger reason for the university contacting you. Granted, I figured it had more to do with getting away from Trent, but this? It's more than anyone could have ever imagined and it's everything you ever wanted."

I give Jess a confused look.

"You were never truly happy in Beaute." Jess begins to count on her fingers. "You needed to get away from Trent, you found your dream job, and you found someone who loves you for you. You can't control everything that happens, but you can control how you handle it. I think you need to take that return flight, march up to his door, and say, "Jaxon Cornelius Parker, you need to listen to me right now."

"Cornelius?"

"It was the first name I could think of. Can you believe that was on Brady's list of potential baby names? Thank God we're having a girl. Do you even know his middle name?"

"Yeah, it's Steven. He was named after his grandf—" I freeze mid-word, thinking back to the day I saw Jax sign a receipt as Jaxon S. Parker. I asked him what the S stood for. It was such a quick moment. I never put it together.

"Aly, what's wrong? Your face just went completely pale."

"Steven Parker..." A burst of adrenaline flows through me and I begin to pace the floor.

"His grandfather was Steven Parker. He never mentioned his grandmother's name or his parents' first names, but...wait! Emmalyn. He always calls his sister Ems." I stop and slap my forehead. "How could I have been so ignorant? Granted, I didn't know they lived in Oregon. I just knew it was somewhere out west." I shake my arms frantically in the direction of where I think is west. "I mean, what are the odds, right?"

"Umm...are you feeling okay?" Jess holds up the call button to the nurse's station. "I mean, you are in the right place if you're having a breakdown."

"Jaxon Parker!" I slap the call button out of Jess's hand. "Nonno Steven's other grandchildren were named Jaxon and Emmalyn. Oh my God! Nonna Grace is his gram!"

I watch Jess's face as she begins to decipher my ramblings. She knows all about my childhood and my fond memories of the Parkers. She even tried to help me find them a time or two. I finally gave up many years ago because I would fall into a funk after our searches came up with nothing. It was like the Parker family just vanished from the face of the Earth.

"Are you sure?" She gasps.

"Like...99.999 percent sure." Silence falls between us as my best friend and I share a knowing look. "I have to go."

"I know," she says with tears in her eyes.

I lean over the hospital bed and give her a squeeze, knowing I need to book my return flight as soon as possible. "I'll be back for the christening...or maybe even sooner if I'm wrong about everything."

"I'll see you for the christening." She pulls away from our embrace and wipes her eyes.

Pulling out the keys to my rental car, I make a beeline for the parking garage. I contemplate calling Jax, but this conversation needs to happen in person. I just hope he will listen to me.

44

Jax

"Sir, I'm telling you, there are currently no available outbound flights headed to any airport in Maine. If you come back on Monday, I might be able to get you on a flight into Boston, but there are no guarantees," the overworked ticket agent at the airport says. He continues to hit random buttons on his computer, and I'm tempted to turn the screen around to see if he is actually looking for a flight or playing some sort of game.

"Boston? But that's Massachusetts." I consider it for a moment. At least I'd be on the East Coast. I would need to rent a car anyway.

"Very good, sir. You know your geography," he deadpans.

"Look, I'm gonna let that sarcastic remark slide, but you don't understand." I lean over the counter, so no one else can hear. "I just found out that the woman I love was literally sent here from Heaven by my gram."

"No!" the ticket agent says in an astonished voice. "Your gram sent you a girl?"

"Yes! And she is currently in Maine. I need to get to her as soon as possible. Can you help me out?"

"No," he says flatly. I slap my hand on the counter in frustration and walk outside to try to call Aly for the millionth time. Her phone seems to be off because it keeps going straight to voicemail.

I walk toward a bench near the doors to the airport, contemplating my next move. I could drive out to Maine, but that would take days. I have Jess's contact information. She was listed as Aly's emergency contact on Michelle's rental agreement. It took a while for Michelle to give me the information, but after pleading my case, she finally broke down and gave it to me. I pull out my phone again and my finger hovers over Jess's name. I don't want to call her because I'm not sure of her condition, but I may have no other choice.

"Are you sure there's nothing available? I'll take anything you have, even a minivan," I hear a tired but familiar voice say. I must be hallucinating because I swear Aly is right in front of me at the Rent-A-Car kiosk.

"I'm sorry, ma'am," the clerk at the kiosk says. "But this is a busy time of year and we're all booked. Have you tried a rideshare app?"

"My phone had a run-in with an escalator. It's completely busted," she says exasperatedly and places her phone on the counter. The clerk winces at the sight.

"Here, you can use mine," the clerk responds, but I'm already on the move before the woman can hand over her phone.

"Need a ride?" I hear myself saying.

Aly's back stiffens as she turns around. Her eyes go wide when her gaze sets on me. "What are you doing here?"

"Trying to get a flight to Maine." I take a hesitant step closer to her. She looks absolutely exhausted and gorgeous at the same time.

"Why we-were you going to Maine?" she stammers.

"Trying to find you." I take another step closer. "I—"

"No! Wait!" she cuts me off with a sudden burst of energy. "This wasn't in the plan. I had a whole plan. She pulls a napkin from the airline out of her coat pocket. "I was going to drive back and knock on your door until you finally opened it. I was going to make you listen to everything I had to say whether you wanted to or not. I even had a speech written." She waves the napkin in the air like a flag.

"Okay." I chew on the inside of my cheek. Even after all the traveling and stress, she's still adorable. It's taking every bit of restraint in me not to just scoop her up and kiss her senseless right now.

Aly fidgets with the napkin then stands a little straighter. "Jax," she says and looks straight at me. "First of all, I am so sorry for not telling you about my name change at work..."

She goes on for about ten minutes, confirming everything that I already put together. I just stare at her in awe as she gives her speech right in the airport. People around us hustle by and announcements in various languages play over the loudspeaker, but Aly stays focused, determined to speak her mind.

"But then," she continues. "Jess called you Cornelius—"

"Cornelius?"

"Yeah, her husband wanted to name their baby that, but I'm getting off track. Anyway, I mentioned your middle name was Steven and then I started thinking that Nonno Steven had two grandkids—"

"Wait!" I can't believe I'm hearing that name come out of that mouth. "You know?"

"I know?" She scrunches up her nose. "I know what? What do you know?"

"What do you know?" I counter back.

"I asked you first. What do you think you know I know? Oh my God, this is insane!" She throws her hands up in the air.

I laugh, put my arms around her waist, and spin her around, catching her off guard. Her hair brushes against my face and the scent of her vanilla-coconut shampoo is euphoric.

"You"—I place a chaste kiss on her nose—"are apparently a very important person in not only my life but the rest of my family's life too."

"You do know," she says, astonished. "How much do you know?"

"Enough." I put her feet back on the floor. "I have a lot to tell you, but I'm sure you have more to tell me."

"So, this means you'll listen?" she asks hesitantly. Shit, yeah, that's the whole reason why things ended in the first place. I refused to listen to her.

"From now on, I will listen to anything and everything you have to say. I am so sorry for the way I treated you. When I saw your ID with that name…it just gave me terrible flashbacks of what Maranda did to me. I couldn't think straight. I couldn't believe you would lie to me. I realize now you didn't. You were going to tell me the day you came home and saw me on the phone with the credit card company, weren't you?"

"How did you…?" She looks at me in disbelief.

"I've had time to think things over. I knew something was up. When I thought back to how you acted that day, it just made sense. Now, about that ride home… Do you still need one?"

"When you say take me home, do you mean your place?" She raises her brow.

"That's up to you, sweetheart." I grab her luggage and nudge her towards the parking lot. I can't get her out of this place fast enough. "I would love to have you back in my home, in my bed, preferably, but if you feel more comfortable with Michelle and Gabby, I will understand that too. It's your decision."

"Jax?"

"Yes?"

Aly puts her arms around my neck and I let go of the luggage to pull her in close. Then she says the words I've been dying to hear. "I want to go home with you."

45

Jax

Aly stares out the window as I drive down I-5 towards the hospital where my sister gave birth to her twins earlier today. This morning was a bit of a frenzy. Emma was supposed to be induced on Monday, but she went into labor naturally on Friday night and gave birth early this morning. I pretty much threw some stuff together and told Aly to get in the truck.

"I'm nervous," she says without lifting her gaze from the window.

"Nothing to be nervous about, sweetheart." I put my hand on her knee and give it a squeeze. "My family is going to love you. Besides, most of them already do."

"I'm not talking about *that* side of the family. I'm talking about *your* side. Maybe we should've waited." Aly chews on the bottom of her lip. "I mean, Emma just gave birth and I'm basically an outsider. Does she really need a complete stranger invading her space?"

"First of all, you are not a stranger, and second, she specifically asked me to bring you."

"She did?" Her body starts to relax.

My family has been chomping at the bit to meet Aly. I've tried to keep them at bay since we got back together. I knew they would innocently come on too strong for her. The twins should be a great buffer in subduing my mom, who can't wait to meet her future daughter-in-law. Her words, not mine, but that's coming too.

We arrive at the hospital a little while later and make our way to the nursery hand in hand. The silhouette of my father standing beside a hospital room door comes into view and I feel Aly freeze beside me.

She breaks away from my hand and walks towards my father. "You look just like Papa Chris!" she says in awe.

A broad smile spreads across Dad's face. "Actually, Chris looks just like me since I'm the older brother."

"Aly, this is my dad, Mark, but I think you already figured that out," I say as I approach them.

"This is crazy!" She shakes her head in disbelief. "If I had seen a picture of you beforehand, I would've known immediately."

"I look more like my mom." I shrug. "None of the Parker men have produced kids that look like them."

"Papa Chris used to joke that I was his biological child since I looked more like him than his own daughters," Aly says with humor laced in her voice.

"Thank God that wasn't true or we'd be in a whole different mess right now." I snort.

Aly looks up at me. "I assure you, I am not biologically a Parker. My parents, aloof as they are, are my actual parents. I had my DNA done back in college just to make sure."

"It's so nice to meet you, Aly." My dad pulls her into a hug. "Emma's nursing the twins right now... I, uh, wanted to give them some privacy."

"So glad I didn't walk in on that!" I announce loudly.

"I heard that!" I hear from inside the room. "I just finished. Get in here!" Emma yells from her bed. I grab Aly's hand and lead her into the room.

Emma is sitting in her hospital bed with two bundles, one in each arm. Her dark hair is up in a messy bun, her eyes have dark circles underneath them, but besides that, she looks radiant for just giving birth.

"Come here!" she says with a grin. "I have one for each of you. The one with the purple headband is Lily and the one with the pink headband is Rosie."

"Oh my gosh! They're beautiful!" Aly gushes at the two little cherubs dressed in soft white onesies with headbands bigger than their heads.

"Here," Emma says to Aly. "Take Rosie. Jax can take Lily. I think she just pooped."

Everyone laughs as the joke breaks any possible tension in the room. Then I scoop up Lily and realize my sister wasn't joking.

Emma throws her head back against her hospital bed and laughs hysterically. "The...look...on...your...face!" She grabs her belly.

"Oh! Give me my grandbaby." Mom grabs the baby from my arms. "Aly, it's so nice to meet you. I'm Eve."

"It's nice to meet you too," Aly replies, and I watch her gently rock Rosie...or is that Lily? Yeah, I'm going to have trouble telling these two apart.

My mom, sister, and Aly begin chatting about the babies and other things. Aly's body language relaxes as she becomes increasingly comfortable around my family. I know my mom is already in love with her. She's all but pulled out the baby pictures of me. Wait...never mind.

"Mom! Can you stop it, please?" I whine. "And who carries actual photographs around anymore?"

"You're old, honey," Mom chides. "We didn't have cameras on our phones back then. Oh! Look! Here is Jaxon in the bathtub! He was just the cutest. The warm water must've relaxed him cause every time I put him in the tub, he would pass gas."

"Mom!" I yell.

"The water would bubble up—"

"MOM!" I yell louder, earning a laugh from everyone in the room. I can feel my face turning a deep shade of red. While I'm embarrassed at my mother's antics, I do appreciate that Aly seems at ease with her.

"Don't worry, Jax." Emma giggles. "Grant's mom pulled out the home videos when I met his parents for the first time."

"Don't remind me," Grant groans.

A gasp near the door has all our heads turning towards the sound. My uncle Chris and aunt Maria stand stone-still, staring at the beauty sitting next to my mother.

"Aly?" Aunt Maria says with a shaky voice.

"Oh my! You're all grown up now!" Uncle Chris says as they bound towards her.

"You're so beautiful!" Aunt Maria says, placing a strand of stray hair behind Aly's ear. You can see the tears forming in her eyes. They pull her into a hug. I can't see their faces, but I can hear my aunt sobbing and muttering something in Italian.

I stand there in awe of everything. How emotional Aly is seeing my aunt and uncle for the first time in years. How happy my aunt and uncle are to have Aly back. You can feel the love radiating through them all.

The sound of laughter from behind me brings me out of my thoughts. I turn to see Emma and Grant whispering and giggling together.

"What?" I look at them.

"Don't you find it funny that your girlfriend refers to your aunt and uncle as Mamma and Papa?" Grant asks with a smirk.

"Huh, I didn't until you mentioned it."

"That's some backwoods type stuff right there and it's hilarious." Grant claps me on the shoulder.

"My brother is dating his cousin!" Emma shouts. My parents and Grant burst out laughing.

"This isn't funny, guys." I cross my arms over my chest, earning more laughs from my family. Aly, Aunt Maria, and Uncle Chris are too deep in conversation to notice.

Everyone talks and coos over the babies until Emma and the twins fall into a peaceful sleep. My aunt and uncle take Aly out to a restaurant to catch up on the last fifteen years. They offered me to come, but I know Aly needs this alone time with them.

Grant and I head down to the hospital cafeteria for some coffee. It's the first time the two of us have had any time to speak alone in what feels like forever.

"I can't believe you're a dad now." I open up a sugar packet and pour it into my paper cup.

"It's crazy! Last night, it was just the two of us and today, we're a family of four."

"I'm happy for you," I say genuinely. "The girls are gorgeous, and Emma seems to be on cloud nine."

"Yeah, I know we're kind of in the honeymoon phase with everyone around to help. It's gonna be tough when it's just the two of us trying to take care of two babies."

"It will be, but I know you'll get through it. Aly and I can babysit, and remember, my parents are just a few blocks away to help." Grant is originally from the Midwest. His parents are planning to come out and visit in about a week.

"Okay, enough about me. How are things going with Aly?" Grant asks.

"Good! Great even."

"I like her. She seems good for you." Grant takes a sip of his coffee.

"She's *too* good for me."

"You think you want to make things permanent with her?"

"I'd marry her right now in this cafeteria, but she's not ready." I concentrate on stirring my coffee.

"You don't think so?"

"I think she's overwhelmed with all the changes. You know the university asked her to come on permanently?"

"No shit! That's awesome, man."

"Yeah, and she loves the job, but that means she has to decide what to do with her home and stuff in storage in Georgia. Then we discovered the connection to my family…" I trail off.

"Now that shit is wild! She's known your family since she was what? Thirteen or something like that?"

"Twelve," I correct him.

Grant lets out a low whistle.

"I'm glad she went out to dinner with my aunt and uncle. I think she needs this time alone with them. I know she has a lot of questions, and hopefully, this visit will give her some clarity."

"Man, I never thought I'd see the day. Aly must be really special." Grant shakes his head.

"What do you mean?"

"In all the years I've known you, I've never seen you so concerned about a woman's feelings."

"True," I agree. "But I've never met a woman like Aly before."

46

Aly

I sit at the restaurant table across from Mamma Maria and Papa Chris, not entirely convinced that this isn't just some crazy dream.

"This is so surreal," Papa Chis says. "I know I'm looking at you, Aly, but I keep expecting to see a teenager sitting across from me."

I nod in understanding. Papa Chris still looks the same, but time has aged him. His dark hair now has flecks of gray, and the creases around his eyes have become more defined. Somehow, Mamma Maria has aged backwards; her bright smile hasn't left her face since we sat down.

"We're sure you have so many questions for us," Mamma Maria says.

"I've thought about this moment so many times. It was so hard when you first left. The letters helped, but then they eventually stopped coming. I stopped writing too because...well, I figured maybe I was being too much of a pest."

"You were never a pest." Mamma Maria reaches across the table and squeezes my hand. "Your letters were quite the lifeline for me. I kept every one of them and read them multiple times. It was so hard to leave you. I felt like I left one of my daughters on the other side of the world."

"I'm afraid I'm the cause of why communication ceased," Papa Chris pipes up with remorse in his voice. "While we were in Japan, I was recruited for a job with Intelligence. I thought it was the right path to take for my career, but I regret it very much. My name got on a hitlist of sorts. As a precaution, we had to move several times. It kills me that I put my family in danger."

"You didn't mean to." I know Papa Chris would never intentionally risk the safety of his family.

"I didn't." He looks down at his plate of food somberly. "Thankfully, nothing ever came of it, but we couldn't risk you being associated with us. I never would've been able to forgive myself if someone had come after you."

"So that's why everyone stopped writing?" Fresh tears prickle behind my eyes. I understand and I don't blame them for anything. But the disheartening memories of looking into an empty mailbox flash in my mind.

"We're so sorry, Aly. It was horrible losing that connection to you, but we couldn't risk your safety. To this day, we keep as much information about us private, just as a precaution."

"I thought you didn't want me anymore." I sob.

Mamma Maria jumps out of her seat and blots my tears with a napkin. "Oh, Aly! We love you. We've always loved you. Tell her, Chris."

"Tell me what?" I sniffle.

Mamma Maria and Papa Chris share a concerned look.

"What? What is it?" I sniffle again.

"I came back to Norfolk a few years later. It was just me on a temporary assignment. I don't remember what year it was, but you were of college age by then. I stopped by your family home hoping that you would be there."

"I went to college out of state," I respond. "I never went back after I left."

"I know that now and I wish I knew that then because I had a very unpleasant encounter with your parents."

"I can only imagine how that went."

"Your parents blamed us for your estrangement. They said we gave you unrealistic expectations of what families should be like. Then they said you were all working on building a better relationship and that we should stay away because we would interfere with the progress you made."

"They were lying." I gasp, although not surprised my parents would say that sort of thing. "My parents are responsible for my estrangement. There was never any progress. I tried several times to connect with them, but they showed no interest. The last time I talked to them was right before I graduated college. I called to let them know about my graduation. I thought that maybe they'd like to see me walk or at least hear about my accomplishments. My father thought I was asking for money in some roundabout way and hung up on me. That was the last I ever heard from them."

"Oh, Aly!" Papa Chris says and two sets of arms wrap around me as I cry harder.

"I graduated with honors." I cry into Mamma Maria's shoulder. "I thought if I kept pushing myself...if I kept accomplishing things, maybe they would like me."

"We love you," Papa Chris says while wiping his eyes. "We love you so much and we're so proud of you. I should've pressed harder with your parents. I didn't think they were being truthful, but I didn't want to ruin any relationship you might've had with them. I'm so sorry."

"It's not your fault. You did what you thought was right."

"*Ascoltami*! Listen!" Mamma Maria says, trying to gain some composure. "We're back in your life now and we will not leave you ever again, do you hear?"

I nod vigorously in agreement.

"Now, tell us, how in the world did you meet Jaxon?"

The subject change instantly puts a smile on my face. I tell Mamma Maria and Papa Chris my story, starting with how I got to Starboard Beach in the first place and ending with Jax and me reconciling in the airport. They listen with astonishment and intensity.

"*Soprendente*! Amazing!" Mamma Maria says once I finish my story.

We make our way back towards the hospital where I spot Jax and Grant sitting outside on a bench. My heart rate quickens at the sight of Jax; walking towards him feels like I'm coming home.

Before Jax and Grant come into earshot, Papa Chris gently tugs on my arm to stop me. "Jaxon is a good man. His life hasn't been easy, which you know. He might have a cold exterior, but there is a warm heart underneath it all."

"I know." I smile.

47

Jax

I cannot explain how much I love coming home from work these days. Aly has officially moved in with me, which means I get to wake up and fall asleep with her in my arms every day. It still pisses me off that we missed out on so much time together, but Aly tells me to just stay focused on our present and future. Speaking of our future, we decided to purchase the house Travis and I are currently working on. We will still be 3rd East residents for the time being as renovations are taking longer than expected. We had to completely gut the Hotel California room, which is now my future office.

"Hey, sweetheart." I wrap my arms around her from behind and kiss her temple. "Are you making those awesome pork chops again?"

"Yeah, we haven't had them since the day you paraded around here naked. I figured it was time to make them again."

I bark out a laugh. "I did not parade around here naked! *You* weren't even supposed to be here. I think you were just sitting quietly in the corner, waiting to catch a glimpse of me."

"While I was sitting quietly in the corner, I assure you I was not expecting to catch a glimpse of your naked ass. Not that I'm not complaining or anything." She turns around and winks.

I lean over her shoulder and grab a pork chop. It's piping hot, but I don't care. It's delicious.

"What are you doing?" she squeals. "You can't just steal an entire pork chop!"

"Just did," I say as I take a huge bite. "These are so great; they taste just like Gram's."

"Well, I'm not surprised since she was the one who taught me how to make them."

"That's impossible." I nearly choke. "Gram took all of her recipes to her grave."

Aly gives me a quizzical look. "What are you talking about? She taught me a bunch of recipes every summer when she came to visit."

"Are we talking about the same woman? Because Gram outright refused to share her recipes with anyone."

"If we are talking about Nonna Grace, then yes, indeed. Every summer, she would spend a whole day with me and we would cook together. She felt bad that I didn't have any grandparents, so she basically adopted me like the rest of your family."

"Why can't you just call her Gram?" I'm curious why Aly uses the names my cousins used instead of the names my sister and I did.

"Because I didn't know her as Gram. My sisters called her Nonna Grace, so that's what I called her too."

I'm still getting used to Aly referring to my cousins as her "sisters."

"Fine," I huff. "So, 'Nonna Grace' taught you how to cook?"

"She didn't teach me *everything*. Like I said, she would spend one day a summer with me. The rest I learned from Mamma Maria or on my own."

A thought hits me. "The oatmeal walnut chocolate chip cookies. Gram—I mean, Nonna Grace—showed you how to make those?"

"Mm-hmm." She nods. "That was actually the first thing we made together. I guess that would be the summer I turned thirteen. I have a lot more of her recipes."

"And the pork chops?"

"I think that was the summer I turned fifteen."

"What else did she show you how to make?"

Aly tilts her head. "Let's see, the cookies were the first thing. She also taught me how to make citrus salad dressing, meatloaf—I haven't made that in a while—the pork chops and—"

I cannot believe what I'm hearing. I drop to my knees and wrap my arms around her waist.

"Tell me she showed you how to make sweet potato casserole. Tell me she showed you how." I start shaking her hips, and we're both laughing now.

"Yeah, she showed me that one too."

I jump up and start twirling her around. "Do you know what this means?"

"Should I?"

"Those were all my favorite foods that Gram made! Except for the sweet potato casserole—that's everyone's favorite."

Aly pauses. Silence falls between us, then she gasps once everything sinks in. "You mean to tell me that while you were out sowing your teenage oats, I was learning how to cook *your* favorite foods?"

"Yes!" I laugh.

"That little conniving grandmother of yours. She was freaking grooming me for you the whole time!"

I throw my head back in laughter, then grab her and pull her into a hug. "You know this means you need to make everything for me."

"You know this means you better be on your best behavior or you're not getting anything."

I kiss her like never before. This woman is my life and I can't wait to marry her.

***

"Is the blindfold really necessary? It looks like you're kidnapping me," Aly says from the passenger seat of my truck.

"My windows are tinted. No one will notice," I assure her.

"Great! So no one can help if you're really trying to kill me. Just know, if you are taking me someplace to do this, I'll—"

"Haunt me, I know."

"Just making sure you are aware of the consequences." She crosses her arms matter-of-factly. "Are we there yet?"

"You're worse than a little kid."

"Am not!" She pouts.

I pull into the turnout for Portside Beach, grateful that the weather today isn't too blistering cold. I could've done this anywhere, but I felt the need to go back to the place where I started opening my heart up to Aly.

"Wait here!" I hop out of my truck and run around to the passenger side. Up ahead, I can see that Carter and Travis carried out their jobs impeccably.

"Can I take this off now?" Aly says once I lift her out of the truck. She sniffs the saltwater air. "We're at the beach? Oh, God! You're going to throw me in with the fish poop again! Is this because I messed with your playlist?"

"That was you?! I thought Travis was the one who switched it all to yodeling."

"Damn! I could've gotten away with that." She stomps her foot.

"Screwed yourself on that one." I pull her in for a hug and kiss the top of her head. It's funny how Aly's little antics used to agitate me. Thinking back, I realize it was probably misplaced anger. Now, I find her little pranks adorable.

"Keep the blindfold on and hold my hand," I direct her. She follows without protest. We walk towards the large flat rock where we sat just a few months ago when we were getting to know each other. This time, I came prepared. There is a large blanket surrounded by battery-operated candles (I knew the wind would kill any regular ones), a bouquet of daisies (her favorites), a thermos of coffee, and a picnic basket full of fresh scones courtesy of Michelle.

I take in the scene, thankful for the friends I never knew I needed. I tap the pocket of my coat for the millionth time, making sure the ring hasn't magically grown legs and jumped into the ocean.

I reach around Aly and untie the blindfold. She blinks a few times, adjusting to the light, and looks around curiously.

"This is the place where I first opened up to you and I figured this would be the perfect place to do it again." I motion for her to sit on the blanket and take her hands in mine. "First, I'm so sorry you missed seeing Gram again by such a short time. I know she would've loved to see you, but she knew you were on the way."

"Umm..." Aly looks utterly confused.

"I know it sounds crazy but let me explain. I told you how I discovered who you were when I found the picture of you with my cousins, but I didn't tell you everything. The night I got the call that Gram was back in the hospital, I knew it would be the last time I would see her. Her body had been weakening for some time; she just couldn't hold on any longer. The family took turns visiting with her, and when it was my turn, she told me something that, at the time, I thought was complete nonsense.

"Gram hated how I handled my life after everything happened with Maranda," I continue. "I was convinced that I would be alone for the rest of my life because I never wanted to feel that level of hurt again. But, during our last conversation, Gram told me that she always knew who I was meant to be with. She said that Pop had been visiting her and they came up with a plan to bring her here, to bring *you* here."

"I'm not sure I understand."

"I didn't either, but I put it all together while you were in Maine." I reach into my pocket and pull out the photograph of Aly and my cousins. I had told Aly about the picture, but I left out the part about the rings until this moment.

"This," I say, holding up the photo, "was not the only thing that was left for us to discover, but I wanted to wait until the time was right to show you what else she left."

I pull out the white gold antique-style engagement ring.

"Is that...?" I watch Aly's eyes go wide. "It can't be!"

"Do you recognize it?" I ask with a little bit of surprise.

Aly responds by nodding. "It would always catch in the sun when Nonna Grace would sit and read outside. I swore you could see that thing sparkling for miles."

I chuckle at her response. "Gram wore this along with her and Pop's wedding bands on a necklace. She didn't have it on the last time I saw her, but I figured the doctors removed it for some reason. Turns out, she had stored it away for us."

Aly opens and closes her mouth, but no words come out.

"Remember what Jess said about your job?" I ask her.

"D-divine intervention," she stammers. "Do you think it was Nonna Grace and Nonno Steven?"

"I do now. It all makes sense. You were hired for a job that you never applied for, you found a roommate who conveniently lived across the hall from me, the water damage to your room sent you right into my place, the recipes..." my voice trails off, wanting to get to the task at hand. "Alyssa Winters..." I get on one knee and take her hand. "I never knew true love and I never cared to know what true love was. But then you showed up out of nowhere and completely turned my world upside down." I pause. "Actually, you turned my world right side up since I wasn't exactly headed in the best direction. My life is exponentially better with you in it. All of my hopes and dreams..." I look into her eyes. "It's like you're the key to them all. Now, God knows I wish we'd met when we were supposed to and I don't know why it took fifteen years for our stars to align, but I will be forever grateful that they did.

"So," I continue. "Would you make me the happiest man in the world and become Alyssa Parker...for real?" I take Gram's ring and slide it on her finger; it fits like a glove.

"I think you're supposed to wait for an answer before you do that," she says through happy tears.

"I knew you'd say yes. I mean, do you really want to disappoint Gram and Pop?" I wink.

"No!" Aly laughs. "I definitely do not!" She leaps forward, wraps her arms around my neck, and presses her nose up against mine. "You're really stuck with me now!"

"There's no one else I'd rather be with."

From this moment on, life is going to be amazing.

Epilogue

Jax, Six Months Later

Today, Aly and I are getting married...again. Yup, you read that correctly. Aly and I had no intentions of waiting to have a wedding; we both wanted to seal the deal right away. However, my family insisted that we should get married at the Parker Family Reunion this summer. That way everyone important to us could be together.

At first, Aly said she didn't even want a wedding, but when Uncle Chris, aka Papa Chris, announced that he wanted to walk his long-lost daughter down the aisle, well, Aly changed her tune. We still didn't want to wait until summer to get married, so Aly and I eloped back in February, just a mere two weeks after we got engaged.

I look behind me to see my parents beaming. My mom's mascara has already begun to leak with tears of joy. Just as I expected, my family adores Aly. How could they not?

My sister and Grant sit to the side of my mom, each of them holding a baby. My nieces are at that cute stage where they smile at everything but still can't walk or talk. Aly calls it the "happy blob" stage, and honestly, it's a pretty accurate description. I still have trouble telling them apart, but Aly can tell who is who just by the sound of their laugh or cry. We try to babysit as often as we can. We need the practice since we're going to have a little one of our own by the end of the year.

We wanted to start a family as soon as possible, so we threw out all birth control the day we were married. We figured it would take a while to conceive. Imagine our surprise when just a few weeks later, we were staring down at no fewer than half a dozen positive pregnancy tests. We were convinced it was too good to be true, but as the months have gone by, it has finally sunk in that we will be parents in just a few months.

Aly's pregnancy has gone well so far. She had a rough battle with morning sickness for a while, but that has finally subsided. She was worried that she wouldn't fit into her dress, but she is only just starting to show.

I look beyond where my immediate family is sitting and notice a bunch of empty chairs. Aly's side of the small venue is packed. "Why are you all sitting on the bride's side?" I ask my cousins. I really don't care who sits on what side, but it looks a little lopsided.

"We all got together and decided we were Team Aly," Mia answers.

"But you're *my* cousins!" I argue.

"And she's *our* sister!" Mia and Lyndsey say in unison.

"God, that sounds so wrong." I wipe my hand over my face as everyone in the venue begins to laugh. I look over at the Justice of the Peace, who appears to be trying to keep a straight face. "It's, umm...it's not what you think. We're not actually related."

"I've been informed." He chuckles.

"No worries, man!" A voice I didn't expect pipes up from the crowd. *Ducking* Jacob. "I'll sit over on the groom's side." He saunters over and takes a seat behind my parents.

"I thought you couldn't make it," I groan.

"I told Aly to tell you that so it'd be a surprise. Surprise!" He does jazz hands and gives me a sarcastic smirk. Soft giggles come from nearly every female in the building, earning them dirty looks from their husbands.

The Justice of the Peace lightly taps me on the shoulder. "I was just told the rest of the wedding party is in place. Are you ready?"

"Of course!" I can't help the smile that spreads across my face. Even though we're already married, it feels more real with everyone we love here to witness our vows.

We kept everything simple. All the men are wearing jeans and button-down shirts. The girls are in sundresses of various pastel colors. I'm not sure what Aly is wearing, since she refused to let me see the dress, but I know it's not a formal, frilly wedding dress—that wouldn't be her style anyway. I also know that no matter what, she will be the most beautiful woman in the room.

Soft music starts to play, and everyone lets out a collective "aw" when Gus, dressed in his own custom-made tux, happily hobbles down the aisle, tail wagging to and fro. Travis, my best man, walks Jess, Aly's maid of honor, down the aisle. I'm proud of Travis. He has become a lot more social lately and I know it's due to Aly's welcoming nature. He and Jess are going to be the godparents of our son. You should've seen Travis's face when we asked him; I'd never seen him smile so proudly.

Carter and Michelle are next down the aisle, followed by Alex and Gabby. The soft music changes and everyone stands to look at Aly on the arm of Uncle Chris. She looks like an angel in an off-white halter top sundress. Her hair is in long waves and she's carrying a bouquet of daisies. Uncle Chris is one proud papa as he walks his daughter down the aisle.

When they reach the end of the aisle, Uncle Chris whispers something to Aly and gives her a quick kiss on her cheek. He winks at me as he returns to his seat, and I swear I see him wipe a tear from his eye.

I turn to face my beautiful bride, who hands over her bouquet to Jess.

"Hi!" Aly says happily when she looks back at me. I'm not sure what the etiquette is for a bride and groom up at the altar, but I don't think it's casual conversation.

"Hi!" I respond. "You look beautiful, sweetheart." I stand back in awe that this woman is my wife.

"Thank you, and look..." She taps the side of her dress. "It has pockets!"

"How's Bean?" Bean is the name we gave the baby before we knew we were having a boy. He no longer looks like a bean on the ultrasound now, but it stuck. His real name is Jaxon Steven Parker Junior and we will call him JJ for short.

"Great! Probably still on a sugar high from all the festivities last night."

Instead of a traditional bachelorette party, Aly had a good old-fashioned sleepover at Michelle's, complete with movies, pedicures, and junk food. No males were invited, but I'm pretty sure Alex attempted to sneak in a time or two. I didn't bother with any type of bachelor party; those days are behind me now.

Someone clears their throat and I realize the Justice of the Peace and everyone else is waiting for us to get started. Aly and I exchange knowing looks and say we're ready. We go about the ceremony, placing our wedding bands that we temporarily took off back on our hands during the ring exchange.

Aly looks out into the crowd. Tears well up in her eyes.

"What's wrong, sweetheart?" I wonder if her morning sickness is flaring up again.

"I just realized that everyone I love is here in some sort of way." She looks down at our hands with our wedding bands that not only symbolize our marriage, but Gram and Pop's blessed union as well.

Later that evening, we dance to our first song. The lyrics talk about how two people finally meet after traveling through life alone. It came on the radio one day while I was working on our house and I knew the song summed up our story perfectly.

I look down at Aly, who is looking up at me with stars in her eyes. "What is going on in that head of yours?"

"My life plan."

"Your what?"

"My life plan. I kind of abandoned it for a while because things got messy. Now, I'm checking my goals off at rapid speed."

"Oh yeah? What have you checked off so far?" I twirl her around on the dance floor.

"Oh, you know, the normal stuff. My academic accomplishments, getting married, starting a family, stuff like that."

"What's the next thing on your list?" I ask and watch her face break into a giant smile.

"Living happily ever after."

Bonus Epilogue

Aly, Five Years Later

"Alyssa Ann Winters Parker, what are you doing standing on that chair in your condition?" my best friend, Jess, scolds me while holding her son, Reece, on her hip.

"My condition?" I snort. "I'm trying to hang the birthday banner," I respond while holding up the superhero-themed decoration. Today is the birthday of our son, Christopher. "And I'm pregnant, not completely incapacitated." Although I realize that it might be a bit harder than expected to climb down since I can't see past my rapidly growing belly. I've learned that you start showing faster with each pregnancy, and thanks to Jax (okay, obviously I'm a willing participant too), I've had four back-to-back pregnancies.

"Didn't you learn anything from what happened to me a few years ago? You need to slow down." Jess taps her foot in frustration. "Stay there. I'm getting Jax."

"Mommy! Mommy! Look what Uncle Travis got us!" JJ and Christopher come running into the kitchen holding water guns.

"Oh, yay. More messy things," I say sarcastically. "You can only use them outside!" I yell as the two boys run after each other. Elton and Tony, our two rescue dogs, gallop on by, hot on the kids' heels. I always wanted a large family, but sometimes I feel like I ended up with a small zoo instead.

"Special delivery!" I hear Carter's voice from the front door.

"I'm in the kitchen," I yell to him.

"Hey, Aly!" Carter appears holding what is presumably Christopher's birthday cake. He places it on the kitchen counter and turns to look up at me. "Should you be standing on a chair in your condition?"

"I'm fine." I roll my eyes and look around him. "Where's Michelle?"

"She's on her way. She sent me in with the cake but mentioned something about running back to get some kiwi bars she forgot."

"Ohh! She's the best!" I rub my hands together, almost losing my balance. I've been craving tropical fruit throughout this whole pregnancy. Funny how I had different cravings with each kid. I craved ice cream and gummy bears with JJ, tacos with Christopher, and anything and everything with peanut butter during my pregnancy with Weston.

"Watch yourself there, Legs." Alex appears out of nowhere and grabs my hips to steady me on the chair. A moment later, I'm weightless as he places one arm around my lower back and the other under my knees, lifting me bridal style.

"Get your hands off my wife," Jax says from somewhere behind me.

"Stop knocking up your wife." Alex walks over to him and unceremoniously dumps me in Jax's arms. "Seriously, dude, I don't remember what Aly looks like not pregnant. Give her a break."

"She doesn't mind!" he calls after Alex as he walks towards our backyard where the party is being held. "You don't mind, do you?" He looks down at me with concern.

"You know I love our growing family." I give him a quick kiss.

"Knock! Knock!" Gabby calls through our screen door.

"In the kitchen!" Jax and I yell in unison.

"I'm not late, am I? I swear I felt like my shift would never end. Then everyone kept stopping to ask me questions when I was trying to leave…" Gabby's voice trails off as walks into the kitchen holding several balloons. She looks at Jax, who is still holding me, and lets out a loud sigh. "Seriously, Jax, I know you get extra overprotective when Aly is pregnant, but she can walk on her own."

I throw my head back in laughter as Jax sheepishly puts my feet back on the floor and turns towards our backyard.

"Umm, Gabby, you know this is a birthday party for Christopher, right?" I look curiously at one of the balloons that says, "Congratulations!"

"I know, but how can we *not* acknowledge your promotion?" She hands me the balloon. "Congrats, Dean Parker."

"Oh, thank you!" I give her a hug. "You're the sweetest."

"Hey! I thought I was the sweetest!" Amelia says, coming up from behind Gabby and playfully nudging her shoulder. "I still can't believe you're my boss now."

"I still can't believe you live here now, and I'm not directly your boss." I shake my head at her. "If you remember, once upon a time, I was your team leader in Beaute."

"Oh yeah! I forgot about that." Amelia's eyes seem to drift. "Sometimes I forget we even lived there."

"That's because all the best people from Beaute live here now." Jacob strolls up to the three of us while holding something behind his back. He recently had a career change and settled here a few months ago.

"Your sister doesn't live here permanently," I remind him. Although Jess and her family come often for visits. They love staying in the detached garage that Jax and Travis converted into a guest house.

"I said the *best* people from Beaute live here." Jacob gives a playful wink and looks around the kitchen. "I thought I heard G.I. Joe in here."

"You just missed him. He went out back."

"Perfect." A devious smile plays on Jacob's lips. He pulls out a giant super soaker water gun from behind his back and pumps it a few times. "I have a little surprise for him."

We watch Jacob saunter off towards the backyard to presumably drench my husband. Those two have developed the craziest relationship, and I'm still not sure whether that's a good or a bad thing.

"I think it might be best if we all head to the backyard," I cautiously walk towards the sliding glass door with Gabby and Amelia following behind.

"*Ciao*, Bella!" Claire comes up to give me a hug as soon as I step out onto our wraparound porch.

"When did you get here?" I hug her back and scan the area behind her. I spot her husband talking with Emma and Grant near Travis, who is manning the grill. Their kids, Maisey and Dominic, are already playing some sort of tag game with JJ, Christopher, Rosie, and Lily. It still blows my mind that our kids are all cousins. Nonna Grace and Nonno Steven would be over the moon to see their great-grandchildren running about.

"We got here just a few minutes ago and let ourselves in through the back." She hooks her thumb over her shoulder, pointing to our gate. "Mamma and Papa are on their way, but they're going to be late. Traffic is awful."

I don't know how they do it, but Mamma Maria and Papa Chris manage to come down from Washington for every event we have. Claire and I see each other the most since she lives the closest out of all of my sisters and we have monthly Zoom meetings to keep in touch with the rest of the family.

"Guess who woke up from his nap." My mom comes up to me with Weston snug in her arms. My parents have done a complete one-eighty over the last few years. I didn't expect a response when I sent them a birth announcement after JJ was born, but something changed in them when they discovered they were grandparents. They contacted me and told me they wanted to be involved. It started off slow. I was hesitant to bring them around for fear it would be a fleeting moment, but they've proven me wrong and have become loving grandparents who visit often.

"Chris and Maria aren't here yet?" my dad asks, putting his arms out to take Weston from my mom. My parents and the Parkers, while not the best of friends, have since found an amiable friendship of some sort. When my parents started coming around, I warned them that I would not jeopardize the relationship I rekindled with the Parker family. If they wanted me in their lives, they would have to accept them too, and to my surprise, they agreed to those terms.

My parents admitted they were jealous of the bond I had with the Parkers but realized they played a key role in pushing me away. The journey to heal all of our hearts hasn't been an easy one, but I'm so grateful for how far everyone has come. Of course, Jax has been my rock through all of this. Without him, I don't think I would've had the courage to set ground rules for my parents.

I walk along our wraparound porch, taking in the beautiful sight of my friends and family talking, laughing, and eating. This, right here, is what I've always dreamed of. Sometimes I still can't believe it's real, but the sensation of a kick in my belly lets me know this is, in fact, my amazing life.

"I know you're excited to meet everyone, baby Grace, but you still need to wait a little longer." I place my hand over my belly. "I need you healthy and strong because we are seriously outnumbered by the males in our family."

The look on Jax's face when he learned that we were having a girl was priceless. Between her overprotective dad and three older brothers, Grace will be lucky if she's allowed to date by the time she's thirty.

"Hey, G.I. Joe!" Jacob's voice has everyone turning their heads in his direction.

"Here we go," I say under my breath as I watch Jacob pull out his super soaker water gun and aim it towards Jax, who is oddly standing next to a set of bushes in our yard. It takes me a minute to realize what he is up to, but it takes Jacob a bit longer. The moment Jacob pulls the trigger, Jax gives some sort of signal. All the men and kids in a ten-foot radius launch a counterattack armed with squirt guns and water balloons. While Jacob and Jax are the main targets, the kids quickly turn on each other and by the end, nearly everyone who wasn't standing on the porch is soaked to the bone.

"I'll get the towels." I laugh while walking back into the house.

And I know just which towel to give to Jax.

Acknowledgements

First and foremost, if you are reading this-thank you so much! It's hard to wrap my head around the fact that I actually wrote a book *and* people want to read it. This has been an amazing experience.

When I told my husband I had an idea for a book, he took one look at me and said, "Do it!" That's when I told him that I already finished it, but I was petrified to share it with anyone. I eventually pushed down my fear and shared it with a few people. With more encouragement from my husband, I took the first step and found a developmental editor. My hands were literally shaking as they hovered over my keyboard while my husband firmly told me to hit the send button. I am so glad I did!

So, without further ado…

A huge thank you to Sue Grimshaw (Edits by Sue). Your advice has been priceless. I was a total wreck when I first sent my work to you, but you were so patient and kind. Because of you, I was able to confidently send Jax and Aly out into the world.

Kelly, my alpha reader and personal cheering squad. You are such a positive ray of light for not just me, but my family as well. Thank you for being you!

Holly, my beta reader. It's crazy to think that we would read each other's poetry in our middle school cafeteria and now, all these years later, you advised me on chapters of my book. I've always admired your honesty and ability to not have a filter. Don't ever change!

Erica Russikoff (Erica Edits)-Holy adverbs! Haha! Sorry about that! Thank you for pointing out ways to make my work stronger.

Emily A. Lawrence (Lawrence Editing)- Wow! You cleaned up my book and made it all shiny and sparkly. Your knowledge of all things related to languages is amazing!

Thank you to Kari March (Kari March Designs) for helping me come up with a gorgeous cover design!

Brittany Holland (The Blurb Whisperer)-I truly appreciate your patience and feedback while we worked together on this stubborn blurb!

Becca Mysoor and her team at The Fairy-Plot Mother- Thank you for coming up with some fantastic quotes for advertising!

To my mom who is no longer with us, thank you for all the trips to the library and instilling a love of reading in me. I know if you were here, you would be telling everyone (whether they wanted to listen or not) that your daughter wrote a book.

A heartfelt thank you to all my friends and family for your support and words of encouragement.

To all the men and women who have served or are serving in our military, thank you for your service!

About The Author

Tracy is a former teacher turned homeschooling mom of three amazing kids. She resides in her home state of New Jersey; however, thanks to her husband's military career, she has also lived in the Southeast and Pacific Northwest. She is a lover of coffee, chocolate, vanilla seltzer, and the Oxford comma. She often writes at her kitchen table with her rescue dog at her feet.

For news and updates on future projects, please go to www.tracymcjames.com or click on the following pages:

facebook.com/TracyMcJamesAuthor

instagram.com/tracymcjamesbooks

pinterest.com/authortracymcjames

twitter.com/@tracymcjames

Made in the USA
Middletown, DE
04 November 2024